ORACLE

SOLAR WIND

C.W. Trisef

Trisef Book LLC

How to contact the author
Website – www.trisefbook.com
Email – trisefbook@gmail.com

Oracle – Solar Wind
C.W. Trisef

Other titles by C.W. Trisef
Oracle – Sunken Earth (Book 1 in the Oracle Series)
Oracle – Fire Island (Book 2 in the Oracle Series)
Oracle – River of Ore (Book 3 in the Oracle Series)

This book is a work of fiction. Any references to historical events, real people, or real locales are used fictitiously. Other names, characters, places, and incidents are the product of the author's imagination.

Written by – C.W. Trisef
Cover designed by – Giuseppe Lipari
Text designed by – Sheryl Mehary
Back cover photography: "Polarlicht 2" by USAF Senior Airman Joshua Strang, and "Internet map 4096" by Matt Britt. Used with permission.

REUNITED NATIONS

"This is an outrage!"

"A catastrophe!"

"A calamity!"

"An international crisis, to be sure!"

"We're all doomed!"

"The planet is under attack!"

"It's aliens, I tell you—aliens!"

"There's no telling what'll happen next!"

"First, there was the mega-quake in the Atlantic—"

"Magnitude 18.3—can you believe it?"

"It's the Bermuda Triangle—what do you expect?"

"Our geologists say the sinkhole is *still* filling up."

"And *we're* still finding bodies."

"Then came the volcanic explosion in the Pacific—"

"Swallowed Easter Island whole."

"And I just vacationed there last year."

"I knew there was something strange about those giant statues."

"And now this!"

"A river through the Sahara Desert!"

"I didn't believe it until I saw it."

"It's draining the Mediterranean Sea!"

"And all the earth's oceans with it!"

"This is the end of the world as we know it."

"Does anyone doubt global warming *now?*"

"The Mayans were right!"

A man stepped up to the podium, looking rather overwhelmed. "Ladies and gentlemen," the man said cordially, but his voice could scarcely be heard over the din of the riotous crowd.

He tried again: "Excuse me—please, please!" But the uproar continued without the slightest sign of letting up.

Tired of being ignored, the otherwise polite man screwed up his face and yelled into the microphone, "Ladies and gentlemen, will you please be quiet!" He banged his white-knuckled fist on the podium, sending a loud booming noise through the sound system and dislodging a small glass globe that had been placed near the microphone for decoration. A hush fell over the tumultuous audience as every pair of eyes turned to watch the globe roll off the podium and then bounce three times on the marble floor. Its tempered glass did not shatter but cracked in a few places before it eventually came to rest.

Now that he had everyone's attention, the frazzled man took a deep breath, readjusted his necktie, and finally began his prepared remarks.

"On behalf of the United Nations, I thank you all for coming to this emergency meeting of the General Assembly, convened this nineteenth day of April, at the United Nations General Assembly Hall in New York City. I believe representatives from all 193 member states are present to discuss the very important matters that are affecting our world."

"The citizens of Italy demand an explanation!" shouted the Italian delegation.

"Our coastlines are devastated!" complained the Greeks.

"And what about our farmland?" the Egyptians added. "The entire Nile delta is ruined!"

"Coasts and farms can be replaced," countered the consulate from Chile. "Easter Island is gone—disappeared overnight!"

"Just like our economy!" the group from the Bahamas joined in. "Tourism to our islands has vanished ever since the mega-quake."

The man at the podium brought his hand to his face and rubbed his forehead in desperation. He had reminded them why they were all gathered together, which resumed the bickering. In all his years as Secretary-General, he had never witnessed so much energy in a meeting of the General Assembly. This nation was blaming that nation—this country taking sides with that country. A gathering that was supposed to be civil and diplomatic looked more like the scuffling you'd find in a schoolyard.

"What do you expect us to do with this river that just barged across our borders?" the Libyans and Algerians wondered. "Our native tribes already don't like us."

"The sea level keeps dropping every hour," Spain and Morocco pointed out. "It's only a matter of time before the Strait of Gibraltar becomes too shallow for ships to pass through—"

"—and every port worldwide becomes inaccessible."

"What should we do?"

"How do we pay for this?"

"What do we tell our people?"

"Who knows what Mother Nature will throw at us next?"

"Why are these terrible things happening?"

"The earth is seeking revenge for centuries of pollution!"

"The time to go green is now!"

"I'm telling you, it's aliens!"

"Mankind must flee to the moon!"

"Who can save us now?"

Suddenly, at the height of the panic, the double doors at the back of the room burst open. Everyone turned to see a man standing in the doorway. At his back was a brilliant light, outlining his strong physique but masking his identity in black silhouette.

Alarmed by such a surprise entrance, the Secretary-General called for security.

"Wait, sir!" the newcomer protested. "It's me: Lionel Zarbock."

The Secretary-General thought for a moment and then, remembering, said, "Ah, yes: Dr. Zarbock, head of the International Atomic Energy Agency—isn't that right?"

"You are correct, sir," Lionel replied respectfully, taking a few steps forward. "I have some very important information to report to the General Assembly, if I may—information that I believe each of you will find most vital to your meeting today."

Feeling relieved, the Secretary-General bowed and said, "The floor is yours, doctor."

Lionel commenced a slow walk towards the center of the room. It was a large hall, built for delivering speeches, with round walls that gradually tapered up toward a wide ceiling. At one end was a dais, the raised platform where the podium stood directly in front of a few chairs for the highest-ranking officials to sit. The rest of the room was filled with tables and chairs, all facing toward the front, enough to accommodate several hundred people. Mirrors lined the walls, and bright spotlights shined overhead.

"Mr. President, Mr. Secretary-General, fellow delegates, ladies and gentlemen," Lionel began in all professionalism, "these are perilous times—uncertain times, filled with headaches and heartaches, times that are bringing death and destruction to our very doorsteps." He was standing well in front of the podium, not far from the first row of seats, preferring to use his loud and natural voice rather than the microphone.

"Over the last several months, we have watched strange events rock our world," he continued. "A so-called earthquake that swallowed part of the Atlantic Ocean and snuffed out hundreds of thousands of lives." He motioned to the representatives from the Islands of the Bahamas, who accepted the condolences. "An entire island in the Pacific that erupted in lava and sank in waves, taking all of its people and history with it." He nodded at the Chilean table. "And, just days ago, a string of events more surreal than the others: the devastating collapse of an Egyptian pyramid, the reversal of the mighty Nile, the draining of the Mediterranean Sea, and the emergence of a Great River in the middle of the

Sahara." He made eye contact with every nation that had been affected by the recent events.

"And now, here we are, gathered together to try and make sense of it all. You know, despite our differences, there is a common thread that unites us all today: we are all victims. We—you and I—are the victims of these heinous acts, committed by an unknown hand. Well, I'm here today to tell you that I know whose hands are responsible for these atrocities. They are not the work of Mother Nature—oh no. They are the result of the selfish actions of one man—a young man, in fact— named Ret Cooper."

Lionel had an absolutely captivating effect on the audience. Every single person—from the delegates to the clerks to the translators—was listening to Lionel's every word, almost in an attitude of worship. The hall, which had hitherto been as clamorous as a zoo, was now as silent as a morgue.

Yes, Lionel certainly knew how to work a crowd. Everything he had to say seemed to be everything his listeners wanted to hear. His words flowed like sweet music. With an age in the thirty-somethings, his dark hair and dark eyes combined to bestow upon him a radiant countenance not unlike lightning. Tall and strapping, he was a man with a commanding presence, and, for whatever reason, you wanted him to like you. All in all, he was a composite character in the prime of life.

"And who is Ret Cooper, you ask?" Lionel pressed on, knowing he had everyone's undivided attention. "Well, let me tell you. I know him quite well, actually. You see, we first met in a place called Sunken Earth." Lionel took out his cell phone, synced it with the hall's projector, and used it to display pictures from Sunken Earth on the large screens up on the walls. Each photo was greeted with "ooh" and "aww" as Lionel showed off his slideshow, solidifying the truth of his words.

"Sunken Earth was the name of the city that once existed underneath the Atlantic Ocean. It was home to an advanced civilization, millions of innocent people, and—" he paused for dramatic emphasis "—the earth element." The crowd replied with grunts of confusion. "Yes, the earth element—the source from which all dirt and soil and minerals on this planet come. It is a small thing that wields immense power. And Ret stole it—he took it right out of Sunken Earth. That earthquake—the one whose aftermath we all have to deal with now—was no earthquake at all. It was the collapse of an underwater civilization."

A hundred whispered conversations filled the air in response to Lionel's revelatory words, sounding like a colony of hissing snakes.

"But that was just the beginning," Lionel resumed, killing the quiet conversations. "Ret moved onto the next element in his greedy quest for power: the element of fire." Lionel walked as he talked. Beginning at the very first table, he looked directly into the eyes of the delegates from Afghanistan and smiled until he knew he had their trust, either out of faith or fear, which didn't take long. Then he slowly grabbed the small replica of that country's flag, which was positioned right next to the placard bearing that country's name, and moved onto the next table, Albania. There, he followed much the same protocol, gaining their trust and then collecting their flag. Algeria, Andorra, Angola—one by one as he continued his narrative.

"And I bet you can guess where the fire element was hiding," Lionel said. "Why don't *you* tell us, Chile?"

"Easter Island!" a pair of indignant voices shouted back.

"Indeed!" Lionel rejoined amid angry grumbles, which only intensified as photographs of the island's demise flashed across the large screens. "But did Ret care? Did Ret show even the slightest ounce of concern for those nearly 900 moai statues that you and I came to adore? No."

More flags: Cambodia, Cameroon, Canada. One of the Canadian delegates was wearing a bowler hat. Lionel removed it from the man's bald head and asked, "May I borrow this?" Intimidated by Lionel's confident character and debonair demeanor, the

Canadian obliged with a nervous nod of his head. "Don't worry," Lionel reassured him, "there's nothing to be worried aboot." The Canadians smiled to hear Lionel employ one of their colloquialisms, and their trepidation quickly turned to trust. With such ease, Lionel had won over the hearts of yet another delegation. He flipped over the hat and used it to hold his growing collection of flags.

"And most recently, our dear friend, Ret Cooper," said Lionel, moving to a new set of pictures, "had the wherewithal to launch a personal attack on the Egyptian pyramids—those iconic symbols of mystery and majesty." The people from Egypt voiced their agreement. "He destroyed the Nile and the Sahara." North African delegates sounded a rallying call. "And now every coastal nation is watching its shores recede ever farther—all for what? So that Ret Cooper could get his precious ore element?"

Haiti. Honduras. Hungary.

Each picture either showed what once was or what now is, reminding everyone of the destruction wrought by this dreadful person named Ret Cooper. With each image, Lionel poured salt into the delegates' already-deep wounds.

Philippines. Poland. Portugal.

"Three elements down, only three more to go," Lionel told them. "He already has the device to collect them, thanks to the Oracle in his pocket, and he will soon know where to find them, thanks to the scars on his hands. The question for us, my friends, is where will he strike next?"

"Could it be you, perhaps?" he said, glaring into the eyes of the Russian representatives who, without hesitation, picked up the Russian flag and presented it to Lionel like a gift. "What destruction will he wreak next? How many more lives will he see fit to extinguish as he continues his rampage across our world?"

"What must we do?" someone shouted.

"He must be stopped," came Lionel's quick reply, "stopped at any and all costs. There's no telling what might happen if he collects all six elements. He'd be more terrible than a thousand tyrants!"

"How? How can we stop him?"

"Send a battalion of UN peacekeeping forces."

"Our nation pledges ten-thousand troops."

"Capital punishment!"

"We can supply a dozen drones."

"No, no," Lionel rebutted, "it can't be done that way. Enough blood has already been spilt."

"Then what do you suggest?"

"Let *me* take care of it," Lionel told them. "I know where the young man lives. I know where he goes to school. I know who his family and friends are. I know his strengths, his fears, his weaknesses. Grant me ready access to your resources, and I will promise to stop Ret Cooper before he collects the sixth element."

Singapore. Slovakia. Slovenia.

"All in favor of pledging unto Dr. Lionel Zarbock free access to each nation's resources," the Secretary-General announced from the podium, "please vote in the affirmative."

"The United States objects to such a resolution," the American delegates promptly declared.

"I can understand your hesitation, my fine American friends," Lionel said. "So let me tell you something else that I'm sure you'll find most intriguing. If everyone would please turn his or her attention to the image on the screen." A satellite image of the world appeared next in the slideshow, with the Atlantic Ocean in the center. "This was the position of the earth's continents just before Sunken Earth imploded and triggered the so-called mega-quake." It looked perfectly normal, as far as anyone could decipher. "Now, let's compare it to the continents' positions *today*, shall we?" When Lionel advanced the presentation, the current slide remained unchanged while a second satellite image of the world came into view, except it was more transparent so that when it was laid over the first map, the onlookers could clearly see any differences between the two images.

And there certainly were differences. And they certainly saw them.

Gasps of shock bounced off the round walls of the assembly hall as everyone learned a startling fact.

"Yes, it's true, ladies and gentlemen," Lionel stated soberly. "The natural movement of the continents has not only been reversed but also greatly accelerated. You see, each element exerts tremendous and continuous amounts of energy, but when one becomes trapped inside the Oracle, it leaves behind a great void in the earth. This sudden power struggle is what causes plates to shift, seafloor to buckle, and volcanoes and pyramids to crumble. So, the void in the Bermuda Triangle pushed the North American continent in a new, southeastward direction while the explosive demise of Easter Island pushed South America into a northeastward one. And all the recent activity in Africa has already sent that continent heading westward."

Such a troubling reality cast a dark cloud of silent terror over the proceedings.

"Well, that explains why our barges have been taking longer to sail to and from the Americas," the Chinese said amongst themselves.

"Maybe this is why the fuel usage for many of our airplanes has been so erratic," the delegates from India debated.

"You've known this for over a year and are just now telling us about it?" the American consulate accused with continued distrust. "Why didn't you tell us sooner?"

"I tried," Lionel confessed. "Do you not remember when I approached this very assembly last year and reported on the condition of all the world's nuclear reactors following the so-called mega-quake? In my remarks, I said that I had reason to believe that the regular movement of the earth's tectonic plates may have been disrupted."

"Did you now?" the American scoffed. Then, calling out to the archivists, "Check the minutes." While the archivists skimmed the electronic archives of past proceedings, the Americans glanced back at the unsettling images on the screen and confidently reasoned among themselves, "How could we forget something like *this?*"

"Actually, as I recall," Lionel grinned, "the assembly dismissed my claim as non-threatening and said it would be investigated at a later date."

Just then, one of the archivists rehearsed the minutes from the former meeting, confirming Lionel's recollections in their entirety. Proven wrong, the American delegates sat down and sneered as Lionel walked away with their Stars and Stripes.

"These are perilous times," Lionel repeated with unfailing vigor, concluding his remarks the way they began. "The current problems that vex your countries are serious, yes, but not nearly as serious as the danger we'll be in if the continents collide into each other. The time to act is now, my friends. With your help, I can stop Ret Cooper and make sure the elements remain under the care of the United Nations. Then, and only then, can we use the great power of the elements to repair in-part the damage that has already been done and prevent any more from occurring. Most importantly, with the elements in our possession, we can keep the continents from crashing into one another and save the world."

Yemen. Zambia. And, finally, Zimbabwe.

"All those in favor of bestowing upon Lionel Zarbock all rights, privileges, and powers that he deems necessary to carry out his stated objectives," the Secretary-General announced, "please vote in the affirmative now."

The votes were cast, the numbers were tallied, and the results were broadcast on the wall for all to see: it was a landslide.

"Congratulations, Dr. Zarbock," the Secretary-General said from the podium amid thunderous applause from the floor. "We expect you to make regular reports of your efforts in this most important matter."

"Indeed, I will," Lionel promised, smiling as he walked from the back of the room up to the front, clutching his hat full of flags. "It is with greatest humility that I accept this responsibility. Given my close association with Ret and his wrongdoings, I feel it is my duty to do my part to help the world in these troubled times. You will not be disappointed. Thank you."

At the end of his impromptu acceptance speech, the delegates again erupted in celebration. Nations that had been accusing one another just moments ago were now embracing each other with rekindled hope. Instead of pointing fingers, they were shaking hands. A room that had recently been divided now stood reunited, all thanks to one man.

Upon reaching the front of the hall, Lionel turned to face his jubilant admirers. He bent down and picked up the small glass globe that had fallen from the podium earlier. Then, with globe in one hand and flags in the other, he triumphantly raised his hands into the air, causing the standing crowd to cheer even louder.

And, from that moment on, and in more than one way, Lionel Zarbock had the whole world in the palm of his hand.

CHAPTER 1

A HOUSE DIVIDED

Ret wasn't himself these days. He didn't feel like his normal, happy self. Neither was he thinking like his normal, hopeful self. In fact, he didn't even look like his normal, abnormal self. Truth be told, he didn't want to *be* himself anymore. So he wasn't.

For starters, he returned from Africa with a lot more baggage than he had brought—the metaphorical kind, the kind that weighs nothing on a scale but tons on your heart. And, stuffed in his imaginary suitcases, he found a slew of unsavory souvenirs. Sitting right on top was a neuroscope, which never failed to bring Conrad to the forefront of his mind, with a blue lotus flower tucked in each pocket to give everything the scent of Lydia. The bulk of the burden came from the sandstone blocks—a whole pyramid's worth of them, each a reminder of the ancient Egyptian structure he destroyed. And, carefully stowed in the zipper pouch, was a scrapbook full of mental photographs that chronicled the upheaval he brought to the Nile River, its delta, and the millions of people who depended on both—just in case he ever wanted to flip through its pages and do some reminiscing on a Sunday afternoon.

Yes, there was so much figurative luggage to keep in check that Ret seriously wondered if he would ever be able to carry on.

Yet, he had one possession that, though perhaps the lightest, seemed to weigh more than all the rest: the Oracle. The glass sphere, no bigger than an orange, now contained half of its six original elements. These were the most painful souvenirs of all. The only thing that remained of the lost city of Sunken Earth was the dirt clod now wedged into one of the Oracle's six sections. Likewise, all that was left of the doused Fire Island was a single flame. But the Oracle's newest addition—a golden nugget—was leaving a legacy as large as a river, and that Great River of ore was now snaking its watery way across the entire width of the Sahara Desert.

It was the river that seemed to wash over Ret's mind the most, especially while they were still in Africa. The continent proved to be a place that was easier to get into than out of. The aftermath of Ret's procurement of the ore element had brought immense chaos to the entire Saharan region almost overnight. Every nation was on high alert. Security was beefed up everywhere. Some governments were calling it a large-scale terrorist attack; others attributed it to a series of natural disasters. A wave of fear was sweeping from east to west as the news of this "Great River" came charging in the same direction. No one knew where it meant to flow. Would it plunge straight through the heart of a major city? Would it collide with an existing body of water and cause wide-spread flooding? The pandemonium was rampant.

In fact, it was enough to convince Mr. Coy that he and his companions needed to distance themselves from the river as much as possible if they ever wanted to return home — alive and not in handcuffs. Soon after their graveside tributes to the martyrs Conrad and Lydia, everyone piled back into Coy's All-terrain Vehicle Extraordinaire (or CAVE, for short) and began to put as many miles between them and the river as quickly as he could. At Ishmael's request, the group bid farewell to him at a remote village in northern Libya where some of his distant relatives lived. Doing so took them in a direction that was pretty much opposite the one in which they needed to go, adding another day or two of travel time to their schedule, but they were in no rush.

At least, that's how they wanted to be perceived, for the fact of the matter was they were in a great rush, hoping to escape before they were found out. Rather than blaze their own trail and cut quickly through the desert, they took the long way—the unsettlingly scenic route along the common roads and highways. But because the entire region was essentially on lockdown, there were roadside checkpoints into and out of each country and major city, and, as expected, the CAVE was stopped at every single one of them. Since it wasn't exactly your average mid-sized sedan, the CAVE was a sitting duck in such situations, and it didn't help that its passengers were five American tourists. People didn't seem to look at (or, more appropriately, *over*look) them in quite the same way as when Ishmael, Lydia, and Conrad had been with them.

As they had made their way west from Tripoli to Algiers, then south from Morocco into Mauritania, and further down until finally Liberia, Ret witnessed firsthand how the whole world was abuzz with talk of the Sahara's new waterfront. Whenever traffic slowed to a crawl in congested downtown centers (which was often), the little English being spoken along the sidewalk always seemed to find his ears, and the subject matter was all the same. Ret saw more than one protest in front of government buildings, and they drove by a few mobs descending on suit-clad individuals with a barrage of demands.

Worst of all, however, were the scenes being broadcast on television. Ret could see them through busy storefronts and small cafés where hordes of passersby stopped to gasp and wince at what was being shown. There was aerial footage of the Great River hurtling ever onward, entire villages first falling with the collapsing sand and then being swallowed whole by the rushing water. There were brief interviews with devastated farmers from the Nile Delta whose crops were failing due to the sudden inflow of salt water from the Mediterranean Sea. There were newscasters from every continent holding microphones up to the mouths of politicians pledging aid and celebrities expressing condolences. What's more, the Great River already had its own hashtag on Twitter. Though only days old, the news was flying on wireless wings to all parts of the earth.

All in all, the horrendous traffic and frequent stops made for a painfully slow and extra-long journey back to Monrovia where Mr. Coy's airplane was (thankfully) still stashed. But, to their dread, then came the tricky business of trying to gain clearance for their private jet to take to the skies. It was not easy, nor very expeditious. But, after a few more days of nearly-stranded patience, the Coys and the Coopers (and their tagalong Leonard Swain) became airborne, flying over the Atlantic Ocean on their way back home, knowing that each thrust of the engines was taking them far, far away from the banks of the Great River.

But there was no escaping it. The flight back to Tybee was full of turbulence—caused not by what was in the air but in the air*waves*. A never-ending stream of thoughts and images was swirling in Ret's mind like a hurricane. Although he was characteristically silent on the outside, there was a great storm of doubt and heartache raging within.

Ret's silence bothered Paige; in fact, it drove her crazy. She knew what it meant: he was thinking. How she wished she could just grab a can opener, pry open that brain of his, and get him to spill his beans. "Just talk to me!" she would shout in her own tin can, "Tell me— tell someone, anyone!—what's going on. Just talk; open up; let me in. Let me help—let me *try* to help, I want to. Share the load. Let me take some of the pressure off before you explode. You can't do this all by yourself. Please, let me help."

But Ret always remained hermetically sealed.

"What do you think's troubling him?" Ana whispered to Paige, nodding her head at Ret. He was sitting across the aisle, staring out the small window at the endless ocean below.

"Who knows?" she sighed with frustration. "Probably just the post-procurement woes."

"The what?" Ana asked.

"Every time he collects an element," Paige explained, "he gets like this afterwards, and I'm sure it gets worse each time. You know how hard he is on himself."

"Maybe he's bummed he looks pretty much normal now," Ana suggested. "Do you think he's noticed?"

"I'm sure he has," said Paige, "but that's one thing he might actually be *happy* about—to not look so different anymore."

They were conversing in hushed tones, as if Ret couldn't hear them, but of course he could. It seemed he was always hearing others talk about him. It privately bugged him that people never came to *him* to talk about him.

"Why *has* he changed so much, anyway?" Ana wondered.

"I reckon it's 'cause there's no more uranium in his blood," Leo joined in. Ana liked how his southern accent was more noticeable when he spoke quietly.

"Uranium?" Paige questioned earnestly. "In his—blood?"

"It was something I overheard Lye saying to him when me and Conrad snuck into the room with the element," Leo told them. "Lye said the reason Ret looked so different was on account of the uranium in his blood. It was while he was using that fission gun on him." Paige winced at the thought. "Lye said the radiation coming from the gun was splitting the uranium atoms in Ret's blood, which is why he was bleeding so much—"

"—Which is why he looks normal now," Paige interrupted, anxious to change the subject away from the thought of Ret's pain, still wishing she had been there to help him. "His uranium is gone."

"Yes, ma'am," Leo concluded.

"So that's why he's been getting sunburned," Ana put together. "And why his hair and eyes are not so...not so..."

"Luminescent?" Leo offered.

"Sure," said Ana.

"Oh," Paige exhaled, sounding deflated. "And I thought it was just because he was sad." She had been rather fond of Ret's eccentricities and was somewhat disappointed to think they might not come back.

Relief filled each weary traveler's heart when the sea finally met land. Coy Manor, that curious cross between a castle and a circus, rose above Little Tybee Island. A large door, hidden in the island's hillside, parted its panels and admitted the plane into the Manor's underground hangar and onto a short runway.

Pauline was standing close by to greet them. Sick with a broken heart, she had stayed home from the adventure this time, opting instead to spend the week at Coy Manor as a sort of guest instructor in its culinary program. The students fawned over her as she shared with them all the tricks of the trade. Her break from all things Oracle had been good for her, as evidenced by the smile on her face as the plane rolled by. Naturally, she had become quite worried when the week ended and her children were still on the other side of the world. Through daily text messages, Ana was able to bring some peace to her fuss-budget of a mother by keeping her apprised of their progress in their days-long quest to escape from Africa.

"Oh, I'm so glad you're safe," Pauline cheered as she embraced Ana. "After you told me what happened, I've been watching the news nonstop. It's unbelievable, what's going on over there. And to think, all from what Ret did."

Ret froze. By far the last one off the plane, he had just stepped over the threshold and onto the landing of the rollaway staircase when he heard Pauline's words. Those last three words—"what Ret did"—struck him like daggers, though the harm had no doubt been unintentional. He closed his eyes, as if it helped in absorbing the pain.

Still sporting his perpetual silence, Ret started down the stairs. Each step, heavy and slow, echoed into the dark shadows of the hangar. Everyone, huddled not far from the last stair, turned to watch. The two parents in the group were standing close to their respective daughters. Leo was also there, to the side.

When Ret stepped onto the cement floor, he stood still, his head down. After a few moments, he spoke for the first time in days.

"I can't do this anymore," he said. His words were as dull and emotionless as the color gray.

No one knew how to respond.

"Oh, Ret," Pauline tenderly cooed, "it's been a long trip. I'm sure, once you get some rest and—"

"—No," Ret countered, a little annoyed as if he had been misunderstood. "I mean I don't *want* to do this anymore."

"Do what, Ret?" Mr. Coy asked softly, though he seemed to already know the answer.

"This." Ret held out the Oracle. There was a slight pause as everyone (except Ret) stared at the sphere. "Here," he said, taking a few steps toward Mr. Coy and extending it to him. "Take it. I don't want it anymore."

In the past, Ret had always given the Oracle to Mr. Coy when they returned home from finding an element, as Ret felt it would be safer in Mr. Coy's possession until he needed it again. But it was suddenly different this time. This time, Mr. Coy feared if he took the Oracle from him, Ret might never ask for it back.

"Take it," Ret restated more forcefully, avoiding eye contact with Paige.

"No," Coy refused, "I will not—"

"TAKE IT!"

Ana had never heard Ret yell like that before. Pauline swallowed a gasp before it escaped. Paige buried her face into her father's side while he remained stone-faced. Leo looked down at his worn-through shoes.

Ret broke down. He slowly fell to his knees and began to weep, his hand still clutching the Oracle that no one else would take.

Mr. Coy stepped over to Leo's side and said softly, "Do me a favor, son, and take the Cooper women across the creek back to their home, will you?" Though surprised, he liked the sound of an adult male calling him "son."

"Yes, sir," Leo obeyed.

Then, turning to Paige, her father said, "You go, too, dear."

The four departed, leaving Mr. Coy alone with Ret. Paige looked back at Ret more than once before the elevator doors closed.

"I never wanted any of this," Ret said, wiping his eyes dry, though he was more mad than sad. "All I ever wanted was to be a normal guy and live a normal life—hang out, play ball, go to the movies. Why can't I have that? Why is my life so different?"

"You can have that, Ret," Mr. Coy told him encouragingly.

"No, no I can't," he quickly countered. "I can't start my first day of high school without making a scene or go to a football game without burying people in dirt or even attend a school dance without things blowing up.

It's a curse. It's like I'm smitten by the universe, or something. My life is not my own. It's being lived for me."

Suddenly, the elevator doors opened with the chime of a bell. Ret and Mr. Coy looked to see who was there, but they saw no one. Leo must have been mindful of them and sent the elevator down for their future convenience.

"No one's forcing you to collect the elements," Coy resumed. "You can still choose not to."

"I know—it's a choice I've made many times," Ret said, "but then a triangle appears on the palm of my hand—or a moai statue or a squiggly river. It invades my thoughts and presses itself against my feelings until I do its bidding. It's like I have no choice. The prophecy says 'one line has the rite,' doesn't it? If that includes my entire family line, then where is everyone? Why do *they* have a choice? Why don't *they* do it from now on?"

"You can't quit now, Ret," Coy pled. "We're halfway there—we're doing so well!"

"'Well'? You call this 'well'? The whole world hates me—and for good reason. How many more people have to die to 'fill the Oracle'? How much more damage must be done to 'cure the world'? 'Cure the world'— what a joke. I'm not curing the world; I'm destroying it—I'm tearing it apart. It's just as Lye said: this world will never change. He's been right all along."

"But we can change it, Ret," Coy urged. "It's changing as we speak. There's now a river in the Sahara Desert, for crying out loud. We only have three more elements to find, and then we can—"

"Don't you get it?" Ret responded, as if speaking to a child. The full expression of his never-spoken thoughts was finding a voice for the first time. "Don't you understand? This isn't about elements. This was *never* about elements, Mr. Coy. It's about people. It's about people's hearts. The Oracle has so very little to do with collecting elements but such a great deal to do with changing hearts. *That's* how you 'cure the world'—by purifying people's hearts, not by filling a glass ball. I used to think it would be my power over the elements that would enable me to eventually cure the world. But what good would it do to use my power over earth to, let's say, push the continents back together—cure the world that way—if people still seek for conflict and war in their hearts? Or what good would it do to use my fire to, maybe, burn away all pollution if people aren't willing to purge their own hearts of unclean desires? Why should I go to the trouble of using my ore to redistribute wealth if people would rather hold onto their greedy hearts? I may be able to move mountains and kindle fire and mold metal, but I have no control over another man's heart. *That's* where the real power is in this world, and from what I've seen of people's hearts, I'm not sure this world *wants* to be cured."

Mr. Coy found himself at a total loss for words. He was stunned by what he saw before him: an obscure boy, unlearned and unadorned, who possessed more wisdom and understanding than all the world's capitols and polities. Surely the Oracle would be hard-pressed to find a better steward than Ret Cooper.

A few floors above the hangar, Leo came bursting back through the main door of the Manor. Out of breath, he dashed across the semicircular foyer toward the elevator. When its doors did not immediately open, he pushed the button repeatedly, confused why it was taking so long since he had just recently used it.

When the doors finally opened, Leo was surprised to find Paige inside the elevator. Like a child caught with her hand in the cookie jar, Paige blushed.

"Oh, hi," she said bashfully.

There was a look of distress on Leo's face as he frantically pressed the button to take them back down to the hangar. Paige was glad he seemed too preoccupied to want to chat with her. Just minutes ago, as the two of them were escorting the Cooper women out of the Manor, she had told them that she would stay behind and that they should go on ahead without her. They obliged and exited the Manor while she hurried back to the elevator to return to the hangar and listen in on her father's conversation with

Ret, knowing it was her best chance yet of hearing Ret share some of his most personal thoughts as never before.

And so, while hiding in the elevator, Paige learned a lot about Ret. She had never even considered some of the weighty material that passed through his mind on a daily basis. She marveled to hear how Ret's anxiety had very little to do with himself. She, at last, had gotten a small taste of the thoughts that kept Ret awake at night, but now, given their gravity, she kind of wished she hadn't.

As soon as the elevator doors parted, Leo lunged into the hangar. After just a few steps, he shouted, "Mr. Coy, sir, you need to see something right away."

Mr. Coy and Ret hurried into the elevator. Not a word was said. Paige glanced at Ret a few times, but his attention remained fixed on his own thoughts.

Leo led the way out of the Manor and across the grounds. As soon as they stepped outside, they saw the first sign of trouble: there was a large but dissipating cloud of black smoke in the sky, not too close to them but not too far away either.

Their brisk walk now turned into a worried run. They followed Leo through the main gate, then down the bluff that led to Tybee Creek. Leo immediately readied the kayak, but the other three stood at the water's edge in shock at what they saw on the other shore: the Cooper home, burned to the ground.

They leapt into the kayak. Leo manned the oar. Wanting to move faster, Ret took it from him and began to cut through the water. The kayak quickly gained so much speed that Ret jumped out a good ways from shore and ran the rest of the way himself, letting the kayak float on its own behind him.

Ret flew up the few wooden planks of their backyard boardwalk that had not been burned. He made his way to the front yard, kicking up ash along the way. He glanced at what used to be their home. Nothing had escaped the flames. It was all gone, now reduced to an ugly heap of charred debris and unrecognizable rubble.

Ret approached the small group on the blackened front lawn. The last of the firefighters were there, preparing to leave. Pauline and Ana were listening to Ms. Montgomery, the widow next-door, whose house had been largely unscathed.

"Oh, it was awful," the old woman told them amid frightened tears. "I was just sitting on the back porch when I saw a creature emerge from the creek." She was obviously very shaken up. "When it got to shore, I could tell it was a man—a hideous, old man with white hair and black robes and...and...oh, that cane! That dreadful cane! He lifted it into the air and, out of nowhere, shot at least a dozen lightning bolts at your home—through the windows, through the doors—one after another. The whole house instantly went up in flames. I ran and called the fire department, but—oh, Pauline, I'm so sorry."

Ret watched from behind as the two neighbors wept on each other's shoulders. Paige and Leo rushed to Ana's side.

Ret walked up the two cement steps that led to where the front door used to be, kicking dead embers away to clear a path. He stared into the ghost-house. The Coopers had never had much when it came to earthly possessions—no more than the essentials, really. But now they had nothing. Ret added it to the growing list of misfortunes that he had caused. He was well aware that Pauline and Ana never had to adopt him. He was a guest in their home. Now, as a reward for their hospitality, they had suffered yet another tragedy. They had already lost their husband and father because of Ret. And now this. What was next? What was *left?*

Through the white and wispy smoke, Ret could see a man standing on the shore. For a moment, he thought it might be that white-haired and black-robed arsonist with "that dreadful cane." But it wasn't; it was Mr. Coy.

Ret trudged across the scorched property toward him. Mr. Coy didn't make it far from the kayak, too overwhelmed by what he saw. Ret stopped in front of him, face to face.

"It was Lye," Ret told him, knowing it was an act of revenge for Ret destroying Lye's Vault. "If you see him, give this to him, will you?"

Ret grabbed Mr. Coy's hand, put the Oracle in it, and walked away.

CHAPTER 2

ANYONE'S GUEST

Fortunately for the now-homeless Cooper family, there was an enormous facility nearby that specialized in caring for the less fortunate. In fact, some of Paige's first words of consolation to her grieving friend Ana were an invitation to come and live at Coy Manor—either temporarily or indefinitely, though she personally preferred the latter. Her father felt the same way; actually, he insisted on it. And so Pauline, without money or roof, gratefully accepted the generous offer.

It didn't take long for the Coopers to feel comfortable enough to call the Manor their new home. Mr. Coy immediately set in motion a plan to build a small house on the west side of the property that would serve as the Coopers' permanent and private residence. Such a project was commonplace in the Manor's curriculum. It gave the students real-world experience in their chosen fields—the sort of hands-on training they would need in order to excel once they left the Manor in pursuit of jobs and careers.

Right there, at the site, instruction was given and then applied. The aspiring architects drew up blueprints that they could add to their portfolios. The future land surveyors came to understand the complications of yet another gradient. Cementers compared aggregate compounds while masons discussed herringbone patterns. The plumbers and electricians worked alongside the roofers and painters. Interior decorators experimented with multiple colors, fabrics, and patterns. The linens were homespun by the Textiles class, and the dishes were hand-made by Ceramics. Standing by were bookkeepers tallying expenses and chiropractors expelling subluxations. The journalists kept the rest of the campus apprised of the progress through daily reports that were featured in the Manor's nightly news.

Each and every one of the Manor's small but varied departments and schools was called upon to participate in "Project: Cooper Home" in some way. It was the unwritten order of things: if there wasn't an obvious need, then they were expected to create one. This is why Coy Manor itself looked so weird—it had a little bit of everything. In fact, by the end of the project, the Coopers' new abode bore a strong resem-blance to the Manor, full of oddities that seemed forced into the design. It was quite a lot to take in during the grand tour.

"Oh, what a lovely decoration," Pauline said with feigned favor when the engineering students showed her the towering wind turbine in her backyard.

"It's not just for decoration," the students beamed. "It's what's going to generate electricity to help power your house."

"Well, if it lowers my utility bills," Pauline told them, trying to look on the bright side, "then I love it."

Then, a little later in the tour, the marine biology students anxiously showed Pauline how they had turned the kitchen's island into a fish tank.

"Well now," Pauline stuttered, "isn't that... different."

"What better place to include our tropical fish than as part of your *island,*" the students cheered. "You do like fish, don't you?"

"Oh yes," Pauline reassured them. Then, eying her new set of pots and pans, she added almost subconsciously, "Braised, especially."

The marine biology students glared at each other and winced.

However, despite the house's occasional unusualness (like the device installed above the shower by the meteorology students, which emitted the clouds, lights, and sounds of a thunderstorm every time the water was turned on), it was a house—a blessing the Coopers gave thanks for in their daily prayers together. As a token of their gratitude (and because Pauline loved to cook), they started a tradition of hosting Mr. Coy and Paige for dinner once a week. She also asked them to bring along a guest, preferably a member of the staff so that they could all gradually get to know each other over time.

"This looks delicious, Mrs. Cooper," Paige said of the chicken and dumplings that Pauline made for their first meal together.

"Thank you, dear," Pauline returned with culinary pride. "Now, we have a rule in this family that we always serve our guests first, so if you'll please hand me your plate…"

She reached out her hand toward Missy, the staff member whom Mr. Coy had invited to join them this week.

"And what is it you do at the Manor?" Pauline asked, taking her plate.

"I mostly just take Paige to and from school," Missy answered politely.

"Then you must be enjoying the extra-long spring break that these three have been taking," Pauline observed, nodding at the Tybee High students at the table.

"Well, yes," Missy smiled, "but Mr. Coy keeps me busy. He's always got something for us to do. Isn't that right, sir?" She glanced at him, having provided the perfect segue for him to share something that the others did not yet know.

"Quite right," Coy took over, "which is why I've asked Missy to start staying the whole school day with the kids—you know, to keep an eye on them."

"You mean she's going to follow us around all day?" Ana wondered with teenage theatrics. "Like our bodyguard?"

"More or less," Coy said between bites.

"Cool," Ana said, shrugging approvingly at Paige.

"I figure she can get a job as one of the supervisors," Coy explained. "Schools always need more narks, don't they?"

"I think that's a wonderful idea," Pauline breathed with relief. "Now that things are finally settling down around here, I think it's time for the children to return to school. I mean, they've been gone for more than two weeks, and there's little more than a month left until the end of the school year." She was directing her words to Missy as a sort of job description. "I've just been worried if it's, you know, safe for them to go back. I'm sure Mr. Coy has told you all about the problems we've had in the past with certain individuals at that school." (Mr. Coy scrunched his face, straining to remember if he had mentioned anything to Missy, though it was obvious he hadn't.) "I mean, Mr. Quirk was more dimwitted than dangerous, of course, but he and Principal Stone still managed to tie me to the front of a speedboat that plunged headlong into bubbling water, which was almost as bad as when Miss Carmen kidnapped us, then took us to the mouth of an active volcano and threatened to throw us in. And now, with our home being attacked—" Pauline was rambling now, more so speaking to herself than anyone in particular.

"Mom," Ana gently prod, trying to bring Pauline back to the table.

"—What I'm trying to say is," Pauline continued, finally taking a breath, "I'm glad you're here. I considered becoming a volunteer myself at the school."

At this idea, Ana discreetly turned to Missy and silently mouthed, "NO!"

Missy grinned. "You don't need to worry," placing her hand gently on Pauline's arm. "I'm sure I can handle things."

There was certainly more to Missy than met the eye. She was not a young person, but neither was she very old. Her wavy, shoulder-length hair was stricken with gray in parts, which her self-esteem told her to embrace rather than hide. Like a well-prepared steak, her tough and wrinkled face was only the outer layer of something rare and tender inside. She was a thick woman, more short than tall, with a build like one of those oversized armchairs you'd find in a mountain lodge, heavy and stable. Mr. Coy summed it up best when he called Missy a "beefy old gal."

As was Pauline's hope, more was learned about this week's guest as the evening wore on. Missy had been raised under harsh conditions in a hostile neighborhood of a large city in another state. Her parents were delinquents and her brothers thugs, so she learned at a very young age how to be tough and fend for herself. She went to work more than school, and her paychecks paid for her family's addictions and legal fees. More than anything, she wanted to beat the odds and make something of herself, but opportunity lived on the other side of the tracks.

Stuck in this endless cycle, she was about to give up on life when she met a delightful woman named Helen. Helen had come to the department store where Missy worked to buy some new clothes. As Helen tried on different outfits, she got to know Missy. Helen was distraught to find such a promising person stuck in such dead-end circumstances. Soon thereafter, Helen began to ask for clothes in a size that felt baggy on her but would probably fit just right on Missy. She told Missy she wasn't much into style and would go with whatever Missy liked best. Helen ended up purchasing bags and bags of apparel and accessories. Then, after Missy finished the transaction, Helen told her, "It's all yours."

Awestruck, Missy listened as Helen told her how she wanted to sponsor Missy to go to college. She would help her apply to an out-of-state school, far from the turmoil of her ravaged home. They would set up a joint bank account to provide her with the necessary funds while she continued to work part-time. And it would all begin as soon as she was ready.

"And boy, was I ready!" Missy recounted to the group at the table. "In the weeks before I left, I became good friends with Helen and her husband." She playfully elbowed Mr. Coy, whose eyes seemed to glisten ever since the name of his wife was said. "I went off to school and studied criminal justice, of all things. After graduating—"

"At the top of her class," Coy added.

Blushing, Missy continued, "—the Coys offered me a job as their, well…," turning to Ana, "as their bodyguard, I guess. They said they needed someone to protect them during their humanitarian trips all over the world."

"She's good with guns," Coy snuck in.

"Sweet!" Ana cheered. "Can you teach me?"

"I'm afraid that's up to your mother," Missy told her, chuckling.

There was something about Missy that Pauline really liked. Actually, there were many things. And so Pauline shocked everyone when she said "We'll see" as she got up to take her dishes to the sink, marking the end of the meal.

Of course, Ret was also present at dinner, though he had neither said one word nor taken one bite. He wasn't eating much these days, claiming he was either not hungry or had lost his appetite. But Pauline knew better; she knew Ret had a cornucopia of things to chew on in his mind. When she saw his untouched plate of chicken and dumplings by the sink, she turned around to confront him, but Ret had already left the room.

The best thing about going back to school the next day was in the "going" part: the Coopers finally got to see how the Coys crossed Little Tybee Creek onto the mainland. Although some residents referred to the creek as the Wilmington River, it fell somewhere in between. It was less than a thousand feet wide and looked more like a snake-shaped extension of the ocean, completely surrounding Little Tybee Island. And the only way to cross it was by kayak—unless, of course, you've ever *Ben Coy.*

The route to school began in the hangar, that big underground room that served as the hub for all transportation to and from the Manor. Until now, however, the Coopers never knew it had an upper level. The descending elevator stopped much sooner than usual, and the three students stepped out, escorted by their chauffeur, Missy. Not far in front of them was the car, just a normal, four-door vehicle. However, it sat in the middle of a wide, circular platform that was suspended in the air, hanging by a series of cables that attached to the nearby ceiling. Connected to the platform was a long bridge that ended at the far wall.

Ana couldn't help herself: "Missy, is this the Batcave?"

Ret took the long way to the car so he could peek over the edge of the platform. The scene below him was dark, so he snapped his fingers and sent a tiny fireball over the edge. It was a long time before it hit the ground.

As with most departures from the hangar, this one began at high speeds with no sign of an exit at the wall ahead. But, as always, a door appeared. Where the suspended bridge ended, a large, rectangular slice of the wall became disconnected at its top and, hinging at the base, fell flat on the ground outside like a ramp. The speeding car flew out of the hangar and into daylight. Launching from the upper reaches of the underground hangar meant they exited at ground level.

What happened next was a feat of mechanical engineering that took less than ten seconds to experience. Ret and Ana watched with great interest as two halves of a long, steel bridge began to rise from the water, each attached at one bank of the creek. They were triangular at first, resembling a still-wrapped Toblerone chocolate bar. Once they had straightened out horizontally, they connected at the middle of the creek, and then the two slanted sides folded outward to become vertical walls. The car quickly crossed a short strip of dirt and then, without any bumps in the road, entered this submerged, walled bridge. It looked like one of those moving walkways you might see at an airport. It rested in the water just deep enough so that the walls running along either side rose just above the surface to prevent water from spilling inside. The bridge was not above the water—it was *in* the water, below the surface—and the walls kept the water out.

From the shore, the only thing a bystander may have noticed was a strip of metal shining from bank to bank, which likely would have been shrugged off as nothing more than a shimmering reflection of the afternoon sun on the rippled water. The presence of a car was completely undetectable at ground level.

They reached the end of the bridge, hit the ramp, and bounced onto a little-used road named Alley Street that came right out to the sand. Ret looked behind them to watch the fold-away bridge close into a tight triangle and then break in half before sinking out of sight. It was yet another impressive display of Coy ingenuity.

"Sure beats the kayak," Ana remarked.

Not until first period (when his teacher asked him if he was a new student) did Ret realize this was his first appearance at school since becoming "normal-looking," as Ana called it. Everyone seemed to take notice. Guys he had never met before complimented him on his new contact lenses and his dyed hair. Girls he had never spoken to told him how much they liked his spray tan. And everyone expressed sympathy for his house that "exploded." It seemed Ret was the talk of the whole school.

"Don't let it go to your head, bub," Ana warned him.

Meanwhile, Missy was having a hard time locating Principal Stone. No one in the front office knew where he was, so everyone referred her to Mr. Kirkpatrick, the assistant principal. When Missy arrived at his office, she found a little man who looked terribly stressed out.

"Excuse me," Missy said politely as she knocked on his door, "I'm looking for Principal Stone."

Without so much as glancing away from what he was doing, Mr. Kirkpatrick replied stalely, "He resigned."

"Oh," said Missy. Although it was news she hadn't been ready for, she was quick on the draw. "Then I suppose that makes you the interim principal, doesn't it?"

"I suppose so," he sighed heavily, buried in a mess of papers. "Just found out this morning. Superintendent called, told me Stone 'went into the wilderness,' whatever that means. Sounds kind of nice right about now, actually."

"In that case, sir," Missy persisted, "I'm wondering if you can help me."

"Can't say I'm surprised," Kirkpatrick complained loudly, ignoring the request for help from the portly woman standing in his doorway. "I've been filling in for that weasel since day one. Worst principal I've ever worked with." He was picking up thick stacks of paper and slamming them on his cluttered desk, sending pencils and paperclips into the air. "Still don't know how he got the job. And now he just up and leaves." His telephone rang, and he knocked it off his desk into the trashcan. "Good thing Kirkpatrick the hero is here to save the day yet again."

"Sir, I'm here to apply for a job as a supervisor on campus," Missy told him.

"What?" he asked, looking up at her for the first time.

"You know, a nark?"

"Oh," he said, rubbing his forehead. "Sure, sure. I can use all the help I can get. Just watch out for the boys' restroom: one of the urinals floods."

"Got it." Missy left the doorway and said to herself, "That was easy. Didn't even have to flash my Uzi."

In the days that followed, the news of Principal Stone's sudden resignation had a troubling effect on the Coys and Coopers. It especially bothered Mr. Coy, who felt a certain duty to protect not only his own daughter but also the mother and her two children who now lived on his property. The fact that Lye had come right in their own backyard and destroyed the Coopers' home put everyone on alert, wondering if or when or how he might strike next.

Mr. Coy even paid a visit to the Stone residence—this time by car—with no intention of going (or breaking) in. He just wanted to drive by and scope things out. So over to Skidaway Island he went, slowing to a stop under the shade of a large oak tree across the dusty street from the main gate of the house. It looked abandoned, its windows dark and its lawn as tall as prairie grass. Using a device that sent out radio waves, he determined there was nothing moving inside the house, and then, switching to thermal mode, concluded the place was cold. The Stones had fled. But why?

Unable to sleep at night, Mr. Coy felt he should contact his good friend, Thorne. They had served together in the Navy years ago. Thorne went on to start his own international business, specializing in the installation and implementation of communications and defense systems. Coy told him he had a sizeable project for him at the Manor if he was up to it. Thorne was intrigued and arrived within a few days.

Thorne flew in on his own plane, a small float-plane that had two buoyant pontoons underneath the fuselage to keep it afloat when landing on water. He came in off the coast of Little Tybee and then taxied up the creek to the backside of the island. Then he moored the plane to the shore and hiked up the bluff to the Manor.

"What is your name?" a woman's voice asked when Thorne approached the main gate.

"Walter Thorne," he replied to the air.

"Please wait while I locate your name on the guest list." Somewhere inside the Manor, a maid was consulting the guest list, a job that once belonged to the Coys' late butler, Ivan. Within seconds, the maid found Thorne's name on the list (which only contained a grand total of four) and said, "Welcome to Coy Manor, Mr. Thorne."

The gate parted, and before Thorne had made it halfway up the long walk, the double doors opened, and Mr. Coy hurried out to greet his old comrade.

"You haven't aged a bit," Thorne observed after a hearty embrace.

"Too bad I can't say the same about you!" Coy ribbed, slapping him on the back. "Gray hair already?"

"That's what two teenagers will do to you," Thorne sighed. "They're not all as wonderful as your Paige, I'm sure."

"Yes, well, you and I both know she gets that from her mother," Coy said. "Come, come; I'll let you tell her in person. You're just in time for dinner. You'll be my guest for this week."

Mr. Coy followed his nose and led Thorne across the grounds to the Cooper home, where Pauline was just taking the rolls out of the oven. Paige was already there, helping Ana set the table.

"They're here," Pauline said when the knock came at the door. "Ana, will you get Ret, please?"

"Sure," Ana obeyed. Then she turned and yelled, "Ret! Dinner's ready!"

"*I* could've done *that,*" Pauline muttered to Paige. "Will you please let your father in, honey?"

"Is that steak I smell?" Coy said as he entered. "Thorne, you're in for a treat. Pauline is almost as good a chef as I am."

"Almost," Pauline humored him as she came to greet this week's guest, wiping her hands on a towel.

"This is Walter Thorne," Coy introduced, "an old friend from the Navy."

"He doesn't look *old* to me," Pauline exchanged with a welcoming smile. "Nice to meet you, Walter." Then, extending her hand, she introduced herself, "Pauline Cooper."

"Please, Ms. Cooper, call me Thorne," he said kindly, taking her hand. "No one's called me Walter since I joined the Navy—hasn't sounded right ever since. I'm not very fond of the name Walter now, actually."

"Very well, *Thorne,*" Pauline said pleasantly. "And this is my daughter Ana and my son Ret."

Thorne's face suddenly clouded over. He stared at Ret with concern, worry even. Everyone noticed and fell silent.

"Ret Cooper?" Thorne asked, as if to make sure he had heard correctly. "Is that your name?" It was a name that obviously wasn't new to him.

Thorne's eyes fell down. He glanced to the left and then to the right. He was looking at Ret's hands hanging at his sides, clearly searching for scars.

Instantly distrustful of this newcomer, Ret's mind gathered all the silverware that was on the table and brought each piece within an inch of Thorne's face. Pauline and the girls let out stifled squeals as the cutlery came whizzing by them. Wide-eyed, Thorne froze with fear, staring at the steak knives in particular.

"Whoa, Ret," Coy intervened, as if calming a frenzied horse. "Let's hear him out before you impale him."

With his brow furrowed in doubt, Ret relinquished the utensils, returning each one to its proper place without ever taking an eye off Thorne.

"Alright, *Walter,*" Coy said with suspicion, purposely calling him by his first name. "What have you heard?"

"You must understand, I mean you no harm," Thorne said respectfully, breathing a sigh of relief. "A few weeks ago, I was in New York at a meeting of the United Nations. I am not a member of the General Assembly but was invited to attend due to my background. It was an emergency meeting, held in response to the events going on in Saharan Africa. We learned what really happened, not only there but also in the Bermuda Triangle and at Easter Island—how each place was hiding some kind of element—and that a person named Ret Cooper was to blame."

"What?" Coy said in shock. "How did they find out? Who told you this?"

"It was some person from the UN community," Thorne recalled. "His name was Lionel Zarbock. Do you know him?"

Pauline's jaw dropped. Paige and Ana glared at each other. Mr. Coy stared at Ret with a face that said "I thought so" more than "I told you so." Ret could feel Mr. Coy's gaze, so he avoided it.

"Yes, we know him," Coy answered, "though apparently not well enough. What else did he say, Thorne?"

"A lot. He had prepared a whole slideshow. He vilified Ret—made him enemy number-one. This guy, Lionel Zarbock, convinced everyone at the UN to pretty much let him do whatever he wants to prevent Ret from finding any more of those element things. Look, Ben," Thorne said, wrapping up, "I'm not sure what this is all about, but I think it's safe to say"—jabbing his thumb toward Ret—"this young man's got some big problems on his hands," which, whether he meant it or not, was very profound.

"Yes, we know," said Coy painfully.

"Lionel," Pauline spoke, as if trying to process an ugly reality, "he betrayed us—betrayed us all! Oh, who can we trust?"

Much to everyone's surprise, Ret left the group and sat at the dinner table. He served himself a generous helping and started chowing down. The others followed, their moods subdued and conversation light. It wasn't long before Ret slid a second steak onto his plate, then another hefty scoop of mashed potatoes and two more rolls. He wasn't starving; he was loading up. You see, he had a plan—a sort of last-resort plan that he had been considering for several weeks but couldn't quite bring himself to carry out. Until now. The news shared by Thorne had pushed Ret over the edge. And so he kept eating until he was nice and full, well aware that he might not eat another one of Pauline's home-cooked meals ever again.

CHAPTER 3

THE ORPHAN'S SONG

Ret was leaving—for good. That was his plan. This Oracle business was far too dangerous, and he cared about his loved ones too much to keep them at risk any longer. Everything was spiraling out of control now, and he was the cause of it, so he would go. Where? He didn't know, just away—far, far away from everyone and everything. Whatever he touched turned to ruin; whatever he did caused someone harm. He, and he alone, was the common ingredient that continued to sour every recipe. And so, he decided, it was *he* who needed to go.

After dinner, Ret went to his room, closed the door, and flopped on his bed. Staring at the ceiling, he could hear occasional groans from his stomach, overwhelmed by its first real meal in weeks. He listened to the sighs and "byes" as the Coys left with Thorne, then to the cling and clang as Pauline and Ana cleaned up. Not much later, he heard the mother and daughter bid good-night to each other and head into their respective rooms.

Ret waited for them to fall fast asleep. He pondered on what he was about to do and wondered if it might not be the best decision after all. He glanced out his window, which he always kept open. The breeze was cool and salty. A full moon hung low in the sky. He watched a thin haze obscure the moon and, for a moment, thought it was leftover smoke still rising from the burned-down Cooper home. It was just the usual fog rolling in from the ocean, but Ret took it as a sign.

He quietly gathered a few provisions and stuffed them in a backpack. He tiptoed from his room and entered the dark hallway. He stopped in front of the cracked door to Pauline's room and peered inside. There was his devoted caretaker. She looked especially lonely, curled up by herself on one side of her large bed. It was Ret's fault her husband wasn't there.

Then he arrived at Ana's door, also ajar. He stole a glance inside. Ana lay sprawled out on her bed, a slight snore disrupting the silence. Ret couldn't help but smile. She had been a friend to him when no one else was. He would miss her quiet optimism and not-so-quiet confidence.

As he left the hall, the tear in Ret's eye advised him to at least leave a note. He knew Pauline would be worried sick, thinking he had been kidnapped or something. So he kept it simple:

I'm going away. I don't know where, but I'll be okay. It's better for everyone. Sorry for all the trouble I've caused. Thank you for everything you've done for me. I'll miss my only family. It's time for all of us to move on.

   Ret

He went out the front door, then locked it from the outside by mentally sliding the deadbolt. He jogged to the Manor's nearest gate, used his brain to bend the bars apart wide enough for him to slip through, and then bent them back into place. He found his trusty kayak and paddled to the mainland (still his preferred way to cross the creek), then briskly walked over a house-turned-ash-heap and didn't look back. He was moving on.

Ret made his way north to the main road with an unusual bounce in his step. He felt lighter, unfettered from the burdens he was leaving behind. Like a recently released prisoner, he breathed in the fresh air and exhaled with freedom. There was no one to hold him back, no strings to tie him down, no Oracle to tell him what to do. He was a new man.

He waltzed further into town. The streets were empty. The only sound that stirred the nighttime silence was the soft and pleasant murmur of the waves breaking on the beach a few blocks away. The digital marquees of the periodic bank or church along the strip told him the time was midnight and the temperature a balmy 62 degrees, which free information he would need to utilize in the future since he purposely left his cell phone out of his meager provisions. He wanted as few reminders of his former life as possible. He was starting over—a fresh, clean slate.

Ret was just about to cross Center Street when he heard a noise. It was the voice of a man, and he was singing. It wasn't the deep, rich voice of a big-bellied man; no, it was soft and smooth and just as beautiful.

Curious, Ret turned east down Center Street and walked a few yards, following his ears. The sweet melody was coming from behind the orphanage. He went around back and saw a young man sitting on the first few steps of the bottommost ladder of the building's fire escape. Even though his back was to Ret, he could tell it was Leo, gazing out over the dark ocean and into the black sky. Ret listened as Leo sang:

> *I fear the darkness in the night.*
> *I'm alone, there's no one but me.*
> *Clearly outnumbered and severely encumbered*
> *By the darkness in all that I see.*

But there's a light—a light in the night!
A light I never saw was there:
The sunshine concealed it, now the darkness
    revealed it.
How could I miss a light so fair?

There are times when I see no hope
For this world of heartache and sin.
Too hard to correct it, so I'll just neglect it,
Too much darkness for light to win.

But there's a light—a light in the night!
I'm not alone; there're legions like me.
And the darker the night grows, the starker each
    light glows.
Oh, these lights in the night—now I see!

Ret was sad when Leo's last word was carried by the wind out to sea. Even though he didn't really understand it, he didn't want it to end. It was a powerful piece of music, its message and melody a balm for the wounded soul.

Finally, Ret said, "That was amazing."

Startled, Leo jolted with surprise and almost fell off the ladder.

"Ret?!" Leo wondered, straightening his glasses. "What are *you* doing here?"

"Listening to you sing," Ret told him, sidestepping the real reason.

"Oh, you heard that?" Leo winced with embarrassment.

"It was beautiful," Ret complimented him.

"Yeah, well, tell that to Mrs. Eisner," Leo said with a hint of scorn.

"Who's she?"

"She's the choir teacher at school," Leo explained, climbing down the ladder to the ground. "For the last two years, I've been trying to get into the school choral group, but every time I try out, Mrs. Eisner tells me I ain't ready—tells me I need to 'suppress the drawl.' And I try to, but it's hard."

"What about country music?" Ret suggested, somewhat in jest.

"Nah, I know what the real reason is," Leo carried on. "It's the other students; I don't think they like me much—you know, me being an orphan and all."

"You're an orphan?" Ret asked in disbelief.

"Didn't Ana tell you?"

"No," Ret said, "I had no idea."

"Well, now you know," Leo said with humiliation. He stepped close to the building and, tapping on the brick, said sarcastically, "Home sweet home."

"What happened to your parents?" Ret inquired delicately, figuring it was likely a sensitive subject. If

Leo had a dollar for every time someone asked him that question, he wouldn't still live at the orphanage. He usually based the depth of his answer on the level of genuine interest he perceived in the asker, so he would spare no details with his good friend Ret.

"They died before I was born," Leo began, taking a seat on the lowest rung of the escape's ladder. "Mom was eight months pregnant with me when she and Dad got in a car accident. They were hit by a drunk driver. Dad died instantly. Mom was in critical condition, so she was flown to the nearest hospital. The doctors told her they could either save her or her child but not both. And, well, we know which one she chose."

"She gave her life for you," Ret pointed out, himself amazed.

"She died during labor," Leo continued. "The doctors barely got me out in time. This is all according to Peggy Sue, of course."

"Who's that? A relative?"

"Peggy Sue? No," Leo chuckled. "She's the director here at the orphanage. She's the one who took me home from the hospital, and I've been here ever since. She said my folks had no living relatives."

"I'm really sorry to hear that, Leo," Ret said.

"It ain't so bad," Leo tried to say bravely, though amid a tear-born sniffle, "especially when you don't know no better. At least I don't have any memories of my parents; then it'd be really hard." Ret had yet another thing in common with Leo. "Peggy Sue—she's been real good to me. And the other orphans—well, I reckon they think I'm some kind of older brother to them. I *am* the oldest one in the mix."

"Are there a lot of others?" Ret wondered, hoping there weren't.

"We're always full," Leo said, almost with pride. "Peggy Sue says she's never seen a night when a bed wasn't being slept in. But we like it that way; we're like a family. It's hard to say goodbye when one of us gets selected."

"Selected?"

"That's what we call it when someone wants to adopt one of us," Leo defined.

"Does that happen often?" Ret asked, hoping it did.

"Not as often as it could," Leo stated. "There are more orphans in the world than people willing to be foster parents, seems like."

"Is that why you've…never been…, you know…"

"Adopted? No," Leo said. "I reckon there're lots of reasons. When I was young, folks didn't favor my story much—too much baggage, would cause too much drama when they had to tell me down the road. Some worried I'd been messed up in the womb from the crash and might have problems later on in life. Then I started growing, but not enough: I was too short, too skinny, wouldn't be very promising in sports. Now I'm just plain too old. The first thing they think when they see me is, 'Why is he still here? There must be a good reason why.' Can't blame them; no one wants a kid who's been a stray all his life—too ingrained, impossible to fix. That's what I hear them say, anyway. We all listen to what they tell Peggy Sue come decision time. They don't know it, but the walls are thin."

"Have you ever tried singing for any of them that come in?" Ret proposed. "I'm sure you'd win them over in a heartbeat if you did *that*."

"Ah, singing," Leo beamed. "My one true love. When I'm feeling down, singing always cheers me up. That song you just heard—it's my favorite. I call it 'A Light in the Night.' Came up with the whole thing myself."

"Really?" Ret said, impressed.

"Sure did," Leo cheered. "Sometimes I get kind of discouraged about life. It's hard to see the good in the world when there's so much bad all the time. I watch these babies come into the orphanage; every one of them has a story, and they usually ain't good ones. True, some ain't as bad as others, but I reckon no story is good when it leaves a child parentless. I watch Peggy Sue take them in, one after the other, and I listen to each story. And do you know what I've noticed? Do you know what they all have in common?"

Ret knew, but he didn't yet know that he knew.

"They all should have been prevented. Not one of them kids *had* to be given up. This one 'has a daddy who hits'—well, dad, stop hitting. Or a young gal comes in and says she wants her precious child to 'have a better life'—well, mom, clean up *your* life. Some say they're too poor; well, *I* say an orphan lives in rags anyway, might as well do so with its own mother. Ironically, *I*'ve got the best story in the house, as sad as it is—and my mom was a heroine, she wasn't *addicted* to it. But my situation could have been avoided, too: if the drunk hadn't gotten drunk. In each case, someone was irresponsible and didn't want to change; someone up the chain was selfish and caused problems for someone else down the road. Someone had a bad heart, and it broke someone else's."

Ret could feel the weight that he was running away from beginning to creep back on his shoulders. Leo's story, with its harsh realities from margin to margin, was exactly the kind of stuff Ret was trying to escape. He wanted to forget that the world needed curing and, instead, try to live his own life.

"But there's a light!" Leo said softly. "A light in the night!" Ret looked at Leo like he was talking crazy. And there, on Leo's tear-strewn face, was a big smile.

"How can you say that?" Ret asked earnestly. "How can *you*, of all people, be so…so happy?"

"Because I'm not alone," Leo continued to quote from his own composition. "There're legions like me."

Ret shook his head, not understanding.

"When dark things happen to us, we have a choice," Leo taught. "We can either hold onto it or we can let it go. If we hold onto it, it will fester inside of us and turn us dark inside. But if we let it go, we can use its energy in a positive way to create something beautiful. Like what my mother did: something truly dark happened to her, through no fault of her own. She could have become bitter and angry. She could have been selfish and saved her own life. But she didn't. She let go of the bad and, instead, did something beautiful, sacrificing herself for her child. She transferred that positive energy to me, and it brings me light even in my darkest nights."

There seemed to be a metaphor at work here, but Ret wasn't catching on. He wasn't in the mood for interpretive poetry. If Leo could relate his discourse to science, *then* Ret would understand.

"So where are you going?" Leo asked, having seen Ret's backpack.

"Oh, I don't know," Ret told him the truth, suddenly ready to be on his way.

"You don't know?" Leo laughed.

"I'm going somewhere," Ret asserted, "I just don't know where yet."

"Are you going to find the next element?" Leo wondered with great interest. "Has a new scar appeared?"

"If it has, I don't care," Ret declared coldly.

"Oh," Leo said, deflated.

"Look, I've got to go," Ret told him, preparing to head off on his way to somewhere. "Thanks, Leo. It was nice talking to you."

"You, too." Then, after Ret had paced several yards away, Leo called out to him, "Hey, Ret: I hope you find your light in the night!"

Annoyed by the continued metaphor, Ret shouted back, "Sure," then muttered under his breath, "whatever."

Ret's sudden departure came as a disappointment to everyone but not really as a surprise. They had all seen a visible heaviness fall over him in recent weeks, so it almost made sense when they learned he was walking away from it all—or hopefully just taking a quick break from it. The girls fully expected Ret to return in no time, equipped with a new life-plan that he had outlined during his few days of fresh air. So, in the meantime, that's what they tried to do as well: put the past behind them and live a normal life.

Everyone except Mr. Coy, that is. He had never favored "normal" very much in his life—too dull, too boring. Now that Ret wasn't around (and had taken his scars with him), Mr. Coy had little hope of getting fresh clues to help him in his now-solo quest to fill the Oracle. He had no way of figuring out which element wanted to be found next or where in the world it was hidden, not to mention how he would collect it without Ret. In fact, Mr. Coy didn't even know what the next element *was*.

But there was one piece of information he did have.

"No. Absolutely not." He shuddered at the thought.

But it was his one and only lead.

"I can't go back there. I won't."

But, no matter how many times he pushed it out of his mind, it kept coming back.

For, you see, Mr. Coy may not have known what the next scar was, but he did know what *one* of the next scars was. It was the scar that had appeared on Ret's hand after they had escaped from Fire Island in the hot-air balloon and were chasing Lye's fleet of ships across the Pacific Ocean. It was the scar that looked somewhat like a Ferris wheel, as Ret had described it to Principal Stone during their question-and-answer session that night at the Crusty Chicken. It was the scar, to Mr. Coy's dismay, that probably shared some connection with the colorful island they saw from the balloon that day — the same island that, years before, had led to the death of his dear wife, Helen; the same island where, just months ago, Pauline, Ishmael, and Lydia had rescued Lionel and seen the brainwashed Jaret; the same island that Lye called Waters Deep.

Ah yes, *that* island: a place Mr. Coy had sworn never to revisit. But now, it seemed he had little choice.

He could either face his fears and set sail for that Pacific isle, or he could stuff the Oracle in a box and hope Ret would return someday.

Compared to the former, the latter didn't sound so bad.

And how appropriate! Here was yet another instance of the Oracle jamming its followers between a rock and a hard place. It had a knack for making people uncomfortable. It didn't matter who those people were — the Oracle would find a way to test anyone to the core. It was as if it knew people — like it could read individual hearts and pick out the weak points of each. In Mr. Coy's case, there was one thing in the known universe that he wished to avoid more than anything else — one thing that he never wanted to rehash: his wife's death, which, as he understood it, had been caused by him. But, never fail, here was the Oracle unburying the hatchet and unstitching the wound, honing in with miraculous precision on the one thing that would try his heart like nothing else could. Had the Oracle asked him instead to climb Mount Everest blindfolded or swim the English Channel covered in shark bait, Mr. Coy would have jumped at the alternative and relished the challenge. But relive his wife's demise? Was there no other way?

No, for such was the way of the Oracle.

Lucky for Mr. Coy, there was always something going on at the Manor to take his mind off such unpleasant thoughts. His old naval pal, Walter Thorne, had recently concluded his brief, consultative visit and promised to return very soon to get started on the grandiose project that Mr. Coy was hiring him to carry out: the installation of a state-of-the-art defense and communications system, capable of protecting the Manor from just about anything. Ever since Lye's brazen attack on the Coopers' home, Mr. Coy had been feeling vulnerable, and now that Lionel had labeled Ret as enemy number-one to governments the world over, he felt doubly so.

Within days, Thorne returned in his floatplane, accompanied by his son, Dusty, a handsome, strapping young man who had finished high school just a few days earlier. Thorne had many reasons for bringing his offspring along. For one, he needed the manpower. Moreover, Dusty wasn't exactly the most motivated adolescent (for example, he didn't have any plans for his future), so Thorne hoped his boy might meet a craftsman or observe a trade while at the Manor that would pique his interest in a field of study. Truth be told, however, Thorne knew his son had a penchant for mischief, so, most of all, he brought him along in an effort to keep him out of trouble.

By Coy's choosing, Dusty was the guest of honor at that week's dinner with the Coopers.

"Welcome to our home, Dusty," Pauline told the lad after his father introduced him. "I'm Mrs. Cooper, and this is my daughter, Ana."

"Hey, baby," Dusty cheered as soon as he laid eyes on Ana. Thorne smacked his son on the back of his head. Mr. Coy chuckled while Ana blushed. Pauline promptly ushered everyone to the table, making sure to seat her newest guest as far from her daughter as possible.

The adults carried the dinner conversation: first, the weather; then Missy observed the approaching end of Tybee High's school year; Thorne gave an update on his work; Mr. Coy asked if the Coopers' home was functioning properly. There was no talk of Ret or the Oracle—just normal, boring stuff.

Paige didn't say much at all, too busy playing with the peas on her plate. Ever since Ret left, she had taken over for him as the forlorn and fasting appendage at the table. She missed him, worried about him. And she didn't like how Dusty was sitting in Ret's seat.

But Dusty didn't seem to care. No, he was busy stealing glances at Ana, who was eating it up. The two of them seemed to be carrying on a conversation of their own, communicated entirely through facial expressions. At one point, Dusty slouched in his chair to see if he could reach far enough to play footsy with Ana. The feet he found felt surprisingly large, old, and wrinkly. Come to find out, they were Missy's.

In the weeks that followed, the Manor's unparalleled defense system began to take shape. Like most other things on the property, it was coming along in true Coy fashion, meaning it had a little bit of everything: guns and garrisons, bullets and bunkers, tanks and turrets. The more modern antiaircraft devices stood within the crenelated battlements of yesteryear. Next to the free electron laser, which produced an energy stream sufficient to sabotage incoming missiles, Mr. Coy positioned a centuries-old cannon from the Manor's antiques department. A medieval catapult looked a little out of place by the satellite dishes. But, as Mr. Coy liked to tell his students, "Anachronisms make for a well-rounded education."

Of course, there weren't any nuclear weapons on the premises; Mr. Coy didn't want such volatile things under his care.

As the project neared completion, Mr. Coy called for a sort of hands-on lecture in the command center. This was the place that served as the gateway to all inter-action with the defense and communications network. There were computers and televisions, servers and routers, and lots and lots of colorful cables. Mr. Coy liked to refer to it as "the brain," which was fitting since he arranged for it to be built inside a protective enclosure that looked like a human skull. It sat deep within the Manor, purposely placed in a spot that would be most difficult for enemies to enter or for their weapons to hit.

Leading the group of students he had invited, Mr. Coy walked out of the elevator and up to the giant skull.

They stopped in front of its two front teeth, which were actually the double doors of the command center's main entrance. To the right of the doors, there was a neuroscope attached to the wall. Mr. Coy stepped toward it and positioned his head between the device's two prongs so that one rested on each temple of his forehead. The doors then promptly opened. Although the students couldn't tell, the neuroscope had scanned Coy's own brain, a secure way to limit access into the building.

The group found Thorne on the second floor, sitting in a wheeled chair in front of an array of electronic machines. He was gazing out the nearby window, which was actually one of the empty eye sockets of the fabricated skull. Coy motioned for the students to fan out and peruse the room, which they excitedly did. They quickly realized this single, remote location made it possible for them to have eyes, ears, and even hands just about anywhere. For example, they could adjust the zoom on the camera at the front gate, fire a grenade from the launcher hidden in the hydrangeas, or engage the emergency mode that sealed off the Manor's every entrance and exit. Or, by rolling across the room, they could watch live footage from one of the cameras hidden in a fake fish swimming offshore, send and receive signals between antennae on earth and satellites in space, or record whispered conversations or store written communications for later analysis. Or, they could simply watch TV, surf the web, and get some hot cocoa from the machine in the corner.

Yet, the command center hummed not only with electrical power but also with another power—an intangible force bestowed upon its users. In very real ways, the system exponentially extended their reach, both physically and mentally. They could control faraway things—change and manipulate them according to their own will. They could intercept things—signals and communications passing by. They could influence certain elements—for good or even for ill. And they could do it all without so much as leaving their chair or having to say "go-go gadget."

In fact, it was a power that became very obvious to the students. They not only marveled at the network's complexities but also at its capabilities. It seemed this power that they were noticing was really an umbrella that included a whole family of related powers. This was at the heart of what the students wanted to know.

"How does a satellite work?"

"What is a radio wave?"

"Can you explain the technology of a cell phone?"

"What is Wi-Fi?"

"Where is the internet?"

After hearing some of these initial queries, Thorne glanced at Coy and said with a chuckle, "These folks sure ask some meaty questions, don't they?"

"They're here to learn," Coy said with a proud smile.

"Well, I don't have *all* the answers," Thorne told him modestly.

"We know, but you have some," said Coy encouragingly. "That's why I hired *you*. We'll appreciate anything you can tell us."

"Alright," Thorne agreed hesitantly, doubting his own knowledge. "You're asking about stuff that's very complicated, but I'll try to put it to you in simple terms, so please don't quote me to any of the people out there who are actual authorities on this stuff." After stating his disclaimer, Thorne took a deep breath and then readjusted his belt under his small gut. Mr. Coy smiled, happy to see Thorne catching the true spirit of the Manor.

Thorne commenced, "The secret to this stuff lies in things that are seen and unseen—understood and not so understood. Take a computer, for example." He sat in a chair and rolled to the nearest computer. "When I write some words on here," he opened a program and started typing a pretend memo, "and then save it and close it," which he did, "what happens to it? Where is it? What is it?"

Thorne wheeled to a different computer and continued, "Let's say I then hop on this computer and retrieve that very same document (since the computers are linked on the same network)." He found the memo and opened it. "Then I go to my email account," he said, opening an internet browser, "and send this file to myself." He turned from the computer and said, "Now I'll get out my laptop to check my email and voila, there it is." He turned around his laptop for all to see the document's icon on the small screen.

"But what *is* it?" he asked. "Is it real? Does it exist? Is it physical matter? It's not ink on paper like a handwritten letter; we can't hold it and fold it and file it away, right? Yet, it must consist of something; why else do inboxes and hard drives fill up? And, if it really is something, then how did it get from the computer to my laptop? There's nothing visibly connecting the two devices, is there? Are there any wires or cables hooked up to my laptop?" He moved his laptop about freely like a magician showing his captive audience that there were no strings attached.

"The secret," Thorne repeated, "lies in things seen and unseen. When I type and save a memo on a computer, the computer encodes it. What that means is the computer has a system (or code) that it uses to assign a value to each different part of the document. So, in this case, it assigns one value to each of the a's, a different one for the b's, and so on even down to the spaces between words. It's like the computer translates it into its own language—a language called a binary code. That means there are only two characters in the code: 0's and 1's. By using 0's and 1's in many different combinations, the computer can assign a unique value to each character." Thorne then quickly executed a series of commands that converted the memo into this binary form he was talking about, which changed the text into a mass of 0's and 1's. "For example," he said, looking at the screen, "this string of code here, 01100001," he highlighted the eight digits, "is computer language for the lower case letter *a*. Each of the eight numbers is called a bit, and eight bits are called a byte."

Recognizing familiar terms, the on-looking students each uttered a quiet "oh" as the information began to click in their minds.

One of them said, "So when a computer says it can hold something like 500 gigabytes, that's how many of those eight-digit bytes of coded information it can hold."

"Precisely," said Thorne.

"Yeah, but what is a byte?" asked another student, in the spirit of the lecture.

"He said it's eight bits."

"I know, but what *is* it? Is it a real, living thing?"

"Yes and no," Thorne grinned. "After I typed and saved my document, the computer encoded it (or translated it) into a bunch of 0's and 1's and then wrote it on its hard drive. Now, the hard drive looks like an old record player: there's a disc with an arm next to it that reaches over to read what's on the disc. The disc in a hard drive is magnetic, and at the end of the arm is an electromagnet. So when I saved the memo, the arm swung out over the disc and passed a current through tiny bits of the disc. The current magnetized each bit either with its north pole up or with its north pole down. (You can change the way a magnet is polarized by changing the flow of the current you pass through it.) So, depending on which of two ways a tiny bit has been magnetized, the electromagnet on the arm either reads it as a 0 or a 1."

"Keep in mind the arm never physically touches the disc," Thorne said. "It gets very, very close, but it doesn't actually 'write' anything on the disc itself. The secret is electromagnetism. The arm can 'write' information on the disc by magnetizing bits of the disc, or it can 'read' information by feeling the way each bit has been polarized. So, to answer your question, I'm not sure if a bit or a byte is real or not. I mean, it is; but, then again, it's not. This memo that I typed is literally just a bunch of tiny bits of a magnetic disc that have been magnetized up or down. So no," Thorne concluded, as if realizing something for the first time, "I guess it's not really physical matter. It's more like a state of being—a state of being that can be changed by an outside force."

"So how did the information wind up on your laptop?" a student pressed.

"Ah," Thorne chirped, still puzzled by his previous thought, "that's another marvel. Let's take a trip into the internet, shall we?" He strode over to a side of the room where there was a closet with a glass door. He opened the door to reveal several racks of complex circuitry. They looked like the innards of a dozen computers, each blinking and humming. A warm air spilled from inside.

"This is the internet," Thorne announced. "Well, a part of it, at least. The truth is, the internet is a lot of places all working together. What you see here is more or less a bunch of hard drives, each storing information that's coming in from all over the Manor. This is Mr. Coy's private data center, but there are data centers all over the world. It's in these data centers where the internet lives. The webpages and blogs and images you see and share on the internet are stored on hard drives like these. The biggest data centers are as big as warehouses, and they're filled with racks like this one — hundreds and hundreds of them. And they're always running, which is why a single data center can use as much energy as a major airport. In fact, some centers even pump water in to keep their systems cool. So the next time someone tells you to go paperless to save the environment, well, doing so might not be as green as they think."

"But I thought the internet was wireless?" someone pointed out.

"Yes and no," Thorne gave his standard answer. "The internet is definitely not entirely wireless. Everything finds itself connected to a cable sooner or later. In fact, there are enormously long cables that cross the oceans."

"Really?"

"Oh yes," Thorne promised. "But that's the *seen* part of the internet. There's an *unseen* part, too. When I send an email from my laptop, my laptop's wireless adapter translates the data into a radio signal and then sends that signal through an antenna. Then the wireless router over there," he pointed to a blinking box on the floor, "picks up that radio signal, decodes it, and sends it through its cables where it becomes part of the internet. So the secret behind this type of wireless communication is radio waves, which are part of the electromagnetic spectrum. The EM spectrum is the range of energy waves that is the backbone of today's Information Age and modern living." Thorne found an online image of the spectrum and brought it up on the screen.

"Radio waves have the least energy but are the biggest, which makes them ideal for carrying data," he said, pointing to the left end of the scale. "As we move along the spectrum, the types of waves increase in energy: microwaves, infrared waves, ultraviolet waves, x-rays, and gamma waves. Visible light, which falls between infrared and ultraviolet, are waves that we can see with our natural eyes. Of course, we don't really see them as waves because they're moving too fast."

"How fast?"

"The speed of light is a dizzying 186,000 miles per second," Thorne answered. "In fact, all EM waves travel at the speed of light. In today's world, there are many waves passing by us all the time; we just can't see most of them. Unlike sounds waves, which need something like air to travel through, EM waves can travel through the vacuum of outer space. They consist of an electric field and a magnetic field that travel together, perpendicular to each other. It might help to compare them to ocean waves. Ocean waves also transmit energy and have two 'fields': one is the horizontal direction the ocean waves are flowing, and the other is the vertical rise and fall of the swells."

"Where do EM waves come from?"

"EM waves are energy," Thorne taught. "They are odorless, tasteless, and have neither weight nor mass, but we *can* feel them sometimes, usually as heat. EM waves are created when charged particles change speed or direction. These charged particles, such as electrons, are microscopic bits of matter that are energized—you know, excited or buzzed. As they move around, they give off their energy before returning to a normal state of being."

"How is information put on an EM wave?"

"That's a great question, the answer to which is beyond my understanding," Thorne admitted. He glanced at Mr. Coy for help, but all Coy did was smile, as if to say, "You're on your own, bud."

"Well," Thorne tried, "if it's anything like how a radio station transmits music, then it has to do with modulating the waves. That's what AM and FM mean: amplitude modulation and frequency modulation, respectively. By changing or varying the height (amplitude) or rate (frequency) of waves, radio stations can create many different channels and send them into the air for your antenna to pick up and translate back into electrical signals."

"So when you send an email wirelessly," one student said, trying to grasp the concept, "there are no real data on the waves?"

Thorne thought for a moment and then told him, "I guess not. Waves are not matter; they're energy, vibrations—a force. But by manipulating them in certain ways, we are able to create a sort of code or language that can be transmitted by them. It's a lot like the bits and bytes of computer storage, actually."

As if trying to find a better comparison to give the students a more complete understanding, Thorne reasoned, "Maybe it's more like the wind. Simply stated, wind is created when air is heated (or energized, excited). As the air heats up, it expands and becomes less dense, causing it to rise above air that is cooler and denser. So, as the warm air rises, cooler air rushes in to fill the space. Of course, we can't see wind, but we can feel it. True, we can see ripples in a flag or dust and debris in a tornado, but our eyes can't see the oxygen and other atoms that make up the air. But, even then, that's not wind—that's air. So what is it that moves the air? What *is* wind?" Thorne was now more speaking to himself, becoming a student of his own lecture. "I suppose it's a force—a result of gravity, perhaps—some force of the natural world."

Thorne was a little unsatisfied with how his discourse was going. It seemed to be leading to more questions. There were some things he honestly did not know the answer to, but there were other things that he couldn't fully explain because *mankind* did not yet know the answers.

"So what's real and what's not so real?" Thorne said, wrapping up his remarks with a broad sigh. "We've discussed some things that are way over my head. I apologize for my lack of knowledge. But you know what? No matter how much we think we know, sooner or later we get to a point where we have to acknowledge there are some things in this world that we just don't understand. Magnetism, electricity, gravity—these are some of the fundamental forces of the universe, and we understand how to use them more than we understand what they are. That's because, by and large, they are phenomena. They are mysteries to man."

Thorne's concluding words got Mr. Coy thinking—not so much about computers and cables, but about elements and Mother Nature's mysteries. He wondered how the Oracle felt toward this seen and unseen energy all around us. The three elements they had already collected—earth, fire, ore—had all been protected by mysteries. Could one of the Oracle's three remaining wedges possibly be for the element of wind? He wished he had Ret and a scar to prove it. Of course, Mr. Coy had *a* scar. Maybe it was finally time for him to face his fears.

"Well, *my* head hurts," Mr. Coy joked, resuming control at the end of the lecture. "Thank you, Mr. Thorne, for leading such a stimulating discussion." Then, turning to the students, "I hope you all took good notes. Class dismissed." The students gradually vacated the room, energized by the things they had just learned.

"This is quite a school you run here, Coy," Thorne said, rubbing his head. "I did my best, but those folks gave me a run for my money."

"Thorne, I need to borrow your plane," Coy told him plainly.

"What for?"

"I need to run an errand," said Coy.

"In a plane?" Thorne smirked.

"It's a long-distance errand," Coy returned smartly.

"Shall I go with you?"

"No," Coy declined, "this is something I need to do alone. But maybe next time."

"Very well," Thorne obliged. He handed over the keys, a little suspicious but well aware that sparing details was Coy's way of living up to his name.

"I'll be back soon," Coy reassured. "Finish up your work and hold down the fort until I return."

"Be safe, Coy."

Mr. Coy gave his old friend an appreciative slap on the back, then took the keys and left the room. Within an hour, Coy had packed a few provisions, visited his Studatory to get a map, and was on his way to a certain island in the south Pacific.

CHAPTER 5

WINDS OF CHANGE

Not long after his midnight chat with Leo the orphan, Ret the runaway reached the city limits of Tybee Island. Even though the small community was the only home he knew, he strode right past the marker without so much as half a glance back. In fact, he quickened his pace, entering on foot the expressway that took him into Savannah just as the sun was rising behind him.

Ret didn't have a particular destination in mind, but he tried not to worry about it. He was turning over a new leaf—many new leaves, actually: one that didn't overthink things, one that didn't agonize over circumstances that were largely out of his control, one that simply went with the flow. It was now his intention to be a completely normal person—run-of-the-mill from here on out—the kind without lofty ambitions or improbable dreams. And although he knew very little about what it must be like to be such a commonplace individual, he was pretty sure the average Joe wasn't stressed out about how to "cure the world."

Deep down inside, however, Ret knew that to graft in a branch with such foreign leaves would betray his core roots. In fact, becoming just another person who refused to challenge the status quo was exactly what this world *didn't* need—it was what it needed less of if it ever wanted to be cured. But, true to his new mantra, Ret tried not to worry about it. Instead, he would graciously let someone else take over the all-consuming task to "fill the Oracle." After all, didn't his entire family line have "the rite" to do so? Ret had already filled it halfway— more than any of his relatives had been willing or able to do. Yes, he had done his part. Now it was time to live his own life.

Using some of the little money he had, Ret boarded a bus that would take him out of town. He rode it to the end of its line, which was in Atlanta, where he spent a day walking around the big, bustling city. It was getting closer to summertime each day, so the days were hot and sticky while the nights were warm and not quite as sticky. He took a nap in a city park before getting on another bus, this time to Birmingham where he, like before, spent the day and got a feel before continuing on.

In Memphis, Ret became a stowaway on a barge that was heading north on the Mississippi River. He marveled at the size of this important waterway, which he had only read about in books. A few days later, when his ride made port in St. Louis, Ret stayed with the cargo and snuck on a train headed first to Indianapolis and then to Columbus.

It was during his time in Ohio's capital city when Ret observed something unusual. He was sitting contentedly on a bench, looking out over the placid waters of the Scioto River with the downtown skyscrapers looming overhead, when a man walked by. This gentleman, wearing a collared shirt and dark slacks, was talking on his cellphone, which was nothing out of the ordinary except for the beam of light that seemed to be shooting out from his phone. The cone-shaped beam started out small and then increased in width the farther it extended away from the man's phone. It was a light shade of red and wasn't exceptionally bright but could still be seen in broad daylight.

Once the man passed, Ret rubbed his eyes and shook his head. Perhaps he was just tired. Maybe his eyes were playing tricks on him. Or, more likely, the flash of the phone's camera had been left on, or it was some special app that turned the phone into a sort of flashlight—Ret had seen that before. Yeah, that was it.

But then it happened again—this time with a woman who had one of those Bluetooth contraptions in her ear. Just as before, Ret could see what looked like a beam of light radiating from the device. He glanced around to see if anyone else was noticing the peculiarity, but they weren't. He reasoned it must be a local thing. And so, trying not to worry about it, he sighed, shrugged his shoulders, and headed for the nearest bus station.

Ret's woes followed him on the road, however. Somewhere outside of Pittsburgh, he saw through the smudgy bus window a metal apparatus in the distance, rising high above the trees. It was one of those communication towers with large drum-looking equipment attached to it, erected most likely for purposes of radio or television. Ret studied it with a stupefied look on his face, for coming from it was not just a single beam but dozens of them, each shooting into the air in all different directions. These rays traveled far across the landscape, out of sight, some so wide that they seemed to fill the entire sky. If they collided with anything, some bounced off like light being reflected on a mirror while others passed through the medium without obstruction. A few even washed over the highway, getting caught inside the bus and bouncing off the walls, but no one except Ret paid any attention to them.

By this point, Ret was certain he needed glasses. He shut his eyes and put his hands over them, hoping a few hours of rest would fix his vision problems. But, even with his eyes closed, he could still see the rays — well, sort of. Of course, he couldn't really see anything, but he could sense things rushing by him at incredibly high speeds. They were like vibrations or tiny, tiny waves, whizzing all around him. And the more he concentrated on them, the more he felt like he was moving with them. He grew a little dizzy and got a little scared. It was like coming under a trance or falling into the twilight zone. For a moment, he thought he was upside-down. He escaped by opening his eyes.

Ret was sure of it now: he was losing his mind. Everywhere he looked, he could see random rays of light. When the bus entered long stretches of rural countryside, the number of beams decreased, but whenever the bus passed through more populated areas, they increased in volume. The thing that convinced Ret he was going insane was the fact that no one else seemed to notice what he was seeing.

Eventually, the bus reached the end of its line, this time in New York City. Ret let all of his fellow riders get off the bus before him; unlike him, they seemed to have things to do and places to go. He watched as they gathered just outside the bus to pose for pictures with the famous Manhattan skyline as the backdrop. For Ret, however, the iconic sight was a nightmarish scene. To his utter bewilderment, the entire metropolitan area looked like it was putting on a laser light show of colossal proportions. There were beams and streams and gleams of light literally all over the place. They were bouncing off buildings, rippling across rivers, and cruising between clouds. Every shade of the rainbow was represented, some colors more prevalent than others. It seemed the metropolis was receiving just as many signals as it was sending. Beams large and small were coming from every angle, even down from the sky above. There was not a single space in the air that was not being filled by this strange phenomenon.

And then something dreadful happened: Ret felt an all-too-familiar numbness in the palm of his hand. He knew exactly what it was the moment he felt it. It was a scar. Ret refused to look at it. Instead, he clenched his fist as tightly as he could, hoping to suffocate the scar until it went away. But the harder he squeezed, the deeper it throbbed. In anger, he slammed his fist against the bus window. The window shattered, and the whole bus shook. The driver glanced back at his one remaining passenger. Ret waved his hand to repair the glass, then hurried off the bus.

The Oracle was turning out to be a lot like a bad reputation: Ret just couldn't seem to get away from it. In the last few weeks, he had traveled some two-thousand miles throughout the eastern United States without any kind of itinerary. He hadn't told anyone where he was going, nor did anyone know where he had been. And yet, somehow, the Oracle had found him. It knew where he was. It wouldn't leave him alone. Didn't it know he was trying to get away from it? Couldn't it take a hint?

Perhaps a subconscious decision made by his empty stomach, Ret ventured into the Big Apple. Manhattan was such a busy, noisy place. Ret marveled at the hordes of diverse people walking the streets, each and every one of them appearing to have something urgent to do. His aimlessness was such a contrast to their purposefulness. "Where is everybody going?" he wondered as pedestrian after pedestrian buzzed by him. He was moseying along at a much slower pace than the flow of the crowd, and he was almost sorry whenever he realized he was slowing someone down—someone who obviously had something much more important to do. More than once, Ret craned his neck to look upward at the seemingly endless skyscrapers, wondering if, in the grand scheme of things, the transactions and redactions that occurred on the other side of their concrete walls really mattered much. Ret came to the conclusion that even if these people *could* see the waves and rays that he could see all around them, they likely would be too preoccupied with other, more important things to even notice them. It seemed the city was in the business of busyness—and whether that busyness was real or imagined, well, Ret probably wasn't educated enough to tell.

Ret tried to flee the din of downtown by seeking out a bench in Central Park. He loved a good bench, a simple place to sit and think while the hosts of mankind walked by. Now that he was going to be a normal person, he wondered what he ought to think about: getting a job? going to school? finding a place to live? what to do this weekend? But no matter how diligently he tried to focus on his new life, he just couldn't concentrate. Voices kept interrupting his thoughts. They were the voices of children laughing, dogs barking, and adults talking. Ret would look around, expecting to find a person behind him or a baby beside him, but no one was ever there. He stopped thinking about himself and instead turned his attention to a pair of kids, playing about a hundred yards to his left. They were throwing a Frisbee, and Ret could clearly hear every word they were saying to each other. He could see the vibrations leaving their mouths and moving through the air. One by one, Ret listened in on the dialogues being spoken all over the park, their sounds carried on the wind. From his remote location on that stationary bench, he could hear every word being said and every conversation being held in the entire park.

Ret plugged his ears. "That'll stop it," he reasoned. But then he heard static—not in his ears but in his mind. As he tried to shake it off, the static started to make noises like the tuning of a radio to a specific channel, and as he sifted through the static, he began to pick up those channels. He heard music and sports talk, commercials and news—all as if he was a human radio.

"What in the world is going on?" he mused with dread, all but certain the Oracle was to blame. He figured he ought to at least look at his scar, which had been throbbing for hours. Mostly against his will, he pried open his left fist, fully expecting to see the image of an antenna that was acting like a lightning rod, picking up everything in the airwaves. And there, in the middle of the palm and to the right of the moai man, was a new scar indeed. It was an empty circle with two straight lines protruding from its edges. One of the lines was coming out from the very bottom of the circle, pointing down, with a sort of pennant or triangular flag at its end. The other line was coming out from the right curve of the circle, but instead of having a pennant at its end, there were four bars or barbs. These four barbs were parallel to each other, equal in length, and all pointing straight down. Together, this line and its four barbs looked like a comb that had a handle and four teeth.

As with all previous scars, Ret had no idea what this new one meant. He could probably argue it had some relation to the beams of light and waves of sounds he was now seeing, but that was just a guess. Perhaps it really was an antenna. But, frankly, he didn't really want to waste any more of his time or energy trying to figure it out.

Just then, a Frisbee landed on the grass near Ret's feet. It belonged to the kids who were playing a little ways off to his left. Ret picked it up and turned to give it to the boy who came to retrieve it.

"Here you go, Jimmy," Ret told him. The boy stood still in shock for a moment, alarmed that a total stranger knew his name, before running off.

When the Frisbee had left his hand, Ret noticed how the new scar looked a bit different. The line with the four barbs had moved from the right side of the circle to the top, while everything else had stayed the same. Still watching the scar, Ret returned to his original seat on the bench, and, sure enough, the line with the four barbs moved back to the right side of the circle.

Now, a developing scar was nothing new to Ret; the Nile lotus scar had come piece by piece, literally line upon line. But a *changing* scar was an entirely new concept. He swiveled to his left and back repeatedly, and each time the line with four barbs mimicked his movement. Then he started walking around Central Park. If he walked straight, the line stayed still, but if he turned, the line turned with him. Even the slightest bend in the road registered on the scar.

At length, Ret realized the scar was acting as a sort of compass. It didn't have a needle that always pointed north like a normal compass, but the line with the barbs always pointed whichever way he happened to be facing at the moment. If Ret turned west, the barbed lined swung over to the left (or west) side of the circle. If he turned east, it moved to the right (or east) side. The line with the pennant, however, never moved. It pointed constantly to the south (which Ret figured out when he turned south and saw the barbed line overlap the line with the pennant).

It would be a few more days before Ret gleaned the meaning of the scar's barbs. By accident, he became part of the crew of a sightseeing tour whose shorthanded director, a rough and tough northeasterner, saw Ret passing by and called on his strength to help handle all of the luggage. In exchange, Ret asked if he could join the outing, which consisted entirely of Chinese tourists. And so, Ret's travels continued. The tour bus hit all the tourist hotspots from New York to Philadelphia to Washington, D.C. As Ret traveled around the region, he periodically observed his scar. He noticed how the number of barbs on the moving line seemed proportional to the number of waves and rays in the air. In the big cities, there were four barbs. In the suburbs, there were three. In the rural areas, there were two or sometimes just one. The barbs seemed to be a means of measuring the activity in the airwaves. The line with the pennant, however, never changed.

By the end of the tour, Ret was convinced the Chinese travelers had taken more pictures of him than of the actual sights. It was as though they had never seen an American before. Ret would laugh to himself, thinking, "You should have seen what I *used* to look like." And it was true: his hair was now more dirty blond than golden yellow, his blue eyes more deep than bright. His skin was fully tanned (and then some), and he hadn't shaved in weeks.

One day, while walking the streets of Baltimore, Ret found a beat up, old bicycle out by the trash in an alley. As his flip-flops were wearing thin, he reckoned he could benefit from a set of wheels. The bike had no chain, which worked fine for Ret since he didn't plan on doing much pedaling anyway. He simply turned the wheel's metal spokes with his mind. He tried to keep away from the big cities, as they were literally a headache for him. Besides the beams he could see and the waves he could hear, Ret involuntarily picked up all kinds of television shows and satellite communications. In midair, he could read emails and text messages, see photographs and webpages, even overhear telephone calls—any and all content that was being shared wirelessly. This was not by choice, of course. He wasn't trying to spy or pry. If there was a way to turn it off, he would have done so a long time ago. He couldn't help it if a beam of light or a ray of energy or a wave of sound bumped into him, which was happening multiple times each second. The truth was, these sorts of things had always been around him, and everyone else for that matter; the only difference now was he could see them all.

Now that he knew something of the scar's workings, Ret reasoned his best bet at getting it to leave him alone was to settle down someplace that was in the middle of nowhere. The more he withdrew from the rest of the world, the fewer waves he would see in the air. The more he isolated himself from people, the less his scar would be agitated. While most people were searching for the good reception provided by four bars, Ret wanted no bars. But where exactly was the middle of nowhere?

The answer came to him in a New Jersey rail yard: Canada. There was a Canadian train on the tracks there, unloading a shipment of lumber. It was perfect: Ret would head far into the north. It was obvious that the scar wanted Ret to go south because the line with the pennant was ever pointing in that direction. So, as if to spite the scar, Ret would wend his way in exactly the opposite direction. That would teach it.

Ret climbed aboard one of the empty boxcars. The train headed northwest, weaving in between some of the Great Lakes as it crossed the international border into Canada. Ret kept track of neither the day nor the time, but he could tell it was the height of the summer season because the sun's path stretched far into the north. The daylight lasted long, and the scenery was beautiful. He kept the boxcar's sliding door ajar just wide enough for him to sit on the edge of the floor and watch the landscape go rushing by. With each click of the wheels along the tracks, Ret could see fewer rays in the air, feel the scar waning in strength, and knew he was inching ever closer to his new life.

With less of man's waves crowding the skies, Ret began to see more of Mother Nature's. He had eyes to see the different wavelengths of sunlight, separating visible light into the colors of the rainbow. He could see the grass and trees absorbing all of these colors but reflecting green. There were heat waves and infrared waves. And then there was the wind moving through it all—not so much disrupting it as merely passing through it. It reminded Ret of some mornings back home when he used to watch the wind blow away the low clouds that had rolled in from the sea overnight, except now he could see the wind as though it was the clouds. It swirled and billowed, rushed and died, filling gaps and flowing wherever it could. It was energy moving through the infinitesimal bits of gaseous matter called air.

It was about the time he saw a "Welcome to Saskatchewan" sign when Ret began to feel lonely— really lonely. Many days had passed. He didn't know where Saskatchewan was, but it sure sounded like a middle-of-nowhere place. And it looked like one, too:

hours would go by without seeing any sign of human civilization, and when he did see something, it was usually just an old, dilapidated barn. Ret was getting anxious for the train to stop, thinking it had taken him far enough. But it kept chugging north.

And so, Ret was left alone with only his thoughts to keep him company, a dangerously depressing set of circumstances. There he was in a dusty old boxcar, riding a train that was speeding toward the northern edge of the earth. Perhaps the onset of delirium, he began to hear a voice in his head, saying:

"What are you doing? You used to have a good life, remember? Pauline loves you as her own son. She took you in—fed you and clothed you—with the precious little she had. Ana adores you. You were the brother she never had. Paige prays for you every morning and night; you couldn't find someone more loyal, except for her father. Mr. Coy has been nothing but helpful to you—a true friend without whose help you would still be researching triangles. Ret, these people are the salt of the earth. They have made great sacrifices. Some even died."

"Why can't *I* be the one who dies? I'd love to put an end to this misery right now. How nice would that be? What an easy out!"

"That may be so for you. But the path of life, if followed right, is designed to lead us to assignments that will stretch our souls, not shrivel them. Some are asked to die for the cause of truth. But most others, including you, are asked to live for it. Ivan and Alana, Conrad and Lydia, the peoples of Sunken Earth and Fire Island—these are they who gave their death. The rest of you have survived to give your life. And, in some ways, asking for one's life is to demand more than asking for one's death."

"What does that even mean?"

"It's naturally not an easy thing to live each day with your private will in subjection to a nobler, harder one. Think of a mother's sleepless nights, a father's evaporating paycheck, or those saintly souls who give day after day of their lives in behalf of a handicapped child or aging parent. It's common for us to think of our time on this earth as 'my life' and not as a life that was given to you for a special purpose. Is a child not asked from his infancy what *he* wants to be when he grows up?—never mind what the world might need him to be instead."

"What do you want from me? I filled the Oracle halfway, didn't I? It wasn't my dream job, but I kept at it for a while. Now it's time for me to live my own life. What if I want to be a doctor or a teacher? Won't that help to 'cure the world'? With the powers I have, I could be the world's greatest geologist or blacksmith or engineer—the possibilities are endless. Why do I have to keep doing this Oracle stuff? I don't want to look back on my life and realize I wasted it—realize I could have been something but turned out to be nothing. Besides, this whole thing has become too dangerous. I had to call it quits, to protect the ones I care about."

"Was Sunken Earth not dangerous? Why didn't you quit after that? And now that you're far from your loved ones, why aren't you resuming the quest for elements? Search your heart, Ret. You didn't leave to save your friends' lives; you left to save your own life— not to prevent your death, but to save your remaining 70 or so years from being totally swallowed up by a will other than your own. The Oracle intends to ask you to put everything you have and are on the table—this you know. With each element, it has been asking for more and more and still more of you. But now you're not sure if you're willing to give it your all. You're holding something back, Ret. What is it?"

"Fine, do you want to know what it is? Here it is: I'm expected to cure this world, but I don't know how to do it, and I'm not sure I *can* do it. I mean, if it was only up to me, then I could do it. But it's not only up to me; it's up to us—all of us. Yes, there are so many problems in this world that need to be fixed, but it's not the problems that are the real problem. The problems are merely symptoms; they're not the underlying illness that's causing the problems. Why can't people see this?

They just mow over the weeds without getting down to the root of the problem. The real problem is not what makes the headlines. No, the real problem is *us*. All of our troubles are merely outgrowths from the evil desires in our hearts. Greed, tyranny, vanity, laziness—these and so many other ills are symptoms of sick hearts. If we cure our own hearts, then the world will cure itself. But how am I supposed to cure someone else's heart? That's a choice that each individual person has to make for himself. And it looks to me like most people don't even care. So that's why I'm giving up—not because I'm selfish, not because I'm afraid—no, because I don't know how to do it, and even though the world desperately needs it, I don't think it really wants it anyway. Look: I've collected three elements, and what do I get for it? A world that hates me for it."

"But people can change, Ret."

"Oh, you mean people like Lionel? You know, my best friend who just turned the whole world against me? Yeah, he sure changed, didn't he? How could he do such a thing? *Why* would he do it? I never met a better person than Lionel—never met someone who was as noble or honest. How can one person be both my hero and my enemy at the same time?"

Suddenly, the train hit a bump in the track. Ret flew from the edge of the boxcar where he had been sitting. He fell a few feet to the ground and then rolled down a short hill. After coming to a stop, he slowly rose to his feet and dusted himself off. He had a few scrapes here and there, but nothing serious. His backpack had broken his fall from the train, which had already sped out of sight.

Ret looked around. He found himself in a great valley. The ground was mostly rocky with a few patches of brush. Mountains surrounded the basin, the tallest of which were still covered in snow. Trees were around but sparse. There was a lake at the other end. Storm clouds were gathering in the distance.

"I wish Mr. Coy was here," he lamented. For a man who was often perceived as someone who didn't quite have it all together, Mr. Coy had a way of somehow bringing it all together—and in a manner that you swore had to have been planned even though you knew it wasn't. It was much more than dumb luck or good karma; it was a special brand of grace, the kind of grace that is earned and cannot be shared. Ret longed for a generous dose of it now.

With a broken heart, Ret put one foot in front of the other. The coarse ground crunched beneath his heavy steps. His stomach ached with hunger; his throat cracked with thirst. Exhaustion filled his thinning face. He was covered in dirt and was as poor as it, too. And he was alone—totally, utterly alone. Gone was his faith in men. Fled were his hopes for humanity. Love by him had waxed cold, for there he was, lost in a barren wilderness, precisely as he once thought he wanted.

He hadn't made it very far across the valley when, in his extremity, Ret fell to his knees. The hillsides rang with perfect silence. The airwaves were empty and still. Ret glanced down at his scar, which had all but faded. Then, being in an agony, he clenched his fists and shook them at heaven. His heart swelled. His eyes wept. His soul refused to be comforted.

With a roar of frustration, Ret slammed his fists against the ground. It made the earth shake. He swung his arms to his sides and sent tidal waves of dirt all around him. With his mind, he reached toward the nearest mountainside and broke off a huge piece of it, then threw it against one of the valley's slopes. The boulder broke into chunks and rolled to the valley floor. One by one, Ret drew the chunks toward him and then punched them like a boxer, causing them to burst into dust. In his rage, he combed through the dust, searching for traces of alkali metals, which he knew reacted with water. He found some, freed them, and showered them over the lake at the other end of the valley. The lake began to erupt with a hundred miniature explosions. Meanwhile, he reached deep into the belly of the earth and forced a lava tube to erupt, which set the valley floor ablaze. Finally, to end the chaos, Ret decapitated a snowcapped mountaintop and held it over the valley. He warmed it until the snow melted, extinguishing the fire and cooling the lava. Then he held the peak over the still-fizzing lake and dropped it. It plunged into the water with a deafening boom that rattled the earth. Fatigued, Ret collapsed to the ground.

Storm clouds veiled the afternoon sun, and it started to rain. Lying on his back, Ret watched the heavens weep with him. Then, directly over the valley, lightning lit up the darkened sky. The thunderclaps followed without delay. Bolt after bolt, the lightning cackled, but Ret wasn't looking at the bolts. He was looking at the energy left behind by the bolts. He could see it, those inordinate streaks of light-purple hues that zigzagged with the power ignited by each lightning bolt. As he was falling into a much-needed slumber, Ret could feel his scar pulsating with renewed life. It was an unwelcomed way to drift off to sleep—a sleep that he hoped he would never awake from.

But he did. He awoke to a dog licking his face.

"Down, boy," the canine's master called. The dog retreated, and Ret heard a man's footsteps coming toward him on the graveled ground.

"You alright, son?" the man asked.

Ret looked up to see who was standing over him. It was Principal Stone.

CHAPTER 6

ONE MAN'S PAST IS ANOTHER MAN'S FUTURE

There were no layovers during Mr. Coy's flight from his Manor on Little Tybee Island to the far-flung Pacific isle called Waters Deep. The journey was long, not only because of the distance but also because of the solitude. For thousands of miles, Mr. Coy was alone with nothing but his thoughts to keep him company. He tried not to dwell on the passing of his wife, but how could he not? Returning to the place of her demise was like traveling to a cemetery to visit the grave of a loved one. Her absence would not be so agonizing for him had their lives together not been so wonderful. But even the good memories stung because Mr. Coy blamed himself for the death of one of the world's most intelligent minds and compassionate hearts.

As heartbreaking as such a trip was turning out to be, there was a separate, though related and much more important, act of heart-breaking that was taking place simultaneously. You see, it was very soon after Helen's death when Mr. Coy strongly set his heart on never, ever going back to the place now known as Waters Deep. He had drunk the dregs of one of life's most bitter cups and, thereby, became bitter himself. In an endless cycle, the bitterness would build up in his heart until, eventually, it would break his heart all over again, and he would become even more hardhearted, which only led to more bitterness. He refused to forgive himself, came to loathe himself. He tried to bury his old self under a new, false self, but the reincarnation was a weird and whacky disaster.

But now, in this gruesome but glorious moment, the true Benjamin Coy was breaking free from the shackles of the past. It was difficult; it was painful; and yet it was all possible precisely because he was doing the one thing he had set his heart on never, ever doing. He was deliberately going against the innermost wishes of his hardened heart, willfully choosing to break it. But, this time, rather than becoming bitter again like it had so many times before, his heart was becoming soft and pure. He was, at last, letting go of his personal will and, instead, yielding his heart to another will, one that was more selfless than selfish. And, as he knew, such a life-saving transplant had been brought about and carried out by the one and only Oracle.

In the floatplane he had borrowed from Thorne, Mr. Coy flew nearly halfway around the globe with a specific set of coordinates as his final destination: 31°42'08"S 172°33'03"W. These were the exact same coordinates that, months ago, Lionel, who was then being held captive at Waters Deep, had included in the letter he had sent asking Ret to come and rescue him. Of course, Mr. Coy never actually saw the letter, nor did anyone find out who actually wrote it. But fortunately, a simple check of the hot-air balloon's electronic navigational log revealed just the information Mr. Coy had wanted to see from the letter that Lionel refused to show him.

It was with slight confusion, therefore, when Mr. Coy arrived at the coordinates and found nothing there. All he could see, in every direction, was open ocean. There was no island (or any land, for that matter), neither was there a ship or platform or any sign of human life anywhere.

Mr. Coy didn't bother checking the map he had brought along, as he remembered from his initial visit with Helen that the mysterious island could not be found on any maps. This was not uncommon of small landforms in the vast Pacific Ocean, where not every single atoll or cay was charted. So, instead, Mr. Coy consulted the plane's global positioning system. He zoomed in as far as the screen would allow, but still there was no sign of any island at the given coordinates.

Mr. Coy reasoned there might be something secret at work here. What he knew about Waters Deep was far less than what he didn't know about it. It was obviously being used, at least in part, as a sort of military base for Lye, since that's where his fleet of ships had been headed. It also likely had accommodations for prisoners, since Lionel had been held there (if, in fact, he was telling the truth). Moreover, the island was oddly shaped and heavily guarded, according to Ishmael's account, and it seemed to share a connection with one of Ret's scars.

But there was one nugget of information that intrigued Mr. Coy more than the others: Waters Deep was the place of the most recent sighting of a certain missing man named Jaret Cooper. Mr. Coy had never contributed much credence to the hope that Jaret was still alive, but now that his survival had been confirmed, Mr. Coy was impressed. And even though it was almost certain he was being manipulated by Lye, Mr. Coy still thought he ought to meet Jaret. In fact, that was the major impetus for his trip. Jaret was his 'in.'

Mr. Coy circled the area, hoping for the vanished island to rise up out of the sea or appear once the sun shone on it at some magic angle. Still nothing. He widened his search, gradually increasing the diameter of the circle he was making in the sky.

It took a few more hours, but he finally found it, a couple hundred miles west of where it should have been. From the air, Mr. Coy could plainly see the odd shape of Waters Deep. It had four slender arms or peninsulas jutting out from its main, circular body. There was a fifth protrusion, but it was much wider and shaped like a trapezoid. It looked like a six-legged starfish with the gap between two of its legs filled in with land. Now Mr. Coy knew why Ishmael had had such a hard time trying to describe the place to him. It was downright bizarre. If Ret had been there, he might have compared it to a Ferris wheel.

Mr. Coy took the plane down, his finger poised to press the ejection button if he noticed any sort of bullets or bombs headed his way. He hovered just above the water as he flew into the space between two of the jetty-like peninsulas. Before the arms met, Coy landed the floatplane on the water and taxied to the rocky edge of the nearest peninsula. After securing his craft, he stood on the wing and paused.

He had been here before. The past played out before his very eyes, whose every blink displayed a new photograph like the click of a slide projector. It was the photo album he was unable to erase from his memory. He saw his hands, younger and stronger, mooring their boat to the island. There was Helen, her instruments in hand, stepping onto those same slippery rocks. He saw her glance back at their humanitarian ship anchored further offshore, worry on her face.

Ben came to himself. His heart was pounding in his chest. He looked out across the ocean, as if to see if the humanitarian vessel was still there. It wasn't. It was all in the past—a past that he kept making the present. He was nervous, an emotion that was seldom his. More than once, he looked back at the cockpit, entertaining the idea of just going home. And, after several anxious moments, that's what he decided to do. Downcast, he climbed back in the plane and was about to turn the key to start the ignition when he heard a voice in his mind, saying:

"What are you doing? Have you come all this way just to turn back? You're right here. You're on the cusp of a bright, new future, one unhampered by the past. You're so close. Now you're just going to give up?"

"I can't do it. I just can't face it again. I miss her. Every single day, I think of her and miss her so much. But she's gone, and it's all my fault. How could I have done such a thing? She was an angel, a gift to mankind, so much better than me. Why? Why did this have to happen?"

"What has happened has happened for a wise purpose. You must learn to forgive yourself, for if you are not able to forgive yourself for what you think you did, then you would not be able to forgive someone else had he or she done it instead, and such would be your tragic flaw. You already forgive others freely: the truth that people can change is the founding philosophy of the Manor. But there is one student at the Manor who has yet to change: you. You must learn that you can change, too. You are not a bad person, though you feel guilty for a part of your past, which you have done everything in your power to rectify. Don't let yesterday hold today hostage. The past is holding you back. Move on. The time to change is now."

"But why couldn't *I* be the one who died? Most days, I wish I had been. Life has turned into misery without her."

"Your life has been spared to carry on the work that she so loved—the work of helping to cure the world. Yes, something bad came into your life, but you took that negative energy and turned it around into something positive: you created the Manor, which has changed hundreds of lives. You could have let that negative energy fester inside of you until it snuffed out the light within. But you didn't. No, you did the opposite. You did what Helen would have done, and you are using her flame to light countless others. Don't you see? You two are still working together, spirit to spirit, in the cause to cure the world."

Mr. Coy recognized the familiar phrase *cure the world*. It was the prophecy's one phrase that Ret referred to most frequently. Until now, however, Mr. Coy had never considered that Helen's work and his continuation of it might be a means of fulfilling such a lofty directive. He had always thought that he had little to do with curing the world; rather, that his contribution was merely to help Ret to do it by finding the elements. Now, however, that perspective was changing. Maybe, like Ret had recently told him, the Oracle had very little to do with elements and quite a lot to do with people.

"I wish Ret was here." But, Mr. Coy remembered, he at least had the next best thing. He leaned across the cockpit and reached into his bag to retrieve the Oracle. He held it in his hands. It didn't open, of course, but it shined back at him. It was such a striking, almost mesmerizing object that, despite containing so much power, exuded an overwhelming sense of peace. Mr. Coy paused to stare at each of the three elements they had collected thus far. From earth to fire to ore, the attractive trio brought back a slew of memories. He missed Ret—his undaunted bravery, his heroic spirit— and wished he was here now to tell him to stop moping and get his butt out of the cockpit.

It was while looking at the Oracle when Mr. Coy saw how the scar over one of the sphere's three empty wedges was glowing. He knew the six markings that were etched around the waist of the Oracle were identical to the six scars that Ret had on his hands. In the past, only when a scar on Ret's hands was illuminated did the corresponding marking on the Oracle also begin to glow. So, as Coy realized, what this meant was this same marking that he was seeing was also burning brightly on Ret's hand.

And what a curious thing it was! It was an empty circle with two barbs or lines extending from it. One of the barbs was stationary, pointing down with a pennant at its end, while the other barb was anything but stationary, twitching and switching often. The mobile barb had perpendicular lines (not a pennant) at its end, but even the quantity of those changed once or twice while Mr. Coy was analyzing it. He recognized the scar as a wind barb, a graphic used in meteorology to show both the direction and strength of the wind.

Mr. Coy smiled to know the quest to fill the Oracle was alive and well. In fact, he let out a hearty laugh and slapped his knee at the irony that even though Ret had tried to run away from the Oracle, it had found him!

Mr. Coy tossed the Oracle in the air a few times, marveling and smiling at it as though he had just caught a foul ball at a baseball game. For being such a small and simple thing, it could certainly bring to pass great things. True, it could crumble great mountains and erupt fiery volcanoes and demolish ancient pyramids; but it could also break hard hearts and bind up broken ones. And, as he looked into it, it seemed to look into him, whispering the reminder, "People can change."

And so he did. In the spirit of Helen and with the vigor of Ret, Mr. Coy threw open the cockpit door, leapt onto the barnacled rocks, and once again set foot on the forbidden island of Waters Deep. A new man, he took in a lungful of salty air and exhaled triumphantly, marching along the peninsula toward the isle's mainland. In true Coy fashion, he did something that most certainly would have been the last thing anyone else would have done having just trespassed onto a heavily guarded fortress where stealth and sneakiness were paramount: he started singing. He wasn't simply humming quietly to himself; no, he was bellowing with the loudest tenor voice his diaphragm could summon. He just couldn't suppress the happiness and relief he felt from letting go of the burdens of his past. And so, arriving at the start of the island's vegetation and waltzing right into it, Mr. Coy's voice rang out across the treetops, singing the familiar lines from the favorite play *Oklahoma!*: "Oh, what a beautiful morning! Oh, what a beautiful day! I've got a beautiful feeling everything's going my way." And even though the day's morning was long gone, somehow everything *would* go his way.

For, meanwhile, deep within the concealed walls of Lye's lair at Waters Deep, a vigilant team of surveillance officers was closely monitoring Mr. Coy's every move. In fact, they had picked up the presence of his plane long before it ever landed at their shores. Thanks to the security cameras hidden all over the island, they watched him get out, then get back in, talk to himself for a few minutes, then get out again and finally come ashore. And now, he was dancing through a grassy meadow, still singing: "There's a bright golden haze on the meadow, there's a bright golden haze on the meadow. The corn is as high as an elephant's eye, and it looks like it's climbing clear up to the sky."

Witnessing this behavior, one of the security officers remarked, "Who is this whacko?"

"I don't know," another replied, "but he sure does have a nice voice."

"Should we eliminate him?"

"He may have seen too much."

"I'll go and get the commander. We can ask him."

Little did they know, however, that such was exactly what Mr. Coy desired. He was purposely trying to be as conspicuous as possible. He wanted to draw attention to himself. He wanted to get caught. So he kept on singing at the top of his lungs, splashing among the hot springs like puddles and waving tree limbs high above his head. When he reached the end of his song, he started calling out for Jaret.

"Yoo-hoo? Oh, Jaret?" he yelled into a hollowed tree trunk, trying to find places where cameras were likely placed. "Come out, come out, wherever you are. I want to speak with you, face to face."

Just then, Mr. Coy's face filled the screen of one of the remote computers. Though he didn't know it, he was doing a good job of finding the secret cameras, and it was quite the entertaining spectacle for the surveillance crew.

When the officer returned with his commander, one of the men at the computer said, "Commander Jaret, you should take a look at this."

Jaret hurried to the officer's side and watched what was playing out on the screen. Their intruder was now performing a series of poorly-executed cartwheels, still demanding to meet with Jaret.

After a few moments of watching the screen with total bewilderment, Jaret asked, almost with sympathy, "What is wrong with this man?"

"We're not sure," an officer answered. "He came alone. He may have found the Deep by mistake. Should we eliminate him?"

"No," Jaret said promptly. "You know how our lord feels about that. Only he can approve of executions."

Suddenly, they heard Mr. Coy say, "Give me a *J*," followed by, "Give me an *a*." He had given up doing cartwheels and was now bending his body to form each letter in Jaret's name. Like an out-of-shape cheerleader, he spelled the whole name and then shouted, "What does that spell? Jaret!"

One of the officers shook his head in disgust and then wondered, "Shall we consult with Lord Lye then?"

"No, he's not here," Jaret informed them. With curious concern, the commander continued to study the character on the screen, who was now performing jumping jacks. Before getting rid of him, Jaret wanted to know how the man not only knew his name but also where to find him. "I'll deal with this."

"What are you going to do?"

"The man is requesting to speak with me, isn't he?" Jaret returned matter-of-factly on his way out. "I'd like to find out what he has to tell me."

It took Jaret a while to locate Mr. Coy, who had apparently ceased gallivanting through the woods and vocalizing his desires, seeing as Jaret could neither see nor hear him. Eventually, however, Jaret found the foreigner taking a break from his tiresome tour and now relaxing in one of the island's many hot springs. Still unnoticed by the wading Coy, Jaret approached the bank of the hot spring, where he found a shirt and trousers neatly folded on top of a pair of shoes.

"You wanted to speak with me?" Jaret called out from the edge.

"Ah!" a startled Coy shrieked, slipping beneath the warm water. When he came up, he wiped his face and said, "Do mine eyes deceive me? Can it really be the famous Jaret Cooper?"

"In the flesh," Jaret replied, not the least bit humored.

"Well, flip my flapjacks!" Coy cheered, slapping the surface of the water with his hands. "What an honor it is to finally meet you! You know, according to the rest of the world, you've been dead for years."

"What are you talking about?" Jaret questioned, still unsure of the mental state of this stranger.

"Don't you remember?" Coy put forth, practicing his backstroke across the spring. "A few years ago, you and your Coast Guard crew went out to help a ship in distress. It was burning and sinking, right in the path of an approaching hurricane, yet you went to its aid by yourself and were never heard from again."

"Who are you?" Jaret asked, suspicious of the man who had finished his swim and was now walking towards him.

"The name's Benjamin Coy," he said, stopping in front of Jaret. The two men stared at each other for a few moments, Jaret suspicious and Coy dripping wet. "You wouldn't happen to have a towel, would you?"

"What are you doing here?" Jaret interrogated, totally unamused.

"Why, I came to see *you,* of course!" Coy cried. "Ever since my first-mate Ishmael told me he found you here during his visit to this island to rescue one of your prisoners, I've been wanting to make such a visit myself just to see you with my own two eyes."

"Wait," said Jaret. "You had something to do with that rescue mission?"

"Well, actually, I had nothing to do with it," Coy admitted, using his socks to dry himself, "but they *did* fly here in my hot-air balloon."

"Hold on—that was *your* balloon?" Jaret asked, dumbfounded at what was going on.

Mr. Coy decided the moment had arrived to stop taunting Jaret with the bait and finally get him to bite: "But, I must say, J, it was pretty cruel of you not to recognize your own wife. I mean, she came all that way, and—"

"What did you say?" Jaret pressed, having heard a word that was of great interest to him.

Coy smirked to see Jaret had taken the bait. "Does the name Pauline ring any bells?"

"You know her?" Jaret asked earnestly. "You know my...my wife?"

"Oh, I know her," Coy said, rolling his eyes, "a lot better than I'd like, too."

"I knew it!" Jaret rejoiced. "I knew I had a wife." Then, with a puzzled look, he asked, "Do I *still* have a wife?"

"And a daughter, last time I checked," Coy

brought him up to speed.

"Yes, my daughter—my little girl!" Jaret cele-brated. "Her name—it's Hannah, isn't it? Or something like that?"

"Minus the h's," Coy instructed.

"That's it—Ana!" Jaret was overjoyed. "How do you know all of this?"

"It's a long story," Coy sighed.

"Ever since that night when I saw my wife," Jaret explained, "you know, when she and your friend came to rescue my prisoner, I haven't been able to stop thinking about her. I didn't remember her when I first saw her, of course, but it wasn't very long after that when bits and pieces started coming back to me. Seeing her face and hearing her name have released a flood of memories that won't stop coming into my mind. Nearly everything I see reminds me of her in some way. So much of what I hear and touch and taste takes me back to a word she spoke to me or an embrace we shared or a meal we ate together. They're all details from some sort of former life I once lived—a life that feels so good and looks so happy and has nothing to do with my current life. I dream of them, Pauline and—" he hesitated, then added "Ana," glancing at Coy to make sure he had the name correct. "All through the night, these scenes play out subconsciously in my mind. Until now, I didn't know if all of these remembrances were real or not. I thought they might just be a product of my imagination, not actual memories from a past I once lived. But now you're here, confirming they are real."

"They're real alright," said Coy.

"Did you bring them with you?" Jaret asked with excitement. "Are they here somewhere?"

"No, but I know where they live," Coy said, thinking of the house he had built for them on the grounds of the Manor.

"Can you take me to them?" Jaret pled.

Grinning, Coy answered, "I thought you'd never ask."

CHAPTER 7

A CHANGED MAN

Ret stared in disbelief at the man who was standing over him.

"Principal Stone?" Ret wondered, squinting amid the sunshine of a new day. Stone's face clouded over in recognition.

"Ret?" he replied, equally shocked. With nervousness, Stone immediately scanned the area, as if to see if anyone else might be around.

Suddenly finding himself in the presence of one of his known enemies, Ret's first inclination was to defend himself. However, he quickly discovered he barely had the strength to move. With uncharacteristic compassion, Stone knelt down to help his former student get up, but Ret recoiled in alarm.

"Don't worry," Stone reassured him, lifting Ret to his feet, "you're among friends." Stone's two dogs gave their welcoming sniffs of approval as they swarmed around Ret's legs. "I didn't recognize you," Stone said as if reuniting with an old pal. "You don't look quite like you used to." He brushed some of the dirt from Ret's shirt and hair.

"*You* would know," Ret jeered, still distrustful. He moved away from Stone's support, but his weak legs gave out.

"Whoa," Stone cried, catching him. "I'd better get you to the house. I'm sure Virginia's got just the right thing to fix you up." Glancing around again, Stone seemed anxious to leave.

There was something different about Stone that was causing Ret to feel especially skeptical. He didn't like the idea of falling under Stone's care, but he didn't have much choice. Leaning on his former principal like a crutch, the two of them set off for a small vehicle parked a little ways off, the dogs trotting in front of them.

"So what brings you to these parts?" Stone started.

"I should ask the same of you," Ret put forth.

"Well, last night Virginia and I were sitting in the living room, watching through the window as the storm rolled in, when, all of a sudden, we saw that mountaintop over there break off and fly away." He pointed up at the decapitated mountain, whose peak Ret had dropped in the nearby lake the previous night. "We thought that was a little strange, so we both agreed I ought to go out in the morning and investigate, and," he chuckled, "who would've guessed I'd find you? Actually, it was Blackie who found you first." He motioned to the dog on his right, whose hair, true to its name, was black. "And that one there," he nodded at the other dog, whose coat was white with a few brown patches, "she's Whitey."

"Come up with those names all by yourself, did you?" Ret jabbed.

"Virginia helped," Stone laughed. "They're just two ugly mutts, but they can spot trouble a mile away."

Stone's new set of wheels was much different from the flashy sports car he used to drive. This one was an old pick-up truck, plain and simple, with chipping paint and a rusted bumper. He helped Ret into the cabin while the dogs leapt into the bed. Then, with one more concerned look around, Stone got in and drove off.

Stone's house wasn't exactly just up the street; in fact, they never even got on an actual road, and, as far as Ret could see, there weren't any. With little speed but plenty of bumps, Stone blazed his own, untraceable trail through the sparse brush. There were no signs of human life anywhere, not even in the air (to Ret's delight). The only energy he could see was coming from gusts of the cool wind and rays of the warm sun. Ret really *had* traveled to the middle of nowhere.

Hidden behind a dense thicket of trees was the Stone residence. It was a small, single-wide trailer, supported underneath by a few stacks of cinder blocks. There was no driveway, no mailbox, not even a front yard—nothing that would give anyone the slightest idea that there was a home in the vicinity.

Stone helped Ret climb the four steps of the ramshackle staircase that led to the front door, then rang the doorbell, which Ret thought was strange until he heard someone inside undoing multiple locks. The door opened just a crack, and Virginia's face peeked out.

"It's me, dear," Stone told her quietly. The crack opened wider. He hurried Ret inside, then scanned the perimeter one last time before shutting the flimsy door behind him and reengaging its many locks.

"Do you remember me telling you about a young man named Ret Cooper?" Stone explained to his wife. "Well, here he is." With a face full of fright, Virginia stared at Ret, then back at her husband.

"Lester, what—" she began.

"Don't worry," he calmed her, "he's alone."

"Are you sure?"

"Yes," Stone reaffirmed. "Isn't that right, Ret?" They both turned toward their visitor. Using his melancholy expression instead of words, Ret confirmed his sad situation of being totally alone. "Besides," Stone added, "the dogs would've sensed the presence of anyone else." Then, as if Ret couldn't hear, Stone requested, "Please, Virginia, I don't know what Ret's doing all the way out here, but he could do with a hot meal and a soft bed."

"Very well," she cautiously obliged, setting off for the kitchen, which was not more than a few steps away in such a small home.

Stone escorted Ret to the only table and eased him into one of its two chairs, behavior which Ret found unusually kind for such a callous principal. Virginia appeared, setting before Ret a steaming bowl of soup and a plate of warm cornbread.

"Ret, I'm baffled that our paths have crossed again," Stone said, sitting down in the other chair, across the table from Ret, "but I'm glad they have. I want to apologize to you—to your family and friends, too, but especially to you—for all the harm I've caused."

"That's nice," Ret told him, stirring his soup and wondering if it had been poisoned, "but I'm sure you can understand why I don't believe you."

"Yes, yes, that's to be expected," said Stone, unoffended, "but you should know I'm not the same man I used to be. I've repented of my past. I'm a changed man."

Virginia returned with two glasses of milk, setting one in front of each man at the table. As hungry as he was, Ret stared at the food suspiciously, remembering a story that Ana once told him about two children named Hansel and Gretel.

"It all started a few months ago when I met with you and your friends at that fried chicken restaurant," Stone began. "We were foes then, of course, but we met on friendly terms to ask each other questions—I'm sure you remember." Ret did, but the cornbread was making his mouth water. "While Mr. Coy was explaining to you the story of how his wife died, I was standing just outside the restaurant's double doors with that massive man, whose name escapes me at the moment..."

"Conrad," Ret said proudly in honor of the martyr.

"That's right: Conrad. I was standing outside with Conrad, who was dutifully awaiting Coy's word to usher me in. Well, thanks to the two-way communications device in Conrad's ear, I could hear everything that Mr. Coy was telling you inside. I heard the entire tale of Helen's death—well, as Mr. Coy understands it, at least." Ret glared at Stone with intrigue and then with complete astonishment when he added, "That's not exactly how it happened, Ret."

Ret kept his eyes fixed on Stone.

"First, you need to understand something about that island, Waters Deep," said Stone. "Lye shares very few of his secrets, and to no one does he tell all of them, so I know very little about the place. But I do know this: the Deep serves as Lye's headquarters—his base of operations—and he goes to exceptionally great lengths to keep it hidden. In fact, he will stop at nothing to ensure no one but his closest allies knows anything about it. It is not on any maps or in any books—he has had all of them checked and revised if necessary. He usually keeps the island situated right on the International Date Line, making it irrelevant to time and calendar, but he also has a way of moving the island around. These are just the security measures that I know of (I'm sure there are many others), but it's enough to illustrate the point that he doesn't want anyone snooping around."

"Naturally, man has stumbled upon the island at various times over the centuries, but you can be sure the Deep sees them coming long before they see the Deep coming. Now, most tyrants would exterminate anything that might come within a certain radius of the Deep—right then and there, no questions asked. But Lye, being the mastermind that he is, understands that such an approach would most certainly give himself away. If a ship were to disappear, would someone not go looking for it? If a plane were to blow up, would a search and rescue team not be sent out? And if a visitor were to die or vanish as soon as he set foot on the island, would his family and friends not call for an investigation? Surely, his secret hideout would be discovered, besieged, stormed, and ruined."

"So he lets them come. He lets them fly by or sail past. And if anyone is curious enough to come ashore, he lets them come, all the while watching them like a hawk. You must understand, Lye has servants every-where—eyes and ears all over this world. There is hardly a government or corporation or organization that he hasn't infected with at least one of his henchmen—like Tybee High, for example. The key is that it is all done in secret. In fact, there are so many levels in the bureaucracy of his secret society that many of his subor-dinates have no idea they ultimately work for someone as menacing as Lye. This is one way he is able to accomplish so much evil because while most of us would never murder, many of us find it okay to lie or steal or accept a bribe, even though doing so might be one step in a murderous plot."

"So if, for example, a barge passes by and takes notice of the Deep, Lye will call for one of his aides to stalk it—if, in fact, he doesn't already have a contact working on that barge or at the port of its arrival. That contact will track, spy, eavesdrop, foster friendship and then betray confidences—whatever it takes to assess the situation. And, depending on the severity, Lye will act accordingly and without mercy."

"Such was the tragic case of Ben and Helen Coy. Lye saw them coming and let them come. He observed their every move: did they snap pictures? did they take

samples? did they write anything down? Lye had his
work cut out for him with the Coys. They had seen far
too much and would surely leave him exposed. But he
had to be careful. If they both suddenly died, then
someone might suspect foul play. But if he only killed
one of them, then the other would likely never rest until
the island was demystified. So which one would he kill,
and how would he ruin the other? The destruction of the
Coys became his top priority. He enlisted the help of his
top aides. Time was of the essence."

Enthralled by the story, Ret subconsciously began
eating the food Virginia had prepared for him.

"As always, Lye raised a silent alarm among his
underground network of aboveground agents. He
needed information on the Coys—clues, tips—any and
all knowledge about what they were doing or where they
were going. With unseen tentacles, Lye wormed his
workers into the Coys' lives, granting him eyes to read
their notes, ears to overhear their findings, and a mind to
learn their plans. Lye has ways of getting his informants
in and out, putting them where they need to be in order
to get what he wants: they tip off the cleaning lady or
impersonate a repairman, bribe the landlord or intercept
the mail, lobby the phone service or stir up a neighbor—
his methods are as endless as the ways to corrupt the
human heart. I know because I've done my share of it
for him. He is the master of deceit and disguise, the

father of lies and lechery, the world's oldest student of the art of evil."

"And in all my years of servitude to Lye, there was only one time when I saw him truly worried. It was when he learned that Helen was decoding the molecular structure of the water samples she had collected from some of the hot springs at the Deep, with the intention of duplicating and mass producing it. None of us knew what the big deal was about that natural spring water, but the fact that Helen had figured it out threw Lye into a panic. Fortunately for him, one of his aides informed him that Helen had administered some of the precious liquid to herself—a small detail that hatched a wicked plot."

"Soon thereafter, Lye poisoned Helen. He didn't do it himself, of course; he had one of his minions do the dirty deed. How? I don't know—spiked her drink, coaxed a waiter, dared a wayward teen. Promise a person whatever *they* want and they're bound to do whatever *you* want. He capitalizes on the unstable hearts of the earth—the weak-willed and wanton-eyed—and corrupts them with bribes of money, promises of power, pledges of prestige, or assurances of revenge. And that's how he was able to reach into Helen's life. He poisoned her, and when she drank another sample of the so-called magic water, he poisoned her again. She fell ill, and when no local doctor could find a cure, the Coys did exactly what Lye knew they would do: they went to their colleague, Dr. Victor Cross."

In dismay, Ret suddenly spoke, "You mean Dr. Cross is —"

"—A fraud," Stone finished, "just like I was as principal. Mind you, Cross *is* a brilliant doctor. He's a board-certified, fully-legitimate, world-class physician, which is why the Coys had associated with him before in their humanitarian work. But Cross also happens to be one of Lye's top-dogs, higher up in rank than I was. I'm not sure how Lye got him to join the cause, but whenever Lye needs to take out someone swiftly and secretly, he usually goes to Cross. So all that time when Mr. Coy thought his good friend Victor was taking care of Helen, Cross was actually ensuring her demise. It was Cross who undid every operation behind the scenes; Cross who nullified every medicine behind closed doors. He did exactly what Lye told him to do."

"But destroying Helen wasn't enough. No, Lye had to figure out a way to bring down Ben. Through his observations, Lye learned of the profound love Mr. Coy had for his wife. Lye knew if he killed Helen, then Mr. Coy would stop at nothing to carry on her legacy and expose the Deep's identity. And so, Lye would ruin Ben by spoiling his love. Lye waited until Helen had finally unraveled the secret of the liquid. He kept her alive just long enough, which was easy since her life was in Cross' hands. When that time came, Helen wrote the information on a piece of paper that she intended to present to her husband. She asked Cross to call for Ben. Cross, whose allegiance to medicine falls second to espionage, figured out what was going on and reported to Lye that the moment had arrived. Then, according to Lye's plan, Cross waited for Helen to nod off, which was easy to do by tinkering with her IV. He took her slip of paper and replaced it with one of his own, having studied her penmanship enough to forge her hand. Then he called for Ben, and instead of reading his sweet wife's decoding of the secret water's molecular structure, he read the Cross-written words of *How could you do this to me?* Then Cross finally pulled the plug on Helen's life, and she died."

Ret couldn't believe what he was hearing. His heart felt sick to learn of such a wretched tale. He grieved for Mr. Coy. The outcome of the whole ordeal was bad enough, but now that he had learned the truth about how it had taken place, it was downright sinister. Helen's death, Coy's tragedy...it was all Lye's fault— and just so he could hide his stupid headquarters! Ret heard Virginia sniffling close by, tearing up as she listened in from the kitchen.

"When it became obvious that the event brought Mr. Coy to the brink of insanity," Stone resumed, "Lye knew he had triumphed. His great threat lay dead, and

her husband was as good as dead. Lye called for a celebration, for the secret society had been saved. That's
when Cross and I took that picture together—the one
that Mr. Coy saw in my former house, where we're
shaking hands. I was congratulating him on the
successful part he played in Helen's demise."

"But that night at the restaurant," he carried on,
"when I heard the account given from Mr. Coy's
perspective, I came to a staggering realization. For the
first time, I realized Mr. Coy and Helen's husband were
the same person—that the man living in the strange
house just across the creek on Little Tybee Island was
the same man whose wife and life Lye had destroyed
years ago. You see, I was not involved in Lye's scheme
to take out the Coys; I never knew them by their real
names because, like most other individuals on Lye's hit
list, Lye had given them code names. It's like I told
you, Ret: it's all about secrets! That's how undetectable
and multi-faceted Lye's secret society is. I mean, for
crying out loud, I worked for the guy and didn't know
what he was up to most of the time. And even though
Lye surely knows by now that Coy is helping you, Lye
never told me his history with Coy. It wasn't until that
night at the restaurant, hearing Coy's story and
realizing it sounded a lot like another one I had heard
of, when I made the connection. And, to Lye's credit, it
was wise of him never to cue me into Coy's past

because, as it turned out, getting the true story broke my heart."

Stone's voice trailed off. He paused for a few moments, his head down. When he looked up again, there were tears in his eyes—tears of pain.

"Shattered it into a thousand pieces!" he wept, throwing his arms up in grief. "Something changed within me that night. I didn't see Helen's death as a victory anymore; I saw it instead as one man's misery. You see, that's what Lye does to you. He brainwashes you, manipulates you. Whether he hits you over the head with his staff or with his lies, he indoctrinates you with his twisted concepts until you live in a false reality. He makes you dead to emotion and puts you past feeling until you feel nothing—not even the coldness of your own heart. He removes you from the pain that his programs cause others until you come to believe there's no such thing as pain—that there's no such thing as right and wrong, that what you do doesn't have any consequences. And you hear and see and do these things so much that you eventually come to believe them yourself. But that night, I began to see things as they really were. I saw all the pain that I had caused and would cause by doing Lye's bidding. I couldn't do it anymore, couldn't live with myself. That's why, when I got the call from those vigilantes who captured you at the delta of the Amazon River, I told them to let you go."

"That was…that was *you?*" Ret asked in surprise, never having learned why those bandits mysteriously turned away that day.

"Yes," Stone confessed, wiping his wet cheeks. "Once I did that, I knew I had to go into hiding. Lye had put me in charge of keeping tabs on you. I was to monitor you at all times and report everything to him. That's why he placed me at your school. He was especially concerned about the scars—which one was active, which one was next. That's why he stationed guards all along the Amazon—each one would act as a buffer against you getting to his Vault before him. He couldn't lose the Vault, Ret; that's where he kept his money to fund his schemes. But I duped him—a total slap in his face. He had no idea where you were, that you would make your appearance at the Vault in a matter of days."

"Then why was he already there when I arrived?" Ret questioned.

"He was?" Stone said, flabbergasted.

"Yeah, he was totally ready for me," Ret recalled.

"So you didn't get the element then?" Stone wondered. This was all news to him since he severed his ties with Lye. "Is the Vault still intact?" A part of Stone hoped this was the case, as it would mean Lye might not be as upset with him.

"No, I got the element, and the Vault is history," Ret told him, "but it wasn't easy. Lye was expecting me."

"Well, I can't say I'm surprised," Stone said. "Someone must have tipped him off, but it wasn't me. No, it wasn't long at all after that phone call from the Amazon when I sat Virginia down and told her everything. In her infinite compassion, she forgave me. I told her we had to leave immediately—go to someplace in the middle of nowhere and live out the rest of our days in hiding or until the threat of Lye was gone. I figured you'd sneak into the Vault right under Lye's nose, then collect the element and, as a result, destroy his treasury. He would be furious, and he would release his rage on *me*. So we left, taking very little with us. We enrolled Charlotte in a retirement community along the way, then bought a trailer and didn't stop until we felt we had reached a place where no one would ever find us. And no one has." He picked up his untouched glass of milk and drank it dry. "Until today." Reaching the end of his narrative, he placed the empty glass back on the table and slouched in his seat with a sigh.

There was silence in the tiny tin trailer for several minutes. Ret sat ponderously, his mind digesting Lester's words and his stomach Virginia's soup. Stone's cheeks were still moist from his tears—tears which Ret wanted to believe were genuine, but, for all he knew, Stone could very well have made up his entire story in an effort to "foster friendship and then betray confidences," which he just said was one of Lye's tactics. It certainly was a good story, but didn't Stone also say his so-called former boss was "the master of deceit"? Sure, he had been kind to Ret today, carrying him into his home and feeding him a meal, but such behavior is faked all the time. Who was to say this pretend principal had really, truly changed?

And, for that matter, what is change? Is it a real, tangible object that we can hold in our hands like the coins in our pocket? Or is it merely a temporary, nebulous concept that ebbs and flows like waves or comes and goes like seasons? Does change actually exist? Can it be bottled and measured or only observed and supposed? The widowed Ben Coy changed because of something that happened *to* him, yet the penitent Principal Stone said he changed because of something that happened *in* him. So where does change even come from? Is it an unavoidable force of fate upon us or a voluntary power of soul within us? Is it a true desire of the heart or a weak wish upon a star? What exactly *is* change? Is it even real?

Perhaps, then, one proof of the reality of an unseen force is its seen effects—not so much the changer as its changes. We know autumn primarily because the leaves are seen changing color, not because of the unseen changing of the earth's orbit. We know old age better because of the seen changes to the body's skin than the unseen changes to the body's organs. We know repentance because we see changes in behavior, not the unseen change of the heart.

And so, for being such an unseen thing, there was a definite change to be seen in the person of Lester W. Stone. His mannerisms were more mild than mean, his words more kind than cruel, his tone more soft than stern. But nowhere was his change more apparent than in his eyes, those windows to the soul. They used to be shifty but now were steady, used to be pointed but now at peace, veiled but now vindicated.

So what is change? Ret still didn't know exactly, but he *could* tell you what it's like. Change is like the wind moving through a field of grain: itself unseen but its influence seen moving through something, working within someone. Change is like the invisible signals of communication: it can emanate from a source and be picked up by an attuned receiver. Change is like the magnetized bits of a computer hard drive: a state of being—an orientation—that is hard to read with the natural eye.

Is change real? "Yes," Ret would say, "yes it is."

Finally, Ret moved to end the pensive silence. He started, "Principal Stone—"

"Please," Stone interrupted kindly, as if displeased with his former title, "call me Lester."

Still employing his sense of propriety, Ret revised, "Mr. Stone, what was it exactly that caused you to change?" Ret's question struck at the heart of what he needed to know if he was ever going to fulfill the mandate to "cure the world." Maybe Stone could offer some insight as a newly changed man himself.

But Stone was at an apparent loss for words. He scrunched his face, looked around, and even scratched his head in search of an answer. Seeing him struggle, Virginia emerged from her hideout in the kitchen and went to her husband's side. She lovingly sat on his knee and wrapped her arm around his back. Stone smiled to find that his answer had literally come to him.

"It was love," Stone said, grasping his wife's hand. His eyes were moist again, his voice stifled by emotion. "It was true love that caused me to change. I saw the immense love that Mr. Coy had for his wife—so real, so pure. How could anyone *not* see something like that? His pain and anguish gave me a glimpse into what lay in store for me if I didn't change course. You see, there is no love with Lye. He'll tell you there is, of course, but it's not real love—it's love's counterfeit: lust. Everything he does is for himself—to satisfy his wants and his desires, never someone else's. That's what lust is: to love self at the expense of others. And that's why

Lye is miserable: because he doesn't know true love." Then, smiling at his wife, he added, "Real love is about others; fake love is about self. And that's what I learned from Mr. Coy that night. I realized Lye's world revolves around himself, but Coy's world revolved around everyone but himself. And when my mind caught hold of such a stark contrast, my guilt and emptiness were replaced by light and hope. I wanted what he had. That night, Mr. Coy rescued me. Please thank him for me the next time you see him."

"I'm not sure when that'll be," Ret informed him. The Stones stared at him with a look requesting explanation. "I ran away. Like you, I needed to escape from all of this."

"Now why would you do a thing like that, Ret?" Stone asked tenderly.

"Because..." Ret stuttered, convicted by his own conscience, "because I was selfish." He was speaking methodically, drawing conclusions from knowledge gleaned thus far on his great northern trek. "Because I let my own useless cares eat away at my love and concern for others." Stone's introspection had spurred Ret's own. "Because I doubted people's ability to change so much that I started to believe they couldn't."

As Ret looked down in shame, the Stones looked at each other with compassion for their castoff guest.

Virginia got up to prepare a place for Ret to sleep for the night.

"Lye must be stopped, Ret," Stone said soberly. "He is raining down his wicked influence over the peoples of the earth. The rising floodwaters largely go unseen, but their damaging effects are very easy to be seen. His might may seem unmatched and his darkness impenetrable, but, in reality, his authority is very limited. He only has as much power as we give him. Not long ago, I was a slave to Lye; I let him have all power over me. But not anymore. Today, his power has shrunk a bit. Today, his dominions are less one heart—*my* heart." Stone rose to clear the table. "People can change, Ret," he told the morose young man with a soft clasp on the back. "I did." Then Stone grabbed the dirty dishes and walked away, his heavy steps booming along the suspended floor.

With the weight of the world on his shoulders again, Ret spilled out of his chair to get some fresh air. He dragged himself to the backdoor, down the makeshift steps, and out into the small clearing behind the trailer. He felt so conflicted—so displeased with his life, with the world, with everything. He felt singled out by the sages—picked on by the planets—knowing what was expected of him but not sure if he wanted to do it. He felt the universe asking him to settle it in his heart, once and for all.

The sun had set on another day, engulfing the world in shadow. And yet, despite the arrival of night, there seemed to be an unusually bright gleam coming from above. Ret looked up, expecting to find a full moon or a starry expanse. But instead of celestial bodies, Ret saw something in the sky that would change his life forever.

CHAPTER 8

LOVE AT FIRST SIGHT (AGAIN)

Mr. Coy's trip home to Little Tybee Island was very different from his initial flight to Waters Deep. Instead of traveling alone, this time he had Jaret to keep him company. The two of them quickly became immersed in dialogue, which prevented Coy from drowning in his own dismal thoughts again. While Jaret's heart was aflutter with memories of his past matrimony, Mr. Coy's heart was soaring on his high hopes for the future, for he had made out like a bandit at the Deep, sneaking away with an important member of Lye's personnel—a commander, no less. It was Coy's intention to free Jaret from his brainwashed condition and make an ally out of him, simply by telling him the truth about the Oracle.

But oh, where to begin! Coy commenced with that day, a few years ago, when it all started for him—when the United States government asked him to investigate an incident off the coast of Florida, involving the sinking of an unidentified ship, the disappearance of a Coast Guard captain, and the washing ashore of some unusual wreckage.

"Yes, yes!" Jaret interjected. "I remember that now!"

Then it was off to Sunken Earth, that surreptitious civilization whose equality Lye had undone in his quest to seize control of the earth element that was protected within the peak of the land's great mountain.

"Sunken Earth!" Jaret cheered. "I think *I've* been there, too."

Next, Coy detailed the cross-country adventure that took them to Fire Island, whose native clans had been decimated by Lye's centuries-old plot to force entry into the volcano's magma chamber and claim the fire element within.

"So that's what that Bubba character was really up to," Jaret learned.

And Coy couldn't leave out the Great River of ore, with its long trail of underground secrets that led to Lye's personal pyramid of wealth where the third element was hidden.

"Lye never said how he lost the Vault," Jaret recalled.

Coy made mention, too, of Ret—his powers, scars, and uncertain origin; of Lionel—his past support but sudden about-face; of Pauline—her previous precautions but newfound trust; of the Oracle itself, even bringing it out of his bag for Jaret to hold for himself. The knowledge to be shared seemed as endless as the miles of open ocean to be crossed.

But Mr. Coy made sure the information exchange was a two-way street. After all, it wasn't every day he found himself in the same cockpit as one of Lye's insiders. Coy was most concerned about what Lye was currently up to—was he already seeking out the next element?

"I don't know," Jaret explained. "He doesn't tell us much, and we don't see him very often. He is constantly on the move. Just a day or two ago, I heard he was somewhere near the North Pole—you know, up in the Arctic Circle."

"Really?" Coy wondered with great interest. "What's he doing up there, I wonder?" He hoped Jaret had more to say.

But again Jaret said, "I don't know," sounding as though he wished he had a better answer, "and who knows if he's still there."

"Hmm," Coy thought. He glanced at the plane's fuel gauge, which told him the tank couldn't afford a detour to the Arctic right then. It would have to wait. "Well," Coy concluded innocently, his mind churning with ideas, "there *is* good fishing up there this time of year."

Through it all, a strong bond was developing between the pilot and his passenger. They asked each other question after question and answered them all. For the commander, the truth seemed to have a familiar ring to it—that is, it rang true to him. Each bit of information was either being aligned or realigned in the hard drive of his brain, according to the real story. Coy's words were filling in the blanks, piecing together the puzzle, and switching on the light bulbs. Jaret vocalized his epiphanic moments with an audible "ah-ha." By the time Coy landed the floatplane near the shore of Little Tybee, Jaret Cooper was a new man—a *re*newed man, that is.

As anxious as Jaret was to see his wife and daughter, Mr. Coy insisted things be done in the proper order.

"First," Coy told him as they approached the Manor's main gate, "we need to get you out of those commander clothes. We don't want you looking like GI Joe for your big debut tonight, do we?"

"Who's GI Joe?" Jaret asked under his breath while Coy instructed the maid on the intercom to open the gate.

Walking through the gate, Jaret had the usual reaction that most newcomers have when they experience the Manor for the first time: shock and awe, with a kind of what-in-the-world-is-this-place look on his face.

In their march to the double doors, Jaret's pace slowed, too busy staring at the varied styles of architecture and the different plants throughout the grounds.

Realizing Jaret had fallen behind to take in the Manor's unique beauty, Mr. Coy smiled with great satisfaction. "Home sweet home," he rejoiced as he pushed open the double doors.

Jaret ran to catch up, crossing the threshold and following Mr. Coy across the semicircular foyer.

Like a child coming home from school, Coy said, "Hi, Mom," waving at the bust of his mother, which was, of course, hidden from view in the middle of the foyer, thanks to the workings of a Black Mirror. Jaret stuttered in his steps, straining to find this phantom matriarch, but he never did.

Coy led Jaret deep into the Manor—down two flights of stairs and then up four, through a zigzagging hallway, down a laundry chute, around a large glass tank, briefly along a tightrope, through five sets of doors, up a ladder, and in and out of a long line of ivory pillars. In the course of his tour, Jaret saw a group of bakers shakily carrying a massive wedding cake; he nearly tripped over a team that was waxing the floor; he crossed paths with a butcher chasing a wild turkey, feathers flying everywhere; he found a pair of electricians Velcro-ed to the ceiling, replacing a shorted fuse; he narrowly dodged a kick to his chest from a ninja; and he almost ran into a moose. What's more, he still had no idea where Mr. Coy's mother was.

When they finally stopped, Jaret asked, out of breath, "What is this place?" He thought it was Mr. Coy who was standing next to him, but, as it turned out, it was an Eskimo man, dressed in a puffy suit that made him look like a hamster that had just been electrocuted.

Now totally beside himself, Jaret shrieked upon seeing the stranger, "Ah!"

Equally alarmed, the Eskimo man shrieked back, "Ah!"

Just then, Mr. Coy appeared and calmly said to a frazzled Jaret, "I see you've met Mo."

"Mo?" Jaret mouthed, surprised to hear such a common name for the exotic man. Mo smiled and waved at Jaret, his hand enclosed in a large mitten.

"Yeah, you know, as in Eski-mo," Coy explained. "He's originally from Greenland, but none of us could pronounce his native Inuit name, so we just started calling him Mo. He's here at the Manor studying fashion, which he says is his passion even though all we ever see him wearing is that snowsuit." Mo blushed behind his fuzzy, fur-lined hood. "So, anyhow, he'll help you pick out some clothes. Then it's off to dinner."

"Dinner?" Jaret questioned.

"Yes," Coy replied. "Your sweet wife puts on a lovely dinner in her home each week, and tonight *you* are the guest of honor. So you'd better look sharp, captain!" Coy moved to leave. "Oh, and Mo," he said, turning back, "let's go with something that's not too Eskimo-ish, okay?" Mo saluted, as best he could in his bulky jacket.

As it turned out, Mo wasn't much help. His only input was a silk scarf that Jaret put on out of pure politeness.

"Nice scarf," Coy complimented when he came to get Jaret.

"Thanks," Jaret muttered. Leaving, the two of them turned to wave to Mo, who, like a great stuffed teddy bear, was grinning from ear to ear to see Jaret wearing the scarf.

Jaret followed Coy to a nearby elevator, which brought them back to the Manor's main foyer within a matter of seconds.

"Why didn't we just take the elevator in the first place?!" Jaret laughed.

"And deprive you of your small taste of the Manor?" Coy returned.

"So what exactly is this place?" Jaret asked as they set off across the grounds toward the new Cooper home. "Is it a...a house?"

"Though my daughter and I live here," Coy said, "most of the Manor is dedicated to teaching and training our students. I call them students, but they're more like family. We've got a little bit of everyone here: some were orphaned or homeless, a few were rescued slaves or ex-convicts, many were peasants from third-world countries. Each one represents someone who needed a second chance in life (or a first one) and was willing to change. So we take them in and give them that chance. After they've learned a skill or mastered a trade, most of them leave to either enter the workforce or go to school. And, once we've helped them become self-reliant, all we ask for in return is that they give back to the Manor in some way, if possible, so that others can benefit like they did." Then, to answer Jaret's question, Coy added, "So yes, captain, it's a house: a house of redemption."

For the rest of the trek to the new Cooper home, Jaret walked in silent amazement. For the last few years, the commander's home had been the forlorn fortress at Water's Deep, which, in some ways, was similar to this place called Coy Manor. Both were large, mostly underground compounds whose happenings were much more than what met the eye. Both were right on the sea, though neither was well known. Each housed dozens of people and served ornate purposes. And yet, in principle, Waters Deep was the exact opposite of Coy Manor: the former was seeking to ruin the world, the latter was trying to cure it.

Finally, the two men arrived at the house.

"Here we are," Coy announced quietly, stepping up to the door. Jaret quickly made sure his shirt was tucked in, then wiped a few beads of sweat from his forehead and started cracking his knuckles.

"You're nervous," Coy playfully pointed out.

"I'm not nervous," Jaret quickly denied.

"Yes, you are," Coy teased.

"No, I'm not," Jaret said, straight-faced. They stood in silence for a moment. Then Jaret turned to Coy and asked, "Is there anything in my teeth?"

"I'm not going to look at your teeth," Coy declined.

"Fine," said Jaret, looking down to make sure his shoes were tied.

Coy rang the doorbell.

Jaret cleared his throat. Then, remembering there was a scarf around his neck, he whisked it off and threw it in the bushes.

There was no answer, so Coy knocked rather vigorously.

Glancing around, Jaret observed with slight confusion, "This isn't the house I remember."

"You're right," Coy whispered, "Lye blew up your old one."

"He did what—"

Suddenly, Pauline's voice rang out from inside: "Come in! Come in!"

Jaret was about to rush inside when Coy stopped him.

"You wait here," Coy instructed. It was all Jaret could do to wait even longer.

Coy opened the door and stepped inside. There was ample evidence that Pauline was cooking in her kitchen: the oven was beeping, the microwave was chiming, a saucepan was boiling over, the range fan was going full blast, there was chopping at the cutting board, the lid of a pot was spinning on the floor, and it seemed every last dish in the kitchen had been dirtied and was now sitting in the sink or on the counter.

"Hi, Ben!" Pauline shouted above the commotion as she rushed to address something on the stove that was smoking. "The kids are on their way. Make yourself at home." Just then, something in the microwave exploded.

Peeking in from the porch, Jaret noticed the chaos and recalled, "Yep, that's my wife, alright." Although Pauline was a good chef, sometimes her scatter-brained thought pattern shone through in her cooking.

"I have someone I want you to meet," Coy yelled.

"Yes, the meat's almost done," Pauline thought he said, "just needs a few more minutes."

"No, I said—"

"What?!" Pauline hollered, unable to hear Coy above the noise.

Back on the porch, Jaret was all smiles, "She hasn't changed a bit!"

Mr. Coy paraded into the crazy kitchen and silenced everything that was beeping, bubbling, or burning. When order was restored, Coy said, "I have someone I want you to meet."

"Oh, well why didn't you say so?!" Pauline heartily obliged, wiping her hands on her apron. Coy rolled his eyes.

"You stand here," he told her, positioning her portly frame a few yards from the doorway.

"This had better not be another one of your practical jokes, Ben," Pauline warned.

"Oh no, quite the contrary, my dear," Coy told her. Then, when the moment was right, he called out toward the door, "Okay, come in."

Just then, Thorne walked in.

"Did you know there's a man standing right outside the door?" he announced.

"Thorne!" Coy howled in frustration. "Step aside!"

Once Thorne had moved away, Coy restated his command, "Okay, *now* come in."

A tall silhouette appeared on the porch, its person concealed by the evening's darkness. Pauline's eyes narrowed without a clue of who to expect. Timidly, Jaret stepped into the house, the soft light revealing his identity.

For a few moments, the entire scene was frozen in time. Pauline stared wide-eyed at her long-lost husband. There, standing before her, was the sand-colored hair, the sun-kissed skin, the broad shoulders. Oh, and the dimple, where was the—ah, there, just below the cheek. His collared shirt hugged his robust chest, and his smiling lips curled her own, for Jaret was staring just as longingly at his wife. With her coarse brown hair drawn back and her grease-splattered sleeves rolled up, there was the woman of his dreams, with even more stains on her apron than he remembered. There, standing before him, were the work-worn hands, the time-tested values, and the love handles he loved to handle. And, in a way, the misery from their years-long separation was well worth it, for, in that moment, they were falling in love all over again.

Finally, the two lovers couldn't stare at each other any longer. With one accord, they rushed together and embraced with a kiss. As they continued to hold each other in their arms, Mr. Coy couldn't help but shed a tear. He went over to Thorne and told him with a hug, "Isn't love beautiful?"

"Yes, it is," Thorne agreed, "but why are you hugging me?"

"I don't know," Coy said, "I just felt like hugging someone."

But the reunion was only half complete, for soon thereafter Ana came running through the door.

"Dad! Dad!" she cried, throwing herself into her father's arms.

"There's my girl!" Jaret rejoiced, picking her up with a royal spin. "What a beautiful young lady you've become!"

"I can't believe you're back," Ana wept with joy. "What…how…?"

And so began a truly wonderful evening. Not far behind Ana were Paige and Dusty, followed by their bodyguard Missy. The food was served and the meal enjoyed, just like old times. And, also like old times, there was a colossal mess in the kitchen to clean up—a chore that Jaret had been dreaming of doing for months.

"Well, Coy," Thorne said, joining him on the couch as the others carried on with all of the catching up they had to do, "looks like you had a good trip."

"Yes, I did," Coy concurred. "In fact, it was so good that I'm ready for my next one."

"Oh?" Thorne chuckled. "And where to this time?"

"Better break out your long underwear," Coy told him. "You and I are going to the Arctic!"

CHAPTER 9

A LIGHT IN THE NIGHT

Ret knew it was much too early for dawn. When he had passed through the small kitchen of the Stones' trailer on his way out the backdoor, he had seen on the microwave that it wasn't even ten o'clock yet. Perhaps the clock had the wrong time, for the scene before him looked like the early indications of sunrise. A couple hundred yards in front of him sat a large hill, much wider than it was tall. It extended far off to the right before it sloped into the flat ground, but to the left it tapered off only slightly before rolling into another hill. There was a faint light outlining the top of the hill so that it looked like the sun was rising behind it. But no matter how much it looked like dawn, Ret knew this was absurd, not only because of the time of day but also because he was looking to the north (not the east, where he knew the sun to rise). He then wondered if there might be a large city on the other side of the hill but quickly dismissed the idea, remembering his remote location.

A few minutes passed, and the mysterious light seemed to be getting brighter. It even slightly flared up a time or two in random places, coming to life like the head of a struck match and then blowing to the left as a wave, all very slowly. Soon, the entire length of the hilltop was a dark silhouette against the unknown backdrop. The light had a green tint to it, and it glowed more than it shined. Unlike a sunrise, the light was having no effect on the night sky, which was still dark as ever. In fact, Ret could see stars immediately around the light—or the glow, or whatever it was. But if it wasn't the sun or a city, what was it?

And then it was gone. In a matter of seconds, it was nowhere to be seen. The light didn't retreat or simply go back down but rather dissolved and faded away, like a firework burning out in slow-motion.

Ret was confused, a little disappointed even. He continued to stare up at the sky. Free from the light pollution of a city, he was granted an untainted view into the cosmos. He saw not only stars but entire systems of them, almost the very colors and clouds of nebulae deep within the galaxy. He located the North Star and traced constellations with ease. The Big Dipper seemed close enough that he could reach out, grab its handle, and pour the ladle. Shooting stars were frequent. The sky was so littered that it really did look like a Milky Way.

Amid so much vastness, Ret couldn't help but feel insignificant and powerless, like sitting in a one-man dinghy in the middle of the ocean. He recalled learning in science class how some stars are so far away that it takes their light many years to travel through space and be seen on earth. And those were just the stars he could see. He knew there were countless others that remained unseen. But even though he acknowledged his relative nothingness in the universe, Ret found consolation in the truth that the Oracle knew who he was. That clever sphere, too perfect to be manmade yet too symbolic to have been forged by nature, was aware of what he was doing and where he was going. It was like it cared about him—like it needed him, even though it could get along just fine without him. In reality, you see, it was Ret who needed *it*.

Ret's star-gazing and soul-searching lasted a good while. There was so much to look at, so much to think about. The night sky was getting ever darker as the earth continued to turn him further and further away from the sun. It was then, in this darkest hour of the night, when Ret saw something out of the corner of his eye. It was the light! The green glow from earlier was back. In total silence, it reappeared on the horizon, far off to the right, a little ways beyond where the hill met the ground. It rose into the air and began to stretch out across the sky from right to left like a great green rainbow. Its arc passed overhead, then maneuvered between the dip in the hills and kept going out of sight into the night on the other side of the horizon.

Ret quickly learned the light had a mind of its own. It wasn't quite bright enough to cast shadows on the ground, but it was alive and moving. It would grow wider, then get thinner, and sometimes fade away in parts, only to come back again. The light flowed through the sky like a slow-moving stream, from right to left, as if it was a cloud of stellar dust being blown by an interplanetary wind. Yet it wasn't far off in the upper reaches of outer space; no, it was much closer than that. The green gas seemed to be passing through the very atmosphere of the earth. Its proximity was a matter of miles, not light-years.

To be honest, it was quite an unusual sight. It was not a meteor shower. There was no comet or asteroid—nothing apparently physical or tangible about it. It contained neither the sun nor the moon. It was not a barrage of shooting stars or a grand coalition of planets swirling together in the heavens. It was just light—a moving stream of greenish light passing through the sky, seemingly without a beginning or an end or even a source. Ret couldn't help but wonder if it was authentic or instead something as simple as a reflection or as mundane as jet exhaust.

Apparently, the light was a night owl. The later it got, the more the phenomenon came to life. Over time, it fanned out into four or five individual bands across the night sky, like massive streamers hung for a party or the strings of some intergalactic guitar. The pale green ribbons were more fuzzy than beam-like, their long edges diminishing gradually rather than ending abruptly. They reached out with a definite curve, convex to the north, and Ret thought it very possible that he was seeing just a small portion of the circumference of a large ring that circled the top of the earth like a giant halo.

But the best was yet to come. As if putting on a show, Ret suddenly saw the steady stream of light flare up on the right. With the shape of a skinny tornado, a bright funnel came into view, far away where the sky met the ground. Like a genie spewing out of its lamp, the light unhurriedly made its way higher into the air, growing bigger and wider the closer it came towards Ret. Without haste, it slithered as a snake and spread out over Ret's head. Like ink dripped in a pool of water, the emerald light moved along its undefined path around the globe. Then, as if there were prisms dangling from the stars, the green glow dashed into dozens of pieces and splashed onto their midnight canvas. It seemed to be the work of a sort of cosmic disco ball, with the fragments dancing in the sky. They lined up like the keys of a piano, no doubt being played by the constellation Centaurus as he was horsing around. When the flare up finally passed on its way to finish its worldwide tour, Ret thought he had been looking at the firmament above through a kaleidoscope. The spectacle truly had been heaven-sent.

Ret spent the rest of the night watching the mysterious light in the sky. Lying on his back, he warmed the frigid ground beneath him to keep away the chill in the air. Eventually, the light began to wane until it disappeared, all without ever making a sound. Not long thereafter, the real dawn began to break in the east, bringing to a close a very thrilling night. Ret retired to the bed Virginia had prepared for him on the couch, where he slept all day. Then, when night had fallen again, he returned to the lot behind the trailer to see if the light would make another appearance.

And, boy, did it. This time it was bigger, brighter, and more animated than the previous night. The radiant stream billowed and curled, swelled and wisped—filling the whole sky, it seemed. Its shades of green were like neon at times, and then it wowed Ret with new colors: reds and purples, blues and yellows. It was amazing. It was stunning. It was unreal. Nearly every moment was different. It was a living, moving thing. Ret longed to know what could possibly be going on to create such dazzling displays.

Again, he watched all night, slept all day, and then returned at dusk for another go. Some nights, the light was very strong and swayed like curtains with many colors. Other nights, it was quite weak and stayed more still in its usual fluorescent green. But it was always there, even if it was barely visible—except for the time when a patch of clouds passed through, temporarily blocking Ret's view of the light above them.

For a week, Ret maintained his midnight vigils, waiting on the light with the kind of devotion that normal people have toward new episodes of their favorite sitcoms. Each night featured something new, ending before dawn in a sort of "to be continued" fashion. Ret loved it.

Of course, the Stones quickly took notice of their guest's newfound astronomical passion. Each night before going to bed, they glanced out the back window to see if Ret was there, and he always was, lying on his back, staring up at the sky. It made them smile to see him take such an interest in a phenomenon they had grown accustomed to over the last few months. For all her worry, Virginia was finding Ret to be quite a pleasant guest. Since he didn't eat much and had recently become nocturnal, it was like he wasn't even there.

It was at the beginning of the second week of Ret's nightly watches when Virginia, seeing him through the blinds again, went out to talk to him. She figured he probably had a question or two about what was occurring in the sky, as had been the case with her when she saw it for the first time. With a creak, she opened the flimsy backdoor, wrapping herself more tightly in her robe against the cool evening air. Her slippers tapped softly on the few steps of the wooden staircase as she made her way down to the pebbled ground.

"Whatcha doing?" she asked pleasantly, as if she didn't already know.

"Oh, just looking up at the stars," Ret told her. He figured the light was something that only he could see, similar to the wind or waves of communication, and he didn't feel like going into a lengthy explanation of what she could not see.

"Must be hard with all that green light in the way," Virginia poked.

"You can see that?" Ret wondered.

"Of course I can see it," Virginia chuckled. "I've seen it many times, actually."

"So you know what it is, then?" Ret said eagerly. "You know how it's done?"

"Well, I know the basics," she admitted modestly.

Thirsty for an explanation, Ret sat up and reached with his mind for a broken footstool he knew was over by the staircase. Made of metal, he pulled it near with hardly a flick of his wrist. On its way, he tightened the loose screws and regrew one of its missing legs. Then he positioned it next to him, conjured a small campfire for warmth, and bade Virginia to sit.

"Wow," she said, awed by Ret's powers, "you could come in real handy around here."

"That's nothing," Ret grinned. "So, about the light…"

"Ah, yes," she said, sitting down, "aurora borealis."

"What?"

"That's what it's called: aurora borealis," she explained, "named after the Roman goddess of dawn, Aurora, and the Greek name for the north wind, Boreas. But it's more commonly known as the Northern Lights."

"Oh," Ret remembered, "I've heard of that. So these are the Northern Lights?"

"These are them."

"Where do they come from?"

"The lights are a result of solar wind," Virginia taught, "which is a stream of ions (or charged particles) continuously being given off by the sun. Because of the sun's rotation, super-hot temperature, and frequent explosions, lots of electrons and protons are able to escape into space. This creates solar wind, a medium that moves throughout space. When these tiny bits of energized matter reach the earth, they are attracted by the earth's magnetic fields and channeled toward the north and south poles, forming a ring around both the top and bottom of the earth. Some solar wind is able to enter the earth's atmosphere, where it collides with gas particles like oxygen and nitrogen. Some of the gas particles become ionized and excited by the solar wind, but when they return to a normal state, they release their energy in the form of light. The different colors of the light depend on which type of gas was involved, its altitude, and how it interacted with the energy it received."

"So *that's* how it works," Ret said with awe. Then, digesting the science, "Hmm…sounds like kind of a raw deal for the gases, don't you think?"

"What do you mean?"

"I mean, the gases are just sitting in the atmosphere, minding their own business," Ret elaborated, "when, all of a sudden, a ton of crazy ions come along and start crashing into them. What a bunch of bums!"

Virginia laughed, "Well, when you put it that way, I guess the ions do seem a little rude, don't they? But look what the gases are able to do with the energy they receive." She swept the sky with her hand. "They create this beautiful sight for us to enjoy."

"But why don't the ions do that on their own?" Ret put forth. "Why do they have to mess with the gases?" Virginia, who was new to Ret's unique brand of deep thinking, could sense the conversation shifting away from the science of chemistry to the science of people.

"You know, Ret," Virginia said with a voice of wisdom, "as we go through life, we are bombarded by all kinds of ions. I don't mean subatomic particles; I mean the unseen forces—positive or negative—that try to influence us for good or for bad. Some ions we welcome; others we avoid; and a few, try as we might, we just can't seem to evade. But even though we can't always choose what happens to us, we *can* choose how we react to what happens to us. And that's how we can put a stop to the cycle of negative energy that we see so much of in the world today. When some of it comes our way, we can either pass it on to someone else and keep the cycle going or we can turn it around into something positive and release it. And when we choose to let it go, a beautiful thing happens." Again, she motioned up at the lights still streaming in the sky overhead.

"So, what you're saying is," Ret summarized, a hint of sarcasm in his voice, "we're all just a bunch of gas?" The remark sent Virginia into a fit of laughter. "You know, my sister Ana says gas is disgusting."

"Lester didn't tell me you were such a comedian," she sighed. "I'm glad you understand what I'm trying to say." Then, putting her elbows on her knees and putting her chin in her cupped hands, she looked up and said, "I've spent a lot of time watching this light in the night."

Light in the night? Where had Ret heard that before? A quick search in his mind turned up Leo. Of course! It was a phrase from Leo's song. Ret could almost hear it again, as if the orphan was sitting on the fire escape now, singing away, his voice being carried thousands of miles by the wind:

> *I fear the darkness in the night.*
> *I'm alone, there's no one but me.*
> *Clearly outnumbered and severely encumbered*
> *By the darkness in all that I see.*

> *But there's a light—a light in the night!*
> *A light I never saw was there:*
> *The sunshine concealed it, now the darkness*
> *   revealed it.*
> *How could I miss a light so fair?*

> *There are times when I see no hope*
> *For this world of heartache and sin.*
> *Too hard to correct it, so I'll just neglect it,*
> *Too much darkness for light to win.*

> *But there's a light—a light in the night!*
> *I'm not alone; there're legions like me.*
> *And the darker the night grows, the starker each*
> *   light glows.*
> *Oh, these lights in the night—now I see!*

It was in this moment when Ret realized Leo's song wasn't so much about light as it was about people. And not just any people—good people. Such was a conclusion brought on by the Northern Lights. Like the lights, there was a steady stream of goodness still alive in the world today, surviving the relentless darkness that threatened to snuff it out. Like the lights, this heavenly band was seemingly small, fragmented, and largely unknown, but it was always there, hanging on, and absolutely stunning. Like the lights, the goodness in people was easy to miss in the light of day, since it stood out best against the night of evil.

It was just like Virginia had said: the lights were about people—people making good choices when confronted with the energies and influences of negative ions.

It was just like the Oracle, how it wasn't so much about collecting elements of the natural world as it was about collecting elements of the social world. The world didn't need the element of earth; it needed the element of good government and honest leadership. The element of fire was worthless compared to the element of self-control and continence. The element of ore would do precious little to cure the world without the element of caring for the poor and keeping greed at bay.

And so it was there, on the far-flung plains of the northern wilderness and under the brilliance of one of the wonders of the natural world, where Ret experienced a turning point in his life. He was done running away. His escape from responsibility was over. The clarion call of duty was sounding in his ears—long, loud, and clear. He would fill the Oracle with Mother Nature's original elements and, along the way, teach the world by example and by precept that it could be cured by fostering certain social elements. He would find strength in the lights—the pure-hearted peoples of the earth—but they needed a voice to sound the alarm and raise the standard. Ret would be that voice—the voice of one crying in the wilderness.

With eagerness, Ret looked down at his scar, something he had tried to ignore for many days. To his delight, it was fully illuminated. The barb with the pennant flag was still at the bottom of the circle, pointing down like always. The other barb, the one that moved in whatever direction Ret was facing, now had a pennant at its end also, which was something Ret had never seen it do before. In the past, this barb had always had one to four bars at its end, but not anymore. What's more, this barb didn't seem to move around anymore either. Ret turned to the right and to the left (to the east and to the west), but the once changeable barb didn't budge. It remained pointed north.

Again, Ret looked to the lights for an explanation. It seemed the scar had an affinity for the aurora borealis.

The barb on top was now fixated on the north, and its pennant was a measure of the extreme activity currently taking place in the airwaves above Ret's head. All along, the scar had intended to send him to the Northern Lights and, in its infinite wisdom, had done so even when Ret was trying to get away from it.

But the barb on top of the circle was only half of the complete scar. Ret now focused on the barb at the bottom of the circle, the one that, thus far, had never moved and was always pointed south. The wheels in his head began to turn.

"Virginia!" Ret cried out with vigor.

Startled by the sudden shout after staring in silence at the lights for several minutes, Virginia fell back in her footstool with a scream of her own.

"Sorry," Ret said more softly, reaching to help her. "Did you say solar wind is attracted to the earth's *South* Pole as well?"

"I did," she recalled. "It's much the same down there as what we see up here, but it's called the aurora australis, or Southern Lights."

"Perfect," Ret whispered, smiling down at his scar. He had a feeling the aurora australis wasn't the only thing he'd find down in Antarctica. He was certain he'd find the Oracle's fourth element there, too.

CHAPTER 10

GOING IN ARCTIC CIRCLES

In preparation for his trip to the North Pole, Mr. Coy was packing all the warm clothing he could find. Even though fall was still a few weeks away in the northern hemisphere, he knew one characteristic of polar climates was their lack of warm summers—at least, that's what Mo the Eskimo told him.

"You'll want to bring a pair of nice, thick gloves," Mo, the wannabe fashionista, advised as he helped Mr. Coy sift through the Manor's costume department. "Oh, and don't forget these," he added, finding some woolen mittens. "And these, too," stumbling upon earmuffs. Next came a colorful assortment of socks, beanies, leg warmers, face masks, goggles, and (of course) scarves. "And all of these," Mo said, dumping his load into Mr. Coy's suitcase.

"Gee, thanks, Mo," Mr. Coy tried to sound appreciative despite seeing many articles he would never wear (especially the leg warmers). "But what's left for *you* to wear?"

"Me?"

"Yes, you're coming with us," Coy informed him. Mo's face lit up, his smile stretching from one side of the fluff of his snowsuit's hood to the other. In his elation, he gave Mr. Coy a big hug, after which Mr. Coy gave him a slip of paper.

"Now, here's a list of things I need you to do before we leave," Coy instructed, zipping his suitcase closed. "I'll see you in a little bit down in the hangar." After receiving a stout salute from Mo, Coy left the room.

Giddy, Mo ran down the list of commands, which didn't take long since there were only two. The first was to pack three weeks' worth of winter attire. He looked at himself in the mirror and thought for a moment. Then Mo, who was always dressed for a polar adventure, said, "Check," and moved on to the next task.

The second assignment was to locate Thorne and accompany him to the hangar. Knowing Mo benefited from thoroughness, Mr. Coy included step-by-step directions of the turns to make and floors to climb in order to find the room where Thorne was living during his visit to the Manor. Coy's instructions would have been fool-proof except Mo didn't know the last letter of Thorne's name was silent.

In time, Mo arrived at the place where Thorne and Dusty were staying, and he knocked on the door (as loudly as he could despite his bulky mittens).

Dusty answered and, giving the strange Eskimo man at his door a quizzical look, said, "Can I help you?"

"Hello," said Mo, employing an official tone as if on important business. "I'm looking for a Mr. Thorny."

"Um, yeah," Dusty snickered, shrugging off the mispronunciation, "it's pronounced 'Thorne.'"

"Okay, but *I* am looking for Mr. Thorny," Mo insisted.

"I know," Dusty said with a bit more laughter, "but the *e* on the end is silent. It's just pronounced Thorne, like a thorn on a rose."

Mo considered this briefly, giving Dusty a suspicious look, and then resumed, "So you are Mr. Thorne. Is there a Mr. Thorny here?"

"Look, dude," Dusty returned, losing his patience with the annoying stuffed animal at the door, "you're not saying it right—"

"It says right here," Mo pointed out with similar frustration, showing Dusty the slip of paper from Mr. Coy, "that I'm supposed to find a Mr. Thorny and escort him to the hangar."

"Yeah, but all I'm saying is—"

Suddenly, Thorne's voice was heard. "You must be Mo," he said pleasantly, stepping behind his son and interrupting the escalating disagreement.

"Yes," Mo told him. "And you are?"

"Why, I'm Mr. Thorny," Thorne said with a smile.

Dusty protested, "But Dad—"

"Let it go, son," Thorne quickly mumbled under his breath. He turned to the messenger and said, "Coy told me he'd be sending you up to get me. Must be time then?"

"Yes, Mr. Thorny, sir," Mo replied, in all seriousness.

"Wonderful," said Thorne, fetching his luggage. Then, sharing a farewell embrace with his son, he cautioned, "Now don't get into any trouble while I'm gone, okay?"

"Yes, Mr. Thorny, sir," Dusty promised with a sly grin, mimicking Mo.

"That's my boy," said the father. "Now then, Mo, lead the way."

"Aye aye!" Then, turning to Dusty, Mo said, "Good day, Mr. Thorne."

Dusty shook his head and gladly closed the door.

Out in the southwestern sector of the Manor's underground hangar—past the runway for the jet, beyond the launch pad for the hot-air balloon, away from the airstrip for the helicopter, and far below the driveway hanging from the ceiling—was the harbor. The yacht was there, the same one that had once gone to the Bimini Road and back, now moored to the dock that was surrounded by jagged rocks. The dark water was rhythmically disturbed by a gentle current, making it obvious that the small inlet was somehow connected to the ocean.

Assuming they'd be making their Arctic voyage in the comfort of the yacht, Thorne strode onto the dock and over to the luxurious vessel, with Mo lugging the luggage behind him. On his way, however, Thorne was startled by the sudden appearance of large air bubbles, coming from the center of the harbor. They grew in size and quantity until, to Thorne's utter surprise, a killer whale emerged from the water. He watched in shock, but the creature was staying as still as he was. A few moments later, he could hear what sounded like the muffled footsteps of someone climbing a metal ladder, and the noise seemed to be coming from inside the whale.

All alarm subsided when, with the squeaky opening of a rusted metal hatch, Mr. Coy appeared at the top of the fake fish's blowhole.

"Ahoy!" yelled Coy. "What do you think of my submarine? I call her the *USS Shamu*."

"You're one of a kind, Coy," Thorne told him, shaking his head and sporting one of those you-never-cease-to-amaze-me looks.

"She's an old boomer," Coy said of the sub, "like the ones you and I used to train in, remember?"

"Oh, I remember," Thorne returned, subconsciously rubbing his lower back.

"The Navy let me have her years ago after they decommissioned her," Coy explained, guiding the submarine closer to the dock. "I've since made a few modifications—reshaped it, reinforced it—and removed the nuclear reactor, of course. Now it's smaller, faster, and safer."

"That and it looks like a whale," Thorne reminded him.

"Ah, the ultimate undersea camouflage," Coy beamed. "A healthy killer whale has no natural predators, you know."

"Camouflage?" Thorne teased. "For all your top-secret missions?"

Ignoring the impertinence, Coy stated, "It never hurts to be a little—*coy.*"

"You didn't happen to modernize its firepower while you were at it, did you?" Thorne hoped.

"I might have," Coy smirked in the affirmative. He extended his hand to help his old military comrade onboard the ship, smiling, "Just like old times, friend."

Then Mo prepared to board, handing over Thorne's bags and proudly reporting to Mr. Coy, "I found Mr. Thorny, sir, just like you asked."

"Mr. Thorny?" Coy muttered.

"Don't ask," Thorne whispered back as he started down the ladder.

"Well done, Mo," Coy complimented him. "Welcome aboard."

It wasn't exactly roomy inside the submarine. It was mostly dark and impressively compact, so much so that Mo thought a more appropriate name for it might be *USS Claustrophobic*. In fact, there was probably more space to be found in Mo's bulbous snowsuit than in the boat's narrow aisles, which he frequently clogged as members of the crew hustled about the cabin in their final preparations before departure. The deckhands consisted of students from the Manor: one who was interested in sonar, another who had a love for marine biology, some who were studying engineering, a few who planned to join the Navy themselves, a pair who really liked torpedoes, and one who came along just to see a penguin in the wild.

Mr. Coy and Thorne took their seats at the controls. It was your typical control room, its walls lined with all sorts of electronics. However, this one was located near the bow, in between the fake whale's two white eyespots, which were actually large windows that had been tinted with a light-colored film. Although the glass was extra-thick, this sub was not intended to dive more than a few hundred feet, which was on par for a real killer whale. Coy was going for as natural a look as possible with his pseudo orca. While the dorsal fin on top aided in steering, the pectoral fins, which could be flapped up and down, were just for show.

As its nuclear reactor had been removed, the vessel moved by way of an electric motor that was connected to a propeller. The power supply began at the whale's exterior, where the long torpedo shafts had been repurposed so that seawater entered and passed through them while in motion. They were like the gills of a fish. Inside these tube-like holes was a series of small turbines, which spun rapidly as water flowed past them. Each turbine was attached to a copper coil within the submarine. When the turbine spun, it rotated the coil among magnets, whose magnetic fields attracted electrons for the coil to collect. This electrical current was then conducted to the motor. Any extra energy was used to charge the backup batteries on board.

Like the pectoral fins, the large fluke in the back also moved but only to scatter the constant stream of bubbles coming out of the tubes, which otherwise would have been a dead giveaway of the whale's mechanical status—either that or made it look like the mammal was constantly passing gas.

The closing of the hatch marked the opening of the journey. The harbor was enclosed on all sides by rocks, but only above the surface of the water. There was an underwater outlet on the far side, granting immediate access to the ocean. So the harbor was almost like a cave, the kind whose mouth is only visible at low tide. Of course, a portion of the wall could be parted, which is how the yacht got in and out, but the submarine simply passed under it.

It was no small voyage they were undertaking. The first day got them all the way up the eastern coast of the United States. On the second, they rounded the island of Newfoundland and started up Canada. It took two days to make it through Baffin Bay. Then they stayed close to Greenland before finally entering the Arctic Ocean.

Even though the purpose of their adventure was to spy on Lye, Mr. Coy had little idea where he would find him or if the dark lord was even still in the Arctic. The whole trip was somewhat of a gamble, based on the vague information Jaret had told him that Lye might be up to something near the North Pole. Coy planned to make the North Pole his first stop, really hoping Lye would be there, for, if he wasn't, Coy didn't know where in the vast Arctic world to begin looking for him.

As they floated toward the North Pole, Mo was on top of the world—in more ways than one. Ever since their course had gotten them near his native land of Greenland, he had been straining to get a glimpse of it, which was difficult to do in a submarine that stayed well below sea level and never stopped to surface. Sitting in the control room with his face plastered against one of the large, oval windows, Mo began to talk to whoever cared to listen.

"Ah, the beautiful Arctic," he said, his voice full of nostalgia, "where there's ice that never melts, winters with no sun, and subzero temperatures that freeze my nose hairs—how I've missed it." Thorne winced at such bleak conditions. Mo continued, "We're a lot different from Antarctica, you know."

"Is that right?" Coy responded, encouraging his student to share his knowledge. "How so, Mo?"

"Well, Antarctica is an actual landmass," Mo answered, his warm breath condensing on the cold glass. "It's an island continent, totally surrounded by ocean. But the Arctic is the exact opposite: it's an ocean that's almost entirely surrounded by land."

"Interesting," said Thorne. "Anything else?"

"And there are no penguins up here," Mo pointed out.

An earshot away, a crewman (the one who had come on the trip solely to see a penguin) mourned, "Aw, man!"

"Antarctica can get much colder than the Arctic," Mo added, "but it's still cold enough up here for the surface of the ocean to freeze. Just look at all the sea ice!"

"Oh, I'm looking at it," Coy said with more worry than wonder. Having arrived near the North Pole, he was currently in the hazardous process of bringing the submarine as close to the frozen surface as he could so that he could take a look around.

"See any leads, Thorne?" Coy asked, employing the proper term for a narrow area of open water within a wide expanse of sea ice.

"There's a fairly large one over there," Thorne informed him.

"That'll work."

With the help of the killer whale's eyes, which were actually cameras, Coy maneuvered the submarine under the long crack in the ice so that only the dorsal fin rose up out of the water. There was a scope on the fin, allowing him a good view of the Arctic world above the water.

Ice. Nothing but ice. As far as he could see and in every direction—ice. And it wasn't the smooth kind of ice that forms when a pond freezes over—the kind that makes for an ideal skating rink—oh no. This ice was rough and jagged. It sat in heaps and mounds. It looked like the abandoned parking lot where snowplows dump their loads. These were not icebergs that had broken off of glaciers; they were ice floes that had formed with the whips and waves of choppy ocean waters. Mr. Coy felt like an ant on top of a poorly frosted cake. The entire landscape was a field of ice, anything but level and uniform. As much as it looked like snow-covered tundra, you had to remind yourself that you were in the middle of the ocean, not on land.

After a thorough look, Mr. Coy pushed away the scope's remote lens and fell back into his chair. He had seen no sign of Lye.

"Well?" Thorne asked, curious to learn what Coy had seen.

"Brr," Coy shivered in response.

"What exactly are we looking for, anyway?" Thorne questioned.

"An old man with a long, white beard," Coy said nebulously.

"Santa?!" Mo exclaimed with the glee of a child.

"No, not Santa Claus," said Coy. Mo seemed deflated.

"No one could live up here anyway," Thorne concluded, further bursting Mo's bubble, "let alone have a workshop. You said it yourself: there's no land, it's just a layer of ice."

"Well," Mo mumbled to himself, "*I* still believe."

And so began their tour of the Arctic Ocean. For days, they followed a simple pattern: travel a fair distance, surface in a crack, look around. But it always yielded the same result: a whole lot of ice but no sign of Lye. Travel, surface, look—ice. One time they saw a polar bear; another, a few birds. But, otherwise, it was travel, surface, look—ice. In a way, the redundant ritual reminded Mr. Coy of when he and Ret traveled down the Amazon River not too long ago, stopping every now and then to look for a golden arch. Except that procedure had been much more productive. And warm.

Sometimes, they arrived in regions where the blanket of sea ice showed signs of breaking up. Mo, whose Arctic knowledge seemed as endless as the ice itself, was quick to point out that they were nearing the time of year when Arctic sea ice reaches its minimum, explaining that much of the younger ice melts during the summer. He claimed it was fortunate that their expedition wasn't taking place during the winter, when sea ice extends far beyond the bounds of the Arctic Ocean, even past the Arctic Circle. Thorne had never met anyone who knew as much about sea ice as Mo did, but the Eskimo's positive outlook did little to boost the sagging morale of the fruitless wanderers.

In time, Mr. Coy began to feel like one of those overzealous explorers from centuries past who saddled a crew and embarked on a crazy mission into uncharted territories, only to be mutinied and never heard from again. He frequently had to remind himself of his objective, which was to find Lye and see if he had any clues as to the hiding place of the next element. But, with each unsuccessful look above the ice, Mr. Coy felt more and more foolish, like he was wasting his time and should just give up. He was coming to the unwelcome conclusion that he couldn't do this without Ret. It was Ret who bore the scars—Ret who possessed the keys—that were necessary in order to gather the scattered elements and fill the Oracle. Little wonder, then, why Lye needed Ret so desperately—or at least his scars.

For meanwhile, elsewhere on the frozen Arctic Ocean, there was an old man with a long, white beard, driving a dogsled across the same fields of ice that the faux whale was roaming under. With a face as cold as death, the musher gripped the sled's handle bars with only one of his claw-like hands, the other firmly grasping a white, spirally-twisted cane. His long robes, whose blackness contrasted brilliantly against the scenery's overwhelming whiteness, flowed freely in the bitter wind. His frail body was apparently unaffected by the freezing temperature. There was only one man on earth with blood like ice: it was Lye.

The evil lord kept his focus on the path ahead, which he was constantly clearing and smoothing to create a flat trail for his team of dogs. Using his apparent power over water, Lye paved a way through the ice, which was technically still water though in a frozen state. The dogs, ten of the strongest and most ferocious canines ever bred, were pulling the sled with great speed, finding little friction on the slick ice.

Once in a while, Lye would take his eyes off the road to check something in the sled's cargo bed. He would bring it close to his face, look at it for a moment, then set it down and sometimes slightly adjust course. It was likely a compass of sorts.

Back in the belly of the whale, the instruments were finally showing signs of activity.

"I'm picking something up on thermal radar," Thorne announced.

"What is it?" Coy asked eagerly, the control room suddenly filled with interest.

"I'm not sure," said Thorne, studying the screen. "It looks like several small bodies of heat, all moving together in a line."

"More birds?" Coy said without hope.

"No, they're going too fast to be birds," Thorne countered.

"Maybe reindeer?" Coy suggested.

With renewed faith, Mo chanted to himself, "It's Santa!"

"I don't think so," Thorne dismissed. "Look how straight it's moving."

"Well," Coy said after inspecting the screen, "I'd say it's worth taking a look."

But the unidentified sledding object refused to stop. It was going north, leaving the coast of Russia and heading toward the middle of the ocean. Mr. Coy decreased the submarine's depth, following close to the ice in hopes of locating a lead and stealing a quick glance, but the unknown creature was simply traveling too fast.

They followed it for many miles. Keeping an eye on their present latitude and longitude, Mr. Coy's heart took courage by the fact that the mysterious mover was leading them back toward the North Pole. Finally, the specimen in question began to slow until it finally stopped—right next to the North Pole. With great stealth, Mr. Coy slowly positioned the dorsal fin into a crack in the ice a safe distance away. Then he anxiously peered through the scope.

There was Lye. He had dismounted the sled and was pacing around, as if surveying the area. He was clearly searching for something—looking high and low, in the sky and along the floor. He even began to chip away at some of the chunks of ice, hoping to find something—anything. After several minutes, he angrily threw up his hands and returned to the sled. Mr. Coy was too far away to see what Lye was rummaging through in the cargo bed. Then, suddenly, there was a small flash of light, and a second individual came into view, standing up in the sled. Mr. Coy was stunned to see who this other person was. It was Ret!

CHAPTER 11

A CRASH COURSE IN
LIFE

The start of the new school year helped establish a sense of normalcy after what had been a very eventful summer. A few days after the reunion with Jaret, the lost-and-found father returned to the Deep. It wasn't the family's preferred choice, of course, but Jaret convinced them it was better for everyone if he pretended to still work for Lye, at least for now. Jaret knew the evil lord would hunt him down if he were to disappear, which would especially endanger Pauline and Ana. He promised to come back and visit whenever he could sneak away. Jaret exchanged extra-long hugs with his wife and daughter before departing.

These days, there was a noticeable difference in the school spirit at Tybee High, not on account of pep rallies but because of the new principal on campus. Despite a thorough search for Stone, the school board had been unable to track him down, so, on the eve of the new school year, they hired his replacement: Ms. Brown, a delightful woman who was as nondramatic as her name. A lifelong educator, she was an older lady who had never married but found great joy in being a caretaker of her students. Compared to her forerunner, Ms. Brown was a breath of fresh air, and no one seemed happier than her assistant, Mr. Kirkpatrick.

For Paige and Ana, junior year would be their toughest yet. Each of their schedules listed plenty of rigorous courses that were sure to challenge their minds and strengthen their preparation for college. Ana, who had an exponential distaste for math, sought help in this subject from Paige, while Paige was aided by Ana in the realm of, what she called, more practical things.

"Put it on your calendar, P," Ana sang as she met up with Paige outside her physics class. "Homecoming is less than two weeks away!"

"Oh, that's all?" Paige winced, noticeably less excited about the school dance than her friend.

"I know we're only juniors," Ana carried on, "but wouldn't it be awesome if one of us was chosen as homecoming queen?"

"Not really," Paige said quietly.

"You *are* going to come with me, aren't you?" Ana asked.

"Well, uh…"

"Paige, you have to come!" Ana pled.

"I want to," Paige told her, "but it's just that I thought Ret would be home by now."

"I know," said Ana with sudden reality, "we all miss him." Then, trying to solve the problem, she offered, "Why not go with someone else?"

"Yeah, I thought about that," Paige sighed, "but it just wouldn't be the same."

"I know!" Ana exclaimed. "You can go with Leo!"

"But who will *you* go with?" Paige wondered.

"I'll ask Dusty," Ana stated. "We'll all go together—in a group." She put her arm around Paige, as if to reassure her. "It'll be fun."

"If you say so," Paige obliged.

Down-to-earth Dusty was an easy sell. Over the last few months, he had been spending a lot of time with Paige and Ana—well, Ana mostly. Since they were essentially next-door neighbors, it was a rare day when they didn't cross paths. Dusty became a regular at the Coopers' weekly dinners, purportedly for the free food but obviously to see Ana, though he was never scared off by protective Pauline always placing him on dishwasher duty. He would go out of his way to find Ana in the Manor or on its grounds, and whenever she and Paige happened to pass by where he was working on the hardware of the communications system, he would ask Ana to hand him a screwdriver or a hammer or (once) a turkey sandwich. The attention flattered Ana but annoyed Paige.

While Dusty was warming up on Ana's range of romance, however, Leo was cooling on the back burner. Now that the Coopers lived across the creek, it was harder for Leo to come around. He didn't see Ana at work anymore because she was no longer employed, finding no need to earn money for gas since the family car had been destroyed in the house fire. So when Ana asked Leo to the homecoming dance, even though as Paige's date, he gladly accepted. It was progress.

For Paige, the best part about the dance was in making her own dress for it. During the summer, she had asked Pauline to teach her how to sew. It was an idea that Pauline surged toward rather than skirted around. Ana showed little interest in the lost art until her mother brought out some old patterns to make different kinds of dresses. They made them all, wearing them to church and other formal functions. And so, when it proved difficult to find a modest dress for the homecoming dance, Paige and Ana decided to make their own.

Ana chose the A-line dress pattern, using a beautiful lavender fabric. She took it down to mid-calf, added puff sleeves, and topped it off with a little flower brooch that she pinned near the collar. For her dress, Paige decided on an empire waist design with bell sleeves. Her ruby red gown went all the way down to her feet. She planned to go in flats rather than heels and wear her blond hair down in her usual long, thick curls.

When the night of the dance arrived, Dusty met the girls at the Cooper home. He looked dashing in his three-piece designer suit, complete with cuff links and a pocket square. Pauline fetched the camera to snap a few photos.

"Oh, here, Mrs. Cooper," Paige said, handing her cell phone to Pauline. "Will you take one with my phone? My dad's still in the Arctic, but he wanted to see how my dress turned out."

"I'd be happy to, dear," Pauline smiled. "What a good father you have."

Following the photos, Missy escorted the trio to the hangar, where the teens got in the car with their undercover bodyguard and departed.

They picked up Leo on their way to the school. Embarrassed by where he lived, he asked them to meet him on the corner down the street from the orphanage. Dusty tried to suppress a laugh when he saw Paige's date. Leo was wearing an old brown coat—double-breasted and made of wool—with black slacks that were a little too short for him. His dress shoes were graying at the toes, and his thin, pastel-colored tie looked like the kind you'd find at the bottom of a used-clothing donation box. With hair slicked back and glasses wiped clean, he was ready for his very first dance, even if he did smell like mothballs.

Compared to their freshman year's winter formal dance, homecoming was pretty uneventful—no Russian spy manning the drink shack, no trespasser raiding the principal's office, not even a bomb scare. Ana spent most of the evening on the dance floor with Dusty, who turned out to be the life of the party. Having graduated from his own high school last year, he walked with a sort of immature maturity that earned him plenty of attention.

Meanwhile, Paige and Leo were sitting at an otherwise empty table on the well-lit and not-as-loud periphery of the hall, each sporting a wildly unentertained expression. Paige didn't like to dance to such music, which worked out great since Leo didn't know how to anyway. With longing in his eyes, Leo watched Ana from afar, that beautiful angel in the pale purple dress. In a way, it made him happy to see her so happy, but being without her made him sad in many more ways.

"You miss her, don't you?" Paige asked tenderly.

"Who? Ana?" Leo came to. "Nah..." he fibbed.

Paige, who couldn't be fooled, gave him a ridiculous glare.

"Yeah, I guess I miss her a little," Leo said.

"You've been staring at her all night," Paige pointed out.

"Okay," Leo capitulated. "I've just never seen anything so beautiful." Then, as if such a compliment for Ana was an insult to his date, he awkwardly added, "Besides you—er, I mean—not that you're not as pretty as she is, but—"

"It's okay," Paige held up her hand. "We're just here as friends, Leo."

Leo sighed, "Look how happy she is with him. And why wouldn't she be? He's tall and handsome, funny and outgoing. When she's got a guy like him, why would she ever need a swain like me?"

"Aw, Leo," Paige sympathized. "Ana really does care for you. Maybe it's for the best that you meet other people. Like they say, absence makes the heart grow fonder."

"Or makes it wander," Leo said under his breath. "You're right. I reckon you would know, huh?"

Paige's heart ached at the thought of Ret.

"Yes, well, at least you can see Ana," Paige observed. "I wish I could see Ret again—or at least know he's okay."

"I saw him the night he left town," Leo remembered.

"You did?" Paige pressed. "What did he say? Did he tell you where he was going?"

"All he said was that he was going somewhere but didn't know where that somewhere was," Leo retold.

That wasn't the answer Paige was hoping to hear.

Just then, Ana approached the table.

"Hey, guys," she said cheerily. "Having fun?"

They replied with two bored stares.

"Where's Dusty?" Leo wondered.

"He stepped outside for a minute," said Ana. "He does that a lot, likes to get some fresh air." Then, addressing Leo, "Would you like to dance for a bit while he's out?"

"Would I ever!" Leo accepted, jumping from his chair. He glanced at his date to make sure it was okay for him to dance with another girl. Paige shooed him away encouragingly. Despite his nervousness, he was overjoyed to take Ana's hand.

They hadn't walked more than a couple steps, however, when Dusty returned.

"Hey, four eyes," Dusty teased playfully, "what're you doing with my girl?" He purposely slapped Leo on the back, causing a cloud of dust to erupt from his coat.

"Oh, Dusty, it's okay," Ana laughed. "Leo and I are just going to share a dance."

"Nonsense," Dusty roared jovially. He put his arm around Ana and pulled her away towards the dance floor.

Looking back, Ana mouthed to Leo, "Sorry."

As the night progressed, Paige and Leo saw Dusty "step outside" on several more occasions. Each time he returned, he seemed a little more animated and sociable than when he left. His demeanor was becoming louder and coarser. Several attendees were getting turned off by his increasingly rude behavior. Ana breathed a sigh of relief when the music ended and the lights came on.

At the conclusion of the dance, everyone spilled out of the school and into the parking lot. Glad to be leaving, Paige and Leo quickly spotted Missy, who was ready to ferry her four passengers home. She helped Paige and Leo into the car and then waited for Ana and Dusty, who had stopped in the crowd to talk to a noisy group of adolescents.

"Come on, Dusty," Ana prodded him quietly, "Missy's waiting for us."

"Why don't you come with me and a few of these guys over to their house?" Dusty happily invited her. "They're going to let me use their car while they run to the store. We can chill at their place for a bit, and then they'll take us home."

"Oh, I—I don't know," Ana faltered.

Several in the group pressured her, "Come on."

"It'll be fine," Dusty roared.

"Okay," Ana gave in. "Let me go tell Missy."

Ana ran across the lot to where Missy was still standing.

"I'm going to go with Dusty over to his friends' house," Ana told her sheepishly, avoiding eye contact. "They'll take me home. I'll be back before curfew."

Missy, who was no spring pig, raised Ana's chin, looked the young girl in the eye, and said caringly, "Miss Ana, I strongly recommend you come home with us, but I'll leave it up to you."

Ana looked torn.

"Come on, Ana!" Dusty bellowed from across the lot.

"It'll be alright," Ana said. "I'll be home soon."

Missy nodded. Ana ran off.

"Where's Ana going?" Paige asked when Missy sat down in the driver's seat.

"To the after party," Missy frowned, watching through the rearview mirror as the rowdy group cheered when Ana returned to join them. She started the car and headed for home.

The group of loitering teenagers split up. Half set out on foot for the convenience store down the street. Ana followed the other half into the car, with Dusty behind the wheel. He turned the key and floored the gas, causing the engine to thunder, much to the delight of his passengers. After doing a few donuts, Dusty turned out of the school parking lot and screeched down the street.

Ana sunk low in the backseat. She was beginning to feel uncomfortable. Dusty was driving recklessly, and his friends were egging him on. They sped up and down the empty streets of the small town with no regard for law or safety.

It was during a hard right turn when Ana felt something hit her foot. She moved her dress aside and looked down on the floor. It was a can of beer, and it was empty. Then she realized the soda can that Dusty kept sipping at and returning to the drink holder wasn't soda—it was beer. She glanced down at the ground around other people's feet and discovered more empty beer cans. Now she knew what Dusty had really been doing at the dance every time he went outside.

Ana found herself in a very dangerous situation. These people were drunk, and Dusty was driving the car under the influence of alcohol. Ana was scared. She should have listened to Missy, not the thoughtless crowd. But it wasn't too late. She would simply ask to get out.

"Um, Dusty," Ana tried to say, but her sweet voice could not be heard above the riot.

"Dusty," she said a bit louder, "I want to get out." Again, he didn't hear, but the person next to Ana gave her a snooty look and laughed.

Finally, Ana yelled, "I want to get out!"

Dusty brought the car to a screeching halt, and everyone went silent.

"What did you say?" he asked, as if suddenly sober.

"I said," Ana restated calmly, "I want to get out." Her request was met with derision.

"Okay, then go ahead," Dusty politely told her. Ana reached for the door and had slightly opened it when Dusty floored the gas pedal. The car lunged forward, and his friends erupted in laughter.

"Oh, I'm sorry," Dusty lied, slamming on the brakes. "*Now* go ahead." Ana hastily tried to exit again, but Dusty took off like before.

Frightened and upset, Ana shouted, "Dusty Thorne, you let me out of this car right now!" From behind, she struck him on his shoulder.

In that instant, Dusty snapped. He went from a social drunk to a belligerent one. He became angry and turned on Ana.

"Fine!" he howled, throwing the car into park. "You want out?" He burst out of his door, got out, and then swung her door open. "Then get out!" He yanked her from the backseat, slammed the doors, and then sped off, his friends celebrating all the more now that their party pooper was gone.

Standing there in the middle of the vacant street, Ana started to cry. She felt painfully foolish. The whole altercation had left her with a sick feeling. The influence that had come over Dusty over the course of the evening was foreign to her. To her knowledge, she had never been around an intoxicated person before, and she would have paid more attention to the early signs of drunkenness had she known what they were. But she was safe now and had learned a great lesson.

Ana started for home. She texted Paige, apologized, and asked if they could pick her up. Paige said they were almost home but would turn around and come get her. Still in her dress, Ana sat down on the curb and waited for her ride. She wiped her eyes dry, so relieved to be out of that car.

A few moments later, a series of quick noises disrupted the nighttime air. First, there was the screeching of tires, then the colliding of metal, followed by the shattering of glass, and finally the honking of a jammed horn. They were the unmistakable sounds of a car accident.

Ana's heart jumped, "Oh no."

She feared the worst and hoped it wasn't true. She immediately left the curb and ran toward the disquieting sound of the car horn. Removing her heels and holding up her dress, she sprinted up the street two blocks until she came to the main road. That's when she saw it. There were two mutilated cars in the intersection. Dusty was behind the wheel in one of them, now in a drunken daze after causing the head-on collision. Ana was heartbroken when she recognized the unconscious driver in the other car: it was Missy.

CHAPTER 12

LYE'S TROUBLES

Mr. Coy couldn't believe his eyes. From the safety of the submarine as it floated just beneath the Arctic ice, he watched through the scope as Lye led Ret by the hand out of the dogsled's cargo bed and onto the ice. Coy wished he could hear what was being said.

"Let me see that scar," Lye hissed. As if Ret couldn't move on his own, Lye grabbed Ret's left hand, opened the palm himself, and glared at the scar. Then he shuffled along the ice, pulling Ret with him and referring to the scar often. He was obviously trying to arrive at a specific spot and needed the scar to help him get there.

Eventually, Lye stopped and rejoiced, "Here it is! This is it! This is the exact spot of the North Pole. Look—look at the scar. Now the barbs are lined up: the moveable barb is overlapping the barb that is always fixed on the south. That's because when I stand in this exact spot, any way I turn is south. I'm on the North Pole—the top of the world. No matter which way I look, it's south." Lye waited for Ret to respond to the great news, but Ret didn't even blink.

"So, Ret," Lye continued, "what do we do next, I wonder?" Again, no response. "Here, you stand here. Maybe you're the one who has to do it." He positioned Ret on the exact spot of the North Pole and prepared for something extraordinary to happen. He stood there for several minutes, hoping for the ice to part or the sky to open or a secret passageway to appear—something, anything—like what usually occurred with elements past. But nothing happened.

With immense frustration, Lye howled, "Then what does this scar mean?!" Despite Lye's vehemence, however, Ret remained as dull as a post.

Mr. Coy couldn't watch any longer. He fell back in his chair in total disbelief. As pleased as he had been to have tracked down Lye, he was stricken with horror the moment he saw Ret with him. Why was Ret working with Lye now? Had he really joined forces with the enemy? How could this be? Coy's heart sank.

"You alright, Coy?" Thorne asked, seeing his friend slip into somber spirits. Coy passed the lens to him but didn't expect Thorne to understand.

"There's the old man," Thorne observed cheerfully

while looking through the scope at the scene outside. "And is that...is that Ret with him?"

"It would appear so," Coy said with sorrow.

"I wish I could hear what they're saying," Thorne said as he looked on.

Back outside, "Bah!" Lye spat with fury, casting Ret's hand away. "Why am I even talking to you? You're not real. You're not the real Ret. You're just a clone. You're just a bunch of skin and bones. You may have some of his blood in you, but you don't have his brain. You don't even *have* a brain. You can't think for yourself. You can't even move without a spark of electricity to bring you to life. The only thing you're good for is the scars, but what good are even those if you don't have the mind to interpret them?"

The clone seemed unfazed by Lye's verbal abuse. It just stood there like an exhibit at a wax museum. There was only one thing about the clone that made it seem alive: its eyes. The clone didn't have blue eyes like the real Ret; in fact, it didn't even have pupils. Instead, there was a small current of electricity surging across the whites of each eye.

"What a waste," Lye rehearsed to himself on his trek back to the sled, pulling the clone along. "I went to great lengths to duplicate Ret—collected a sample of his blood while he was unconscious at the Vault, hired the brightest (and most expensive) minds in science, painstakingly cultured his clone for months until I finally had my own set of scars—then I traveled all the way out to this miserable place, by dogsled no less, and all for what?" Lye pushed the clone onto the cargo bed, then raised his cane and took back the spark that he had previously bestowed. The clone's eyes went blank, and the lifeless mass folded to its former resting place.

"Of course there's no element up here!" Lye continued to rant. "There's no land up here—no continent. This isn't even real ground," he booed, stomping on the solid floor of ice. "The elements hide themselves deep inside the earth, not the ocean!" Thoroughly miffed, Lye leaned against the handlebars to contemplate his next move. He sighed, "This was so much easier with the real Ret."

With the drama benched, Thorne relinquished the lens. Finding it free, Mo took a turn.

After a few minutes, Mo said with uneasiness, "Uh, I think he sees us."

"What?" Coy asked incredulously.

"He hasn't taken his eyes off of us for a few minutes now," said Mo.

It was true. Lye had noticed the dorsal fin a long time ago, but, in his excitement upon arriving at the North Pole, he hadn't given it much thought, assuming it was nothing more than a whale. But as he was sitting on his sled, still groping to find anything out of the ordinary that might be a clue to finding the next element, he was growing more suspicious of the lone fin with each passing minute. He realized the fin hadn't moved in a long time. In fact, he had never heard or seen the whale come up for air. What's more, he thought it strange to find a whale so far north, especially alone. Perhaps it was lost or stranded. Or, as Lye concluded, it was dead.

"Should we leave?" Thorne asked, his voice a worried whisper.

"Hold on," Coy instructed, watching for Lye's next move, hoping he would just look away.

Knowing the carcass would provide a hearty meal for his dogs before embarking on the long journey back to land, Lye decided to reel in the dead animal and serve it up on an icy platter. He gathered the water around the whale and lifted it out of the ocean like a giant raindrop. The former silence and stillness of the desolate Arctic was ruined by the sound of great slabs of ice breaking and crashing. The dogs sprang up in alarm as they felt the floor shake. Lye moved the bubble to the side and then set it on an intact section of ice, which cracked slightly but held together despite the heavy load.

The setting inside the submarine was a bit shaken up. Coy and Thorne were gripping their seats with white-knuckled hands, and Mo had done a face plant into the eyespot's window.

"Nobody move," Coy breathed with uncharacteristic caution.

Lye studied his catch. Its exterior was coarse and plated, not smooth and velvety as he thought a killer whale's skin ought to have been. He stepped forward for a closer inspection. He could see sheets of metal and rows of bolts. He stopped near the nose and tapped on it, which was like knocking on a tin roof. With growing distrust, he knelt down and wiped the frost from a portion of the eyespot, where he found Mo's face smashed against the window. Mo fluttered his fingers to politely wave at the stranger. Lye's suspicions were confirmed: Shamu was a sham.

Knowing his secret was shattered, Mr. Coy entered defense mode. A panel under each pectoral fin slid open, exposing the barrel of a machine gun. The firearms erupted in shots, swinging back and forth in a half-circle motion, the bullets creating wide arcs of divots that were purposely perforating the ice sheet. At the same time, a large torch at the killer whale's mouth began belching forth flames, quickly melting the ice all around it.

Though not Coy's target, Lye ran for cover, dashing back to his sled to assess the situation. He had just made it back when, as Mr. Coy had hoped, the battered and melted ice around the submarine gave way, returning the sub to the sea. Coy threw the controls into overdrive and took off.

Lye didn't take kindly to spies (besides his own, of course). Although he didn't know who these snoopers were, he feared they had seen too much, especially considering their quick getaway. Although he preferred to keep his enemies alive so he could ruin their lives and feed off their misery, sometimes it was easier just to eliminate them and move on, especially when, as in this case, the public would simply ascribe their disappearance to being "lost at sea."

The first step in the execution of the fugitives was to halt their escape. Standing a few steps from his sled, Lye grasped his cane with both hands, raised it high above his head, and then jammed it into the ice. He sent a tremendous bolt of electricity into the icy ocean waters, letting the power flow for a good while. Although his view of the ocean was blocked, Lye could feel the electricity surging far and wide throughout the water, being conducted by the ions of dissolved salts.

It made for quite a surreal sight under the water, with several auxiliary bolts branching out from the main one.

"Whoa!" Thorne shouted upon seeing the ocean light up behind them.

"That can't be good," Coy assessed, maintaining his usual collectedness.

"What?" Thorne wondered. "What is it?"

"The old man's cane is some kind of superconductor of electricity," Coy explained. "I don't fully understand it; I just try to avoid it."

"I can see why," Thorne remarked.

It didn't take long for the fleeing submarine to get caught in the chaos. First, the lights inside the sub began to flicker. Then, when the overwhelmingly metallic sub got struck by a bolt, the power completely died, and the sub went pitch black.

"Ah!" Mo screamed like a little girl.

A moment later, the backup batteries kicked in, restoring the power but at a much lower level.

"What's going on?" Thorne cried out.

"Where are my engineering students?" Coy bellowed in the dimness.

"We're here!" came their immediate replies.

"I need you to inspect the circuitry," Coy ordered. "Check the breakers, the fuses, the wires—whatever the problem is, fix it. And fix it fast. We don't have much time."

"Yes, sir!"

"We don't have much time?" Thorne asked.

"The backup batteries are mostly to keep us from sinking and being crushed to death," Coy answered. Mo swallowed hard. "Besides, I don't think the old lightning striker's done with us yet."

And he wasn't. Lye freed his cane from the ice,

pointed the top low to the ground, and began to move it in small circles. The sound of sloshing could be heard as the ocean below began to crash against the ice under his feet. The sled dogs, sensing some kind of disturbance, huddled together to whimper. Lye gradually enlarged the circles he was tracing in the air. Soon, water could be seen splashing up through the leads in the surrounding area. Lye was creating a massive whirlpool.

Stalled in the sea, the submarine was powerless against the swirling waters, getting sucked in like a bath toy toward a tub's drain. The crew members could feel themselves making a never-ending turn as they were dragged farther and farther toward the churning center. Soon, they were spinning on the inside of the funnel. Most of the ice at the top had broken away, now that it had no water beneath it, but Lye had saved one section, allowing him to look over his creation and continue to stir it as a witch would mix her cauldron.

"Got any ideas, Coy?" Thorne said, trying not to panic as he held onto his chair as if on a carnival ride.

"I'm thinking," said Coy calmly, scanning the many buttons before him.

"They didn't train us for anything like *this* in the Navy," Thorne commented.

Mr. Coy settled on the *harpoon* button. He reasoned it might just work. He'd only have one shot but only if his students got the power reengaged.

"Come on…," Coy whispered encouragingly as if the students could hear him, hoping to see the power gauge come alive.

Lye smiled to see the submarine swirling helplessly deeper and deeper into the ocean. He wondered if he should let it keep sinking and thereby be crushed by the pressure or if he should just get on with it and blow them to bits now.

"Come on…," Coy said with more anxiousness, his finger poised to push the *harpoon* button.

There was little room for error, for Lye had decided to cut to the chase and blast his foes to smithereens. From his icy perch above the whirlpool, he raised his cane into the air, preparing to strike the sub with a deadly bolt.

But the students came through. Full power was restored just in the nick of time.

"Yes!" Coy cheered, smashing his button of choice. A large, steel harpoon shot from the side of the sub, not out across the empty center of the whirlpool but away from it in the other direction. Mr. Coy hoped the harpoon had enough line to reach the ice that had remained intact around the periphery. It did. As soon as it became lodged in the ice, Mr. Coy reeled the sub in, pulling it free from its whirling doom.

Once they reached the open sea and could

overpower the force of the whirlpool, the crew cheered, celebrating their miraculous escape.

"Only Ben Coy *saves* a whale with a harpoon," Thorne said merrily, slapping his friend on the back. Coy breathed a sigh of relief himself.

But it was all premature. Lye, the world's sorest loser, was willing to move ocean and earth to get his way.

The mood in the submarine had relaxed considerably, everyone a bit relieved to be heading home. They were coming up on Canada's Queen Elizabeth Islands, the first landmasses after being at sea for many days. They were preparing to navigate through the islands when unsettling signs of unusualness returned. The sub had not changed its depth, but the water level above them was getting lower and lower. There was also a growing sense of drag working against them, slowing their pace.

Like before, it was the work of Lye. He had harnessed the enormous kinetic energy of his whirlpool and transformed it into a gigantic wave, with him and his dogsled fixed on a piece of ice, riding it like a surfer. It was truly a colossal sight, so big that it was draining the water in front of it to feed itself.

"That man has got to be, without a doubt," Thorne marveled, "the most stubborn old guy I have ever seen. What's your plan, Coy?"

"I'm open to suggestions," said Coy, feeling like a parent whose child always comes with problems but never any solutions.

"Can this thing fly?" Thorne proposed.

"You know, Thorne," Coy returned, "that's the one thing this puppy doesn't do. Any *other* suggestions?"

"You could try Fury and Hecla," Mo spoke up. Coy and Thorne exchanged puzzled glances. "The Fury and Hecla Strait," Mo explained, matter-of-factly. "It's a narrow channel that leads to Hudson Bay. A wave that big would never make it through."

"Mo, you're a genius!" Coy said happily, liking the idea. "I'm glad you're here."

Instead of heading east to use the much wider waterway into Baffin Bay, Mr. Coy took the submarine west toward the much smaller Fury and Hecla Strait. Lye followed in hot pursuit, his wave swelling larger every minute. It was a monster, consuming the water in its path and using it to add to its stature, leaving a trail of destruction in its wake as it crashed into and washed over the uninhabited landforms. The sea level continued to drop in the trough at the foot of the wave, forcing the sub to sink deeper to keep from being exposed.

"There it is!" Mo pointed, seeing the narrow opening of the strait. The water in the strait was shrinking fast, so much so that the submarine threatened to scrape the bottom. They could see the naked sides of the strait, exposed by the receding tide.

"Thorne, do you see that red button over there," Coy said, "the one under the words *lateral torpedoes?*" Thorne said he did, showing sudden enthusiasm. "When I give the word, I need you push that button as fast as you can."

"With pleasure," Thorne grinned, cracking his knuckles.

Seeing the approaching strait and sensing a plan, Lye decided to make his move. He began to strike the water with lightning, lighting it up in parts to learn the exact location of the meddlesome submarine he wished to destroy.

"Ready…," Coy said, Thorne's trigger finger at the ready. Then, as soon as they crossed into the strait, Coy yelled, "Fire!"

Thorne pummeled the button, launching a barrage of torpedoes from the sides of the submarine. They shot out laterally across the strait and exploded into its bare sides, which had become towering cliffs of mud now that the water level was so low. With each detonation, more and more sections of the hillside collapsed, initiating a series of landslides on both sides of the strait. By the time the sub made it through to the other side, they had turned the strait into a wave-breaking shoal.

As if running ashore, Lye's tsunami collapsed. With no more water to funnel into itself, the base collided into the mudbank and fell to pieces. In a great garbled mess, the wave crashed onto the strait, swallowing the ice floe and engulfing Lye and his sled in a quagmire of dirt and debris.

Upon exiting the strait, the submarine passed into the large Foxe Basin en route to the even larger Hudson Bay. From the safety of the depths below, they watched the muddy remnants of the fallen wave flow out over the surface. When they did not see Lye emerge from the aftermath, the true celebrating commenced and continued all the way home.

The same could not be said for Lye, however. The victorious submarine was long gone by the time Lye staggered to shore, dragging the clone behind him. Exhausted, the elderly man collapsed on the ground. With shaky fingers, he reached inside his robe and retrieved a small flask, which he opened and pressed to his lips. He took a few gulps and immediately sprang back to life.

Only two of the ten dogs survived. The wooden sled was mangled but also floated to safety, washing up several yards away. Lye made do with what he had, regrouping his reduced team, which was his only mode of transportation. He had other, more efficient ways of getting around, but not when he had the dead weight of the clone to lug around.

Night was coming on. Lye let the dogs roam the vicinity to scrounge up a meal while he sat down next to his clone, pondering his next move.

Lye was losing his touch. He had fallen on hard times recently. It all started with the destruction of his Vault—his entire life savings, gone in a flash. Ore had been the most expensive element yet, and, for the first time in thousands of years, he was in need of cash. And it was all downhill from there. Not long after losing the Vault, Stone abandoned him, leaving him understaffed, and then Ret disappeared, forcing him into the business of collections. Moreover, when you factor in the events of the day—his Arctic vacation a total bust, getting outsmarted by a phony whale (twice), eating it big-time on the world's tallest wave, the subsequent mud bath (talk about dire straits), not to mention eight dead dogs (man's best friend, you know)—heck, if Lye wasn't the worst person on earth, you might be tempted to feel sorry for the guy.

He certainly wasn't getting any sympathy from the clone. Lye wondered what he was going to do with the almost worthless and completely unintelligible mass of cells. Thus far, it had been about as useful to him as a department store mannequin. But the clone was about to redeem itself.

All of a sudden, the clone came to life. Without receiving any help from Lye, it rose to its feet. Startled, Lye looked to see what was going on. Instead of there being sparks of electricity in the clone's eyes, there was a stream of green light running through them. Standing still, the clone had its head cocked upwards, as if looking to the sky, prompting Lye to do likewise. There, in the darkening sky, Lye could see the initial bands of the Northern Lights. He was well aware of the aurora, but he had never before seen the clone come to life by itself.

Suspecting a connection between lights and clone, Lye eagerly inspected the scar. The stationary barb was on the bottom of the circle, pointing south as always. However, the other barb—the moveable one—was on the top, pointing north, which confused Lye since the clone wasn't facing north at the moment. He moved the clone in all directions, watching for what effect this might have on the moveable barb, but it never changed. With its pennant, the north barb looked like a firmly-planted flag, officially marking the Northern Lights as the right spot. And if that was what the north barb meant, then the south barb clearly pertained to the Southern Lights in Antarctica. A satisfied smile curled Lye's pale, thin lips: now he was on to something.

Just then, as if coming into consciousness on its own wasn't enough, the clone started to walk away. Amazed by his clone's newfound zest for life, Lye followed after it. He quickly called the dogs back, harnessed them to the sled, and gladly let his clone lead the way.

The trek started off slow. The clone walked at a steady but unhurried pace. Except for a random berm or occasional patch of grass, the landscape was mostly flat and overwhelmingly barren, allowing the clone to blaze its trail without obstruction.

The clone's pace gradually quickened until it started to run. As the night wore on, the deserted wilderness became enveloped in profound darkness, which caused the Northern Lights to shine ever brighter, casting a dim but welcome gleam on the otherwise obscure ground. The clone maintained a southwest direction. It was running toward the lights, following the dancing arc as a treasure hunter might seek out the end of a rainbow.

Lye didn't have much time to analyze the lights, however, for he was too busy trying to keep up with his clone. There was neither snow nor ice on the ground, making for a rough ride on the dogsled. Occasionally, they would come to a small lake or pond, the waters of which Lye would part to allow him and his guide to pass through on dry ground without abatement.

With the lights getting closer and shining brighter, the clone's speed grew in intensity until it entered a full sprint. Unlike the world's greatest athletes, the clone never stopped. It never took a break to rest or get a drink. It didn't need to, for it was drawing its energy from the energy in the sky. All it required was a little solar wind. The lights' power was the clone's power, and the stronger they shined, the faster it ran.

Until the early morning hours, that is. Not long before dawn, as the lights began to fade from view in the face of the morning sun, so did the clone's stamina. The clone's pace slowed from a fast sprint down to a respectable run until it returned to a brisk walk. When the lights finally closed their curtains for the night, the clone stopped, its eyes went blank, and it fell to the earth.

Anxious to keep going, Lye manually brought the clone to life with a spark, hoping it would pick up where it left off, but it just stood there. It needed the lights. When night fell and the lights could be seen again, the clone promptly awoke of its own volition and resumed its trip.

Lye wanted nothing else than to know where his clone was going. What was its destination? He really hoped it wasn't planning on going all the way to Antarctica on foot.

Nevertheless, Lye again followed all that night. As they continued to journey southwestward, the terrain became more difficult to traverse. The hills rose steeper, the waters sunk deeper, and the plants grew thicker.

Near the end of the night, when the clone's stride slowed back down to a walk, they came to a thicket of trees. Without even glancing back at its maker, the clone plunged into the grove, which was too wooded for Lye to follow in the sled. Leaving the dogs at the edge of the trees, Lye chased after his clone, hoping he wouldn't lose it.

Soon, Lye caught up to it. The clone had arrived at a clearing in the middle of the thicket and stopped at the edge of the trees. The Northern Lights were almost done for the night but were still present in the sky. The clone's eyes still showed green, and it hadn't collapsed into unconsciousness yet. Lye knew the clone had finally arrived at its destination, for, if it hadn't, it would still be walking.

The clone was staring dead ahead. Lye turned to see what it was looking at. There, in a grassy area surrounded by trees, sat a little tin trailer.

CHAPTER 13

A HUNGOVER JURY

Ana was the first bystander to arrive at the scene of the accident. She rushed to Missy's contorted door, but it was jammed. Then one of the rear doors began to open, and Ana heard two seatbelts being unfastened.

Stepping toward the backseat, Ana asked urgently, "Is anyone hurt?"

"I'm okay," Paige responded, though she sounded a little shaken up.

Then Leo's voice was heard, "Same here."

There was no reply from Missy. Ana reached through the backseat and gently tapped her on the shoulder.

"Missy, are you okay?" Ana said, her voice unsteady. "Missy? Missy, say something."

Ana placed two of her fingers on the driver's neck and was relieved when she at least found a pulse. She felt so powerless to free the poor lady from all the warped metal and shattered pieces of the totaled automobile.

Paige and Leo slowly exited the car, both a little in shock from what had just happened.

"I'm so glad you're okay," Ana told each of them, followed by a desperate hug.

"I'll call the police," Paige said.

Meanwhile, the other vehicle was showing signs of life. A bit larger in size, it had not received as much damage as the car it collided into. The first occupant to emerge was Dusty, spilling out of the driver's seat like a seasick sailor. One by one, the other riders followed, all in a suddenly-sober stupor as they tried to understand what was going on.

Within minutes, the police arrived, bathing the scene in sporadic splashes of red and blue from their flashing emergency lights. A fire truck and ambulance were also close behind. Ana stood arm in arm with Paige and Leo as they watched the personnel get to work.

The firemen swarmed the car where Missy lay unconscious. One of them cleared the remaining glass while two others brought out hydraulic tools. With the Jaws of Life, they pried open the driver's door, only to find Missy's legs crushed under the dash. Within seconds, they cut the cabin frames and pulled back the roof like the lid of a tin can. With great care, they extricated Missy from the mess and set her on a stretcher. Medical attention commenced before they even started rolling her toward the ambulance. They loaded her into the back, closed the doors, and sped off.

Meanwhile, some of the police officers were conducting interrogations. As much as they tried, Dusty and his friends couldn't hide their drunkenness. After a few simple tests, the officers brought out their handcuffs.

"No, wait!" Dusty protested when he felt the cold clasp of each handcuff come full-circle around his wrists.

"Ana, help me! Please!" Dusty continued to beg as the officers forcefully guided him and his friends into the cop cars. "Paige, Leo, someone—please!" Ana looked away in grief. The officers shut the doors and left to take the criminals downtown.

While waiting for the tow truck to remove the two crashed cars, the remaining police officers spoke with the three teenage civilians who were huddled together off to the side. Ana gave her account as the only witness while Paige and Leo were checked for minor injuries. The officers instructed them to call their parents to come and take them home. With heavy hearts, Ana called Pauline while Paige texted Mr. Coy, who was on his way home from the Arctic. Leo, however, stood in somber silence, thinking it a cruel (albeit unintentional) irony that the officer would tell him to call his parents at a scene like this. It wasn't the first time the orphan boy had been involved in an accident caused by drunk driving.

Escorted by a member of the Manor's staff, Pauline showed up in no time, taking the three distressed youth in her arms as a hen would gather her chickens under her wings. As they watched the final shards of broken glass being swept from the street, the four of them wished their worry and fright could be swept just as easily from their hearts and minds. They returned home, where they had a long night together, sharing their thoughts and tears.

The first thing Mr. Coy did when he got back from the Arctic was visit Missy in the hospital. She was in bad shape—or, as the nurse told him, "critical condition." Although not in a coma anymore, she still wasn't quite her fully conscious self. The head-on collision had left her with several broken bones, a couple bruised ribs, and a severe cut to the head. She lay in her hospital bed like a mummy in a sarcophagus, nearly her entire body wrapped in white bandages. Mr. Coy dropped off his bouquet of yellow roses and only stayed a few minutes after that. Missy was asleep, and he wasn't very fond of hospital rooms anyway.

The first thing Thorne did when he got back from the Arctic was visit Dusty in the city jail. He was in bad shape — or, as the warden said, "lacking remorse." Dusty was in a downcast mood, of course, but only because he feared the trouble he was in, not the trouble he had caused others. During his father's visit, Dusty never asked about Missy or anyone else involved in the accident. He was only interested in himself, begging his dad to pay his bail and end his time behind bars. With tough love, Thorne told his son he'd think about it.

Two chairs were empty at the group dinner the week following the accident. Pauline prepared a hearty beef stew, hoping the warm broth would help to stave off the chilling events of the past few days. Coy reported on his visit to the hospital, explaining Missy's stable condition. Then Thorne discussed his visit with Dusty, expressing dismay at how his son did not seem to have learned his lesson. Such impenitence was disturbing to all at the table, and it gave Mr. Coy an idea, the details of which he hammered out with the group for the remainder of the meal.

The next day, Mr. Coy went down to Tybee Island's little jailhouse. It was more like a correctional facility than an actual prison, a place where under-age or small-scale offenders paid their penalties through service if no one came to bail them out.

"Good morning, Ben," the warden welcomed him. "Here to rescue another prisoner from a life of crime, are you?" Speaking in somewhat of a smart-alecky manner, the warden was referring to the occasions when Mr. Coy would drop in to talk with the inmates to see if there were any who sincerely wanted to change and might be interested in coming to the Manor.

"You know me too well, Jim," Coy replied in the affirmative.

"Have you come to see one louse in particular or the whole lot of them?" Jim asked.

Always disappointed by the warden's hardness, Coy smiled, "Just one today: Dusty Thorne."

"Oh, his old man was here just a few days ago," Jim recalled, sifting through his assortment of keys. "That boy's a mess—still a minor and already causing trouble. Mark my words, Ben: that boy's a bad egg. He'll make a fine career criminal."

"We'll see," Coy said unconvinced as he followed Jim through a sturdy door.

They entered a long hallway with cells along each side. As Jim walked by, he purposely banged on the bars, alarming the inmates who were behind them. Mr. Coy's pace slowed. He knew several of the prisoners. He called them by name and asked them how they were doing. To his delight, they remembered him, too, and without contempt.

"Ya know, Ben," Jim bellowed as he strutted down the aisle, his proud voice echoing against the stone walls, "it's a noble thing you try to do with these scumbags, but an intelligent man like yourself should know a leopard never changes his spots."

"Well then," said Coy optimistically, catching back up to Jim, "it's a good thing there aren't any leopards here, isn't it?" Several cheers emerged from behind the bars.

Jim leaned in close to Mr. Coy and said softly, "Come on, Ben, stop wasting your time."

Mr. Coy smiled and told the cold man, "I don't want to change the spots, Jim; I want to change the leopard."

The old warden was silenced. He had never thought of it that way before.

A few more steps brought them to Dusty's cell.

"Now you let me know if you need anything," Jim told Coy after unlocking the cell. There was a little less rudeness in the warden's voice, a little less swagger in his walk as he paced away.

"Good morning, Dusty," Mr. Coy said cheerily, stepping into the dingy cell.

"Hey," was all the young man said, hardly looking up as he lay on the bed.

"I've come to pay your bail," Coy told him.

"Really?" Dusty replied with great enthusiasm, immediately sitting up.

"Under one condition," Coy said sternly.

"Sure," Dusty welcomed.

"I'll be holding a trial of law at the Manor in a few days," Coy explained, "and I need you and your friends from the other night to come and help me."

"Done," he thoughtlessly accepted.

Mr. Coy studied the eager lad for a moment and said, "Very well then." They gathered his very few belongings and left to find Jim.

The warden seemed subdued as he watched Mr. Coy fill out the usual forms and write out the hefty check. Mr. Coy knew the procedure well, as he had gone through it with Jim on several previous occasions. It was during this instance, however, when Jim realized for the first time that none of the prisoners who were bailed out by Mr. Coy ever returned to his jailhouse to serve time for another crime.

"Good day," Jim pensively told them after all the paperwork had been taken care of.

"Till next time, my friend," Coy beamed, knowing he was finally beginning to leave an impression on the warden. Then he put his arm around Dusty as they strode out the door.

"Thanks," Dusty said somewhat insincerely as they pulled away from the jailhouse.

"You're welcome," said Coy, "but remember my condition."

"I know," Dusty asserted. Then, realizing he didn't know, he asked, "Remind me of the specifics again?"

"I need you and your friends—all of them from the night of the dance—to come to the Manor," Coy restated.

"When?"

"Next Friday at twelve o'clock noon."

"Where exactly?" Dusty inquired, knowing something of the building's intricacies.

"The courtroom," said Coy. "If you have trouble finding it, just ask someone."

And so it was that, while Dusty and his friends were wandering the Manor that next Friday just before noon, they needed help locating the courtroom. Since his friends were totally bewildered by the Manor, Dusty was the one who flagged someone down and asked for directions.

"Oh, I'm on my way to the courtroom right now," the arborist said, having just come from the grounds where he had been trimming trees. "You can follow me."

Dusty and his friends went out on a limb and followed the man, even though he smelled like sawdust and was splattered with sap. The newcomers marveled at the heights and depths of Coy Manor. The further they progressed, the more crowded the corridors became. Soon, the halls were filled with people from wall to wall, all moving in the same direction as the teens and their tree friend. They eventually came to a grand entryway and followed the throngs of people through its large double doors.

The courtroom was alive with chatter. Dusty scanned the gallery to find some empty seats for him and his friends, but nearly every chair was taken. There was even a balcony that wrapped around the back half of the ceiling, but it was filling up fast.

"What are we doing here?" one of the friends asked Dusty with an air of annoyance.

"Yeah, can we go now?" another whined.

"Let's just watch the first few minutes and then leave," Dusty told them. "That way I can say we were here. Come on, we'll stand in the back by the door."

When the last of the spectators finally filed into the courtroom, a man rose at the front of the room. He had been standing against the wall, dressed like a security guard.

"Hey, Dusty," one of the friends said, "isn't that your dad?"

Dusty squinted at the guard. Sure enough, it was Thorne.

"My dad's the bailiff?" Dusty said in shock.

Once the crowd quieted down, Thorne loudly proclaimed, "All rise for the honorable Judge Coy."

The audience promptly rose to their feet as Mr. Coy entered the courtroom from a side door at the front of the room. With a regal look on his face, he walked with a dignified gait, his long black robes dusting the polished floor. He was wearing a peruke, that white wig from eras past with curls on the sides and a plaited tail in the back. He climbed the few steps onto the raised judge's bench and sat down in the large leather chair.

"The audience may be seated," Thorne announced.

"Is this some kind of joke?" one of the friends whispered to Dusty, who just shrugged.

"I welcome you, one and all, to our trial today," Judge Coy began. "As we begin, I'd like to make a few introductions." Motioning to Thorne, Coy said, "You've already met our bailiff, Walter Thorne," who slightly raised his hand. "Our court reporter is Pauline Cooper." Hearing her name, Pauline strode through the side door and took her seat at the reporter's desk, where she prepped her fingers to start typing away on the stenograph.

Coy continued, "My daughter, Paige, will serve as proxy for the plaintiff," Paige entered the room, "and the plaintiff's case will be argued by Leonard Swain." Leo followed, joining Paige at the counsel table nearest the jury box. Both of them, as well as Pauline, were dressed professionally and looked their parts.

"Yeah, this is a joke," Dusty reassured his friends, preparing to depart.

"I will introduce the defendant in a moment," Mr. Coy informed. "Today's defense attorney is Dusty Thorne."

Dusty froze. His friends discretely turned to look at him.

"Don't move," Dusty told them through his teeth. "Maybe he doesn't know we're here."

"I see you, Dusty," Mr. Coy said, "standing by the door at the back of the room." Whispers filled the air as the audience members turned to look. "Come on, now," Coy coaxed, "we need you to argue the defense."

Too late to escape, Dusty started up the long aisle of the gallery toward the front of the room, every eye watching him.

"Oh, and bring your friends with you," Coy added. Dusty looked back and bade his friends to follow. With hesitation, they obeyed, and together they all crossed the bar and stood before the judge.

"Dusty will sit at the other counsel table," Coy instructed, pointing at the desk next to where Paige and Leo were sitting. Then he said, "The rest of you will sit there," directing their attention to the jury box. None of them moved.

"What's the matter?" Coy interrogated. "Never seen a jury box before?" Still, there was no movement. "You're the jury," Coy told them. "This is a trial by jury—Article III, Section 2, of the U.S. Constitution. Read it sometime." It was like talking to a bunch of rocks.

With a bit more firmness, Coy leaned forward and ordered, "Take your seats."

After a futile glance at Dusty, they entered the jury box.

"Now then," Coy said, moving on, "bring in the defendant."

That was the bailiff's cue. Thorne stepped into the side room to retrieve the defendant. The audience strained to get a glimpse of who this person might be. Dusty watched with great interest to learn who he would be defending. Everyone was surprised, therefore, when Thorne returned holding an empty glass in one hand and a beer bottle in the other.

Thorne walked across the well and set the empty glass on the defense's table. He opened the bottle and let the cap fall to the tabletop, sending a few sharp chirps through the silent courtroom like the bouncing of a small coin. While his son looked on with great vexation, Thorne filled the glass three-quarters full, the yellowish liquid foaming nigh unto the brim. Then he placed the bottle down next to the glass and returned to his post against the wall.

It was all Dusty could do to restrain himself from taking a sip.

"I hereby call to order this trial on the sensibleness of alcohol as a beverage for human consumption," Judge Coy convened.

"Are you serious?" Dusty interjected, considering the case an act of foolery. "You can't do this."

"Sure I can—I'm the judge!" Coy shot back. "And I've got the wig to prove it."

"But you're not a *real* judge," Dusty said. "This isn't a *real* court."

"Well of course this isn't an act of actual litigation," Coy acknowledged.

"Good," Dusty said, having proved his point. "Besides," he added, getting up to leave, "alcohol is perfectly legal."

"Did you not hear what I said?" Coy questioned. Dusty stood still. "I said we're trying the sensibleness of alcohol, not the legality of it."

"Oh," said Dusty, his quick escape halted.

Coy challenged, "We're putting alcohol on trial—"

"Is that right?" Dusty accepted with sudden interest, sporting a look of defiance as he sat back down.

"—And *you* are going to defend it."

Cracking his knuckles, Dusty said, "Bring it on."

CHAPTER 14

LYE'S REVENGE

The phenomenon of the aurora borealis had proven to be a source of enlightenment for Ret. His nightly observations of the Northern Lights had an energizing effect on him—recharging his batteries, so to speak—and it ignited a curiosity within him to learn the exact nature of the next element he was starting to control. Was it the air in the wind or the energy that blew it? Could he only manipulate existing electromagnetic waves or create his own? Was it light as a whole or the individual frequencies within light? The possibilities seemed endless.

As the days passed, Ret added a sort of early-morning practice session after each night of watching the lights. When the aurora again became indiscernible among the superior rays of the rising sun, Ret would set out in search of a secluded area where he could experiment with his power over all things in the air. He came to favor one place in particular, about a mile from the trailer, where a pair of hills provided a measure of privacy, even though not much besides an occasional fox or moose stirred the stillness of Canada's northern reaches.

As Ret quickly discovered, the element of wind was but an umbrella that encompassed a host of other components. He could work the wind, of course—start and stop it with ease—but he could also influence anything with energy. Like a human prism, he could diffract light to single out specific colors, even meddle with frequencies and wavelengths to turn one color into a different one. He could refract light, too, bending it and varying its velocity so as to create optical illusions, like when a slanted pencil looks broken in a glass of water. When the sun finally peeked above the mountaintops, Ret rerouted some of the heat waves to come his way.

Despite his remote location, Ret was able to get a few channels—radio, television, and the like. Some mornings, he would sit back and look at the signals being rained down from satellites orbiting the earth, but there was seldom anything good on. So he'd often switch to the wide-waved radio signals stretching across the sky and search for a good instrumental station. Every now and then, the microwaves of a wireless telephone conversation would stream by, but Ret tried not to tap in. But oh, the sounds! Ret's ears picked up any and all disturbances to the molecules in the air. From the bird flapping its wings to the ant carrying its things, Ret could pick up sound waves near and far and amplify them like a microphone or throw them against a wall to create an echo.

At first, this bombardment of lights, waves, and noises was tremendously overbearing, an overload for the senses even for Ret. With some effort, however, he developed the capacity to tune in or tune out the sights and sounds all around him. It was a skill he hoped to fully master once he collected the actual element, the procurement of which was a topic that Stone brought up frequently.

"Have you figured out anything more about the next element?" Stone would usually ask whenever Ret returned to the trailer after one of his morning practice sessions. Then, after Ret shared any news, Stone would typically reply, "Keep up the good work," adding a caution not to give away their position.

Ret regularly reassured them that all the activity he conjured could only be seen by him. The last thing he wanted to do was disrupt the lives of Lester and Virginia Stone. Theirs was a simple existence, disconnected from the outside world. They had neither telephone nor tele-vision—anything that might create a signal or leave a trail. They produced little waste, rationed their dehy-drated foodstuffs, and passed the time by reading together. Although they had virtually nothing, they had each other, and that was all they wanted.

Little did they know, however, that their secret way of life had recently been discovered by the one person they wished to avoid most: Stone's disgruntled ex-boss. Lye was perplexed when his clone stopped in front of the random trailer in the clearing of the thicket. Experience told him the situation called for patience, not impulsiveness. Rather than make a mad dash into the mobile home, he would first hide out and observe. And so, as soon as the night's lights were gone and the clone's eyes went blank, Lye dragged it back to the dogsled on the outer edge of the woods and then concealed himself in a spot with a good view of the trailer.

Imagine Lye's surprise when, not much later, Ret came around the corner from behind the trailer, crossing the front lot on his way to practice his powers after another night of watching the lights. Lye almost gasped out loud. He marveled at the incredible odds of the happenstance but quickly ascribed the once-in-a-million coincidence to the clone. Of course! The clone was a part of Ret—like an extra finger—an appendage that was somehow connected to its host. It was trying to get home.

This stunning revelation could only be interrupted by the bafflement Lye experienced when he saw the trailer's curtains being drawn by—Virginia? Virginia Stone? Lye was astonished beyond all reason. A few minutes later, Lester walked through the room. A wicked smile began to form on Lye's face. His blood started to boil with revenge. He had found Stone.

Perhaps the clone wasn't so worthless after all.

It was Lye's patience that made him the most evil villain of all time. As much as he wanted to strike then and there, he knew he had to play his cards right. There was Ret to consider. Lye would need to attack in his absence, not only because the young man's powers were an increasingly even match for his own but also because the clone had to go undetected. The clone had proven its usefulness, and it was very possible that Lye no longer needed the real Ret anymore, which was the desired outcome that had been the brainchild of the clone.

So Lye forbore. For a few days, he spied on the Stones and their third wheel. He noted what time Ret left each morning and how long he stayed away. He watched when Lester went out to the truck or when Virginia fed the dogs. Other than that, Lye witnessed firsthand how the hermits purposely didn't get out much.

Once he had their habits memorized, Lye formulated his plan and pounced.

It was all too perfect.

Lye knew he had less than half an hour to drag the lifeless clone back through the trees before Ret, as usual, came striding across the clearing. Lye watched him leave and then waited several minutes until he knew he was far enough away. With Ret gone, Lye was free to do whatever he wished with the Stones.

Lye hadn't quite emerged from the shadows of the thicket when the Stones' dogs began to growl. Before they could even bark, however, Lye vaporized the water in their bodies, reducing each canine to a wave of steam and a pile of hair. Then he cordially walked up the front steps.

There was a knock at the door.

Sitting at breakfast, Lester and Virginia stared at each other. Lester got up from the table, walked to the door, and looked out the peephole. One glance at the hideous face staring back at him sent Stone into a state of complete and utter terror.

"Who is it, Lester?" Virginia asked. Her husband was stiff with shock. "Lester?" Then, with growing anxiety, she pressed, "Lester, who's there?"

Although he knew he was an unwanted guest, Lye rolled his eyes when no one opened the door. He had heard the approaching footsteps and seen the peephole become overshadowed, two tell-tale signs that someone was home but wasn't going to answer. Nevertheless, the spurned visitor forced his way in. With a clap like thunder, Lye zapped the thin door, blowing it from its hinges and launching it into Stone, who crashed into the wall opposite the front door. Virginia let out a startled scream and ran for the kitchen.

"Hello, Stone," Lye hissed.

"Get out of my house," Stone demanded as he extricated himself from the cheap wall.

"You call this tin can a house?" Lye insulted, walking over the threshold.

"What do you want from me?" Stone asked, backing up with each of Lye's steps.

"You left," Lye stated simply, blowing the recliner out of his way. "You and I both know no one just leaves."

"I'm done helping you, Lye," Stone asserted, bumping into the table behind him. "Now get out of here!"

"I wish I could," the white-haired wretch lied, "but I'm afraid you know too much."

Just then, Virginia appeared from behind Lye and, with all her might, hit him over the head with a cast-iron skillet. Lye reeled in pain from the blow. Then Stone grabbed the wooden chair at his side and smashed it over Lye's back, knocking him to the floor.

Lester grabbed Virginia's hand and fled to the bedroom. Winded, Lye shakily rose to his feet, a trickle of blood dribbling down the back of his head.

He yelled in anger and instantly flooded all the water pipes until they burst, breaking walls and drenching everything.

"I warned you, Stone," Lye snarled as he began a search of the trailer. "I gave you a chance, but you walked all over me." By process of elimination, Lye knew the Stones were hiding in the bedroom at the end of the short and narrow hallway. "You pledged your life to me, remember? You belong to me." He slowed as he turned the corner into the room. "Now I've come to take what's rightfully mine."

As soon as Lye entered the room, Stone yelled defiantly, "I don't think so," and then fired a round from the rifle he was holding. Virginia jumped at the startling bang. The bullet struck Lye's left breast, right in the heart. He fell back against the wall, slid to the floor, and rolled over onto his side.

After reloading the rifle, Stone cautiously left his wife in the corner to check on the dying man on the other side of the room. Gasping for air, Lye reached into his robes and pulled out a flask, then uncorked it and took a desperate drink to save his life. With the barrel of his gun, Stone nudged Lye onto his back.

"And I thought a man like you didn't have a heart," Stone eulogized, seeing a moist and slightly reddish hole in the chest of Lye's robes.

Defying death thanks to the mysterious liquid in his flask, Lye suddenly lunged from the ground and pinned Stone against the wall.

"I'm no man," Lye breathed into Stone's horrified face. "I'm your lord."

Stone tried to move but couldn't. Even when Lye let go and took a step back, Stone remained still and immobile.

"Unfortunately for you," Lye explained, "about sixty-percent of the human body is water." It looked like Stone was having a convulsion, so valiantly did he struggle to release himself from the influence that was being exerted over the water in every cell of his body.

"Stop it!" Virginia cried, rushing toward Lye.

"No, *you* stop it!" Lye returned, holding up his other hand to immobilize Virginia in the same manner as her husband.

"You may put down your weapon, Stone," Lye calmly informed him. "Guns are of no use against me." Still restraining Lester, Lye smiled, "Here, let me help you." Lye unclenched Lester's fingers, and the gun fell to the floor. "Now, Virginia, if you will kindly go in here." Lye flung her into the small bathroom just outside the bedroom and closed the door on her. Then he passed his cane along the edges of the door, melting the frame so as to seal her inside. She immediately started wailing on the door, trying to get out.

"And, Stone, if you will please come with me," Lye said. Knowing he would likely resist, Lye relinquished control of Stone above the waist but maintained power over his legs. Lye dragged him feet-first out of the room. Stone reached for the gun but couldn't grab it in time. Then, as he passed the bathroom, he touched Virginia's fingers, which were reaching through the only crack she could find along the bottom.

"Virginia!" he yelled, trying to latch onto the sides of walls and the legs of furniture as Lye pulled him along.

"Lester!" she screamed back, rapping against the skinny door.

Lye exited the trailer and marched down the steps, Stone helplessly following behind despite his best efforts to pull on cords and tug on rugs. Lye dragged him out to the center of the clearing and brought him to his feet.

"What are you going to do to me?" Stone asked, unable to move his feet as Lye slowly paced around him in a circle like an animal taunting its prey.

"First, I'm going to put you in your place," Lye told him, forcing Stone to bow by bringing him to his knees.

"How does it feel to know no one would ever willingly bow to a fool like you?" Stone mocked, grabbing two fistfuls of dirt and hurling them into Lye's face.

"Bah!" Lye howled, wiping his eyes.

"No one ever obeys you out of love, Lye—only fear!" Stone continued. "You're a loser, Lye—nothing but a cheat and a fraud. And you will fail!"

"Hold your tongue!" Lye ordered, forcing Stone's tongue against the roof of his mouth so that he couldn't speak.

"Before I take you back to the Deep, where you will live out the rest of your miserable life as one of my prisoners," Lye said, "I'd like to discuss your severance package." He abruptly spun Stone around to face the trailer. "Sounds like your wife is still in there." Virginia's cries for help could still be heard, and the trailer was shaking a bit from her futile attempts to escape. "Maybe you should go and help her."

Immediately feeling Lye's invisible hand release his legs, Stone ran for the trailer. He had gone just a few yards, however, when Lye reached into the sky with his cane and sent a brilliant bolt of lightning directly into the metal home. The trailer instantly exploded, sending Stone hurtling backwards in a wave of heat and debris. A fireball consumed the lot, sending a pillar of black smoke into the air.

Not far away, Ret heard the roar of the explosion. He looked around and saw smoke rising above the thicket where the Stones lived. Gravely worried, he entered into a full sprint back to the trailer.

"VIRGINIA!" Stone exclaimed, reaching toward the unforgiving flames. "Virginia!" Even through the tears in his eyes, he could see the trailer and everything inside it had been incinerated. Only a pitiful pile of ash remained. With his face in his hands, Stone knelt and wept.

A few moments later, he felt a cold chill come over him as Lye came and stood beside him.

"Tears are prohibited in my presence," came the killer's terms as he whisked away the drops of water that were in and around Stone's eyes. "You can cry all you want in my dungeon."

Stone's agony momentarily gave way to anger. He clenched his fists and, rising in one rapid motion, took one to Lye's face.

"Murderer!" Stone bellowed, delivering another dizzying blow to the ugly old man. Lye staggered in pain. He attempted to lift his cane but Stone kicked it out of his hand.

"No!" Lye lamented, promptly going to retrieve the twisted stick. But Stone continued jabbing at him, a one-two punch followed by an uppercut. Lye flew a few feet and landed flat on his humped back. Wasting no time, Stone leapt into the air to come crashing down on his foe, but Lye caught him and held him in mid-air.

"Come on, you coward!" Stone demeaned. "Use your hands! Fight like a man!"

But Lye preferred his powers. With fury, he straightened Stone spread-eagle, dangling him inches above the ground, and gradually withdrew some of the water from his body. With drops of water dotting his skin, Stone quickly looked drenched in sweat. Then his clothes became wet. Like turning a grape into a raisin, Lye maniacally maneuvered much of the water out of Stone's body until he became dehydrated and passed out.

Lye dropped Stone like a rock and set out to locate his cane. He found it and was preparing to reach down to retrieve it when a mighty wind rushed into the clearing. It was strong and sudden. When Lye looked around to see what was going on, he saw something flying toward him. Without enough time to react, the figure plunged into Lye with the force of a rocket, catapulting the elder into the woods. Lye crashed through multiple trees, snapping their thin trunks and sending wood splintering into the air.

"What was that?" Lye wondered to himself, struggling to rise after sustaining some severe injuries. He looked up and saw Ret checking on Stone. "Oh, no," Lye feared as he took another swig from his flask, "not Ret." Lye was about to make a run for it when he remembered he didn't have his cane. Now that Ret was on the scene, Lye was willing to leave Stone behind, but there was no way he was leaving without the First Father's cane.

Lye snuck to the edge of the clearing and made a beeline for the cane. Ret, who had just barely revived Stone back into consciousness, laid him down gently and moved to cut off Lye. As they both darted toward the cane, Ret created a small gully in Lye's path, causing him to fall in, and then closed it around his torso, trapping him halfway in the ground. Lye struggled to free himself. Then, desperate to regain his cane, he mentally felt around in the earth beneath him and located a large underground well. He channeled its water upwards, causing the ground to rumble. Sensing this, Ret held the earth together everywhere except immediately around Lye, forcing the water to erupt directly underneath him. As if he was sitting atop Old Faithful, Lye's geyser burst to the surface, launching him out of the ground. He flew into the charred remains of the trailer, enveloping him in a cloud of soot and ashes.

Ret picked up the spirally-twisted cane. Like touching an electrical current, it shocked him, and he dropped it. He reached for it again, this time anticipating the shock, and latched onto it. It made him feel a little fuzzy, like there was a charge running through his bones. It was the first time he had ever touched the cane, since it had always been in Lye's careful possession in the past. He studied it closely. It looked more like a tusk grown by an animal than a staff hewn by a man, and it flared slightly at the top as if it had once been attached to something.

A stifled plea for help halted Ret's concentration, "Ret!" He spun around and saw Lye suspending Stone in the air.

"Give me the staff, or Stone dies," Lye stated in all seriousness, his robes soiled by soot and ash. Ret could see drops of precious water dripping from Stone's body. Ret quickly obliged, tossing the cane at Lye's feet.

"Now hand over Stone," Ret demanded.

Lye bent down and picked up the cane. A look of relief flooded over him. Then, going back on his word, he retained Stone and hurled a lightning bolt at Ret.

In the blink of an eye, Ret ripped off the tailgate of Stone's pick-up truck and held it up to shield himself from Lye's attack. The bolts ricocheted off the sheet of metal, skittering into the forest and burning holes through its canopy. In between each shot, Ret peered around his shelter. He could see Lye running away, still holding Stone a ways in front of him.

Ret thought he should give his budding power over wind a trial run. From the safety of his blockade, he began to stir the air around Lye. He could see the dark lord's robes beginning to flutter, so he stirred faster. Soon, Lye started to spin, and his world morphed into one big blur, causing him to lose track of Stone and release him. Ret accelerated the wind until it grew into a miniature tornado. He blew it into the woods, and he could hear Lye hitting the trees and branches as he spun in circles. The twister picked up leaves and other debris, giving it definition as Ret swirled the air even faster. Higher and stronger it soared, drawing in some of the lingering smoke from the fire. With a final gust, Ret released his creation into nature, letting Lye get carried away in the whirlwind.

Despite their distance, Ret could clearly hear the sound waves that were carrying Lye's departing words, "Ret won't always be around to save you, Stone!" He sounded terribly out of sorts, coughing from all the dust and smoke in the chaotic wind storm. "I'll find you— you know I will!" Faint sounds of choking took over as the whirlwind drifted out of sight.

When the threat of Lye had blown over, Ret turned his attention to his dear friend, Lester Stone. The now-widowed man was a wreck, even more so emotionally than physically. He lay lifeless on the cold ground, his eyes open but his heart crushed. A large part of his being had perished with Virginia. His condition mimicked that of the trailer, which now had been reduced to little more than a blackened spot of earth. He had lost the will to live.

Ret knelt by his side and picked him up.

"Please, Ret," Stone petitioned, his voice devoid of hope, "just leave me here to die." He could hardly move, so Ret positioned himself under one of Stone's arms and dragged him along. The scene was reminiscent of one that took place just a few weeks ago, when Stone had discovered Ret on the ground close to where he had fallen from the train and carried him away.

"Where are you taking me?" Stone inquired as Ret set him in the front seat of the truck.

"You and I both know another man who lost his wife to Lye," Ret said, referring to Mr. Coy. "Maybe he can help you."

Ret got in the driver's seat. He didn't have the key, so he simply used his power over metal to start the ignition. He pulled out of the lot and entered the narrow path through the thicket.

"Learn from my mistake, Ret," Stone said between sobs, staring inconsolably through the side mirror at the cremated remains of his wife. "There is hardly a choice in life that affects only the man who made it."

It was a long, sad drive to Coy Manor.

CHAPTER 15

DUSTY'S SENTENCE

Back in the courtroom at Coy Manor, the trial on the sensibleness of alcohol was just getting underway.

"The floor is yours," Judge Coy told the prosecution.

"Thank you, your honor," Leo graciously accepted, rising from his chair to begin his opening remarks. "Ladies and gentlemen of the jury," he addressed the coarse crew in the jury box, "numbers tell a story, so allow me to provide a few for your consideration."

"According to a World Health Organization global status report for the year 2011," Leo read from a paper in his hand, "the harmful use of alcohol results in 2.5 million deaths each year."

"I object!" Dusty interrupted. "It's not alcohol's fault if someone uses it 'harmfully.'"

"Overruled," Coy told the defense.

Leo resumed, "According to a 2009 study cited by the National Institute on Drug Abuse, alcohol abuse costs the United States $235 billion annually in crime, lost work, and healthcare."

"Again, I object!" Dusty repeated, purposely trying to get on their nerves. "That figure is about alcohol *abuse*, not alcohol *use*."

"Overruled."

"And, finally," said Leo, "according to data released by the U.S. National Highway Traffic Safety Administration, a total of 10,322 people died in drunk driving crashes in 2012."

"I object!" Dusty stated a third time. "You can't blame alcohol if someone who has been drinking gets behind the wheel."

Observing Dusty's selective hearing, Leo slowly repeated the statistic to emphasize its gravity: "In just one year, drunk driving killed 10,322 people in this country. That's an average of one person every 51 minutes—28 people each day. Can you believe that? And it's an increase of 444 from the previous year. More than two dozen people—some guilty, some innocent—die every day in this country for no good reason. It's a massacre—one that happens daily—but does it ever make the headlines?"

"That's why there are laws against drunk driving

and underage drinking," Dusty submitted.

"Which you defied," Leo inserted.

"We're not talking about me," Dusty sneered, his ego bruised. "We're talking about alcohol, and the *fact* is alcohol doesn't kill people—people kill people."

"Even though the World Health Organization says alcohol kills 2.5 million people a year," Leo reminded. "And how many people do you think get behind the wheel drunk specifically to kill another person? Did you get in your recent accident on purpose?"

"Of course not," Dusty admitted. "If that's what this is all about, then fine: I'll stop drinking until I'm old enough, okay? Can we go now?"

"As if age has anything to do with it," Leo remarked. Then, returning to the jury, "As I said before, numbers tell a story, and the story of alcohol is one that never has a happy ending. Can anyone tell me one good thing that has come from human consumption of alcohol?"

"It sure does *me* a lot of good!" one of the jury members joked, sending a wave of laughs through the box.

"Case in point," Leo muttered to himself, shaking his head.

"Always a 'good' time!" agreed another. "Just like the billboards say!"

"Yeah, nothing but 'happy endings' here!" cried a third, only adding to the jury's hysterics.

"You call handcuffs a happy ending?" Leo rebutted.

"Not if you don't get caught!" another said.

"And the hangovers? The health risks?" Leo pointed out.

"It's always worth the fun!" one more claimed.

"Yeah, Dusty, why don't you pass that bottle around already?" asked the friend closest to him who had been eyeing it ever since Thorne brought it out.

"Order! Order!" Coy exclaimed from the bench, slamming his gavel on its wooden pedestal. The party in the jury box settled down.

"Look," Dusty spoke up, "I understand what you're trying to do here. But this is a free country, and alcohol is perfectly legal."

"It wasn't always legal in this country, however," Leo said. "Such was a battle that was fought and lost many years ago, and we have been paying for it in health, money, and blood ever since. But we're not here today to squabble about laws. My purpose is to instill sobriety not by virtue of the law but by its own virtues."

"If you think alcohol is bad, then don't drink it," Dusty stated. "But I don't think there's anything wrong with it, and I'm entitled to my opinion, aren't I? It's like the industry always says, 'Please drink responsibly.' That's all there is to it, okay? Case closed."

"Ah, 'Please drink responsibly,'" Leo iterated, "the ultimate copout! The makers of alcohol are well aware that unfortunate consequences are sure to follow those who consume it, so that statement is their nifty way of removing themselves from any and all accountability. But, in reality, any semi-intelligent person would realize that such a statement is flawed. It's an oxymoron. It contradicts itself. It doesn't make any sense."

"For what does alcohol do? It first and foremost makes the drinker less responsible. It makes him less responsive to everything around him. It deadens pain and lessens embarrassment. It induces a less rational state of mind, leading him to do and say things that his normal, responsible self would not do or say. It temporarily removes the stresses and obligations in life—work, spouse, offspring—the things he is responsible for. It makes him unfit to drive or operate machinery—why?—because his mind, his judgment, and his reflexes have become less responsive. Sometimes a drinker will find himself in a place and not know how he got there, or with people whom he does not know, or having done something that he doesn't remember doing."

"You can drink without getting drunk, you know," Dusty informed him.

"So why drink at all then?" Leo carried on. "If one drink doesn't do anything—if it fails to wipe away cares or create a buzz—then why drink it? A drinker will never be more responsible than before he takes his first sip for the night; every sip thereafter, he becomes less and less responsible. Do you really expect a person in that state of mind to, as they say, 'know his limits'?"

"That's why you're supposed to be responsible and pick a designated driver," Dusty argued.

"And that makes perfect sense, doesn't it?" Leo disagreed. "Sure, be a responsible person by asking a friend to be responsible for you while you become irresponsible. You see, it's the principle of the matter. There is nothing responsible about making yourself irresponsible. So when they tell you to 'please drink responsibly,' what they're really saying is 'please become irresponsible, but do it responsibly.' Such a directive is simply impossible and outright hypocritical, and a kingdom divided against itself cannot stand."

Leo's words were having a sobering effect on Dusty and his friends. He was trampling on their tipsy hearts, their flippancy replaced with resentment.

"Alcohol is not bad, in and of itself," Leo taught. "It can be quite useful for cleaning and sanitizing things, for example. But when it is taken into the body, it wields an influence—it exerts a force. We already know this; it cannot be denied. This is why the crime is appropriately named 'driving under the *influence*.' The influence of what? The influence of alcohol, of course. But what is it exactly? Can it be seen? Is it a tangible thing? Is it even real?"

The jury was speechless.

"I'd like to call Ana Cooper to the witness stand," Leo transitioned.

Thorne stepped to the front of the room and pulled open the side door. Ana strode through and took her seat at the witness stand near the judge's bench.

"You were with Dusty the night of the accident, were you not?" Leo questioned the witness.

"Yes, sir," Ana answered.

"Did you observe any change in Dusty over the course of the evening?"

"Yes, sir," she said again.

"Would you please describe the change you saw?"

"Now that I know what he was up to," Ana recalled, "I remember sensing a difference in Dusty after the very first time he returned from stepping outside. He began to say things that were rude and do things that were kind of unusual for being out in public."

"Can you give us an example?" Leo requested.

"Well, he made a crude joke about how a heavy-set girl looked in her dress," Ana remembered, "and he started to do some dance moves that were borderline inappropriate. But he didn't seem to be aware that he was causing people to feel uncomfortable."

"Would you say he had become unresponsive to their feelings?" Leo asked.

"Yes, sir."

"I see."

"And it took me by surprise because I never knew Dusty to be mean or offensive," Ana said. "At the time, I thought maybe he was just getting into the music or something. But each time he left and came back, he returned with more energy—a foreign energy that made him not himself. By the end of the night, he had become a totally different person. And then, when I told him to let me out of the car, he really changed. It was like I became his enemy by not approving of what he was doing. The Dusty who left me on the street that night was not the same Dusty I showed up at the dance with."

"Thank you," Leo told her. "You may step down."

On her way back through the side door, Ana passed by Dusty, his head down in disgrace as she recounted the events of that homecoming night.

"Seen or unseen?" Leo put forth. "As we have just heard, the power of alcohol remains unseen in the bottle but most certainly can be seen working within someone. You see, it needs a vessel—something that it can take control of—and when a man voluntarily ingests it, he gives it free license to take control of him. And so the irrefutable fact remains: the influence of alcohol is very real."

"Within that bottle," Leo said, pointing to the defendant on the table, "there are lurking demons that will kill common bacteria when applied topically but will destroy common sense when consumed orally. You and I may not be able to see these drinkable devils, but it is impossible not to see the havoc they wreak—not only on the drinker himself but also on the innocent souls who get in his way. Even the smallest dose will change a man—give him a buzz that erodes his reason, hijacks his freedom, and turns him into a puppet whose strings move with the whims of a liquid. Only a period of restraint can give the body the time it requires to purge itself of these microscopic monsters. Is it any wonder, then, why they are often called 'spirits'?"

It was getting more difficult to refute Leo's points. With the well-sharpened ax of truth, he was striking at the root of the issue, not merely trimming its foliage. The glitz and glamor of beer and liquor were now identified as nothing more than foolishness and ignorance. What the jury had chalked up to be an arena of fun and games had been accurately depicted by Leo as a pastime with no winners. It was the principle of the matter, not the lawfulness of it, that was changing hearts in the courtroom.

"I know what I did was wrong," Dusty said at last, his tone starting to show the remorse that his father had been praying would come into his heart. "I'm sorry for what happened to Missy." A feeling of hope began to fill the courtroom. But then he left every listener dumbfounded with one sentence: said he, "I never would have done that to her in real life."

Mr. Coy couldn't believe what he heard. Leo stood as still as a statue. Pauline looked up from typing with a face of shock. Thorne scrunched his forehead in utter disbelief. Paige's jaw dropped. In profound silence, everyone stared at Dusty.

"What did you say?" Judge Coy asked from the bench, hoping he had misheard.

Unusually timid, Dusty repeated the sentence, "I never would have done that to Missy in real life."

Mr. Coy's heart sank to know he had heard correctly.

Despite the collective mood of stillborn hope, Leo turned to the bailiff and said, "Bring in the evidence."

Still in shock from his son's statement, Thorne again walked to the side door and held it open. Ana slowly reentered the courtroom, this time pushing a wheelchair in front of her. There was a mass of white bandages sitting in the wheelchair. Within those bandages was Missy.

A pin drop could be heard as everyone in the courtroom watched Ana roll the evidence to the plaintiff's table, granting the defense table a nice, long look. Ana positioned the wheelchair right next to Paige and then took a seat on the other side of Missy. Both girls put a hand on their bodyguard's hands, though only the fingertips of which were uncovered. Missy was awake but clearly incapacitated.

Leo took a few steps back from where he had been pacing in front of the jury box. He held out his right hand, pointing at Missy. With tenderness, he asked Dusty, "Is this not real?"

Dusty's head fell in shame. He had not known the extent of what had happened to the driver in the car that he crashed into, until now. He stole a glance at his friends in the jury box, but their heads also hung low. Convicted by their own conscience in the face of such indisputable evidence, they sat with broken hearts.

"Is this not 'real life'?" Leo lectured. "Are these bandages fake? Is this woman's pain pretended? Do you think that collision never really happened? It may not seem real to you; you may not have done it on purpose; you may not have been your true self at the time; but I can assure you, *this*," pointing once again at Missy, "this is real. This is not a 'happy ending'; this is not a 'good' time; this is not being 'responsible.'" Leo walked to the defense table and picked up the glass of beer. "In fact, who is responsible for that poor woman's situation: you or this?" Leo moved the glass in fast circles, swirling the yellow liquid. "Tell me, Dusty: was it worth it?"

Dusty looked up with tears in his eyes.

"Tears can't change the past, Dusty—this I know very well," Leo said without sympathy, as if the two of them were the only people in the courtroom. "I shed tears every night, wishing my parents hadn't been killed in a drunk driving accident. The other orphans where I live also shed tears every night, each a victim of someone else's poor choices. You may claim it's just a drink—that the danger is in its misuse. But I say there is danger to be found in every drink, that any use is misuse. And so I say to you: stay completely away from it. Its present use was never its intended use. There is no responsible way to do it, no matter how little you drink or how strong you think you are. There is no fun to be had when you play in harm's way. All who try to drown their problems in alcohol quickly find out their problems grow gills. Don't let the sad story of alcohol be your story, too."

"Let it be known," Leo concluded with all boldness, stepping away from the counsel tables to address everyone in attendance, "that I am an enemy of all drunkenness—that I lend my voice to the cause of personal responsibility. There has never been, nor will there ever be, a good reason why anyone should ever drink alcohol. There is only evidence against it— evidence which grows more heinous and bloody with every person killed, every liver poisoned, every child abused, every baby defected, and every life scarred.

These are the terrible realities of our world's chemically-induced fantasies. How long will we allow our selfish hearts to keep us blind to an evil that is so fundamentally false?"

"Let's get a grip, not a glass. Let's rise above the letter of the law and embrace the spirit of it. Let's give three cheers for no more booze. Let's get our buzz from selfless service, not selfish striving. Let's get over being under the influence of alcohol and start being an influence for good." Then, turning to face the judge, Leo finished, "Your honor, I rest my case."

No one stood taller in that courtroom than the little lawyer named Leonard Swain. The case he presented before the jury was the product of seventeen years of pain and sorrow. The boy had been born an orphan, cradled in crisis, and raised without regard. He sought no vengeance on the drunk who drove his parents to their death. It was not that person's fault; the tragedy had been unintentional. The blame, therefore, belonged less to the body behind the wheel and more to the influence steering the body. And so, before the boy could yet speak, Leo had it in him to make known the evil energy of inebriation and be an outspoken voice against any use of the mind-controlling substance known as alcohol.

A screech filled the courtroom as Dusty pushed back his chair. Wiping the tears from his face, he stood with newfound resolve and grabbed the glass of beer.

With the jury watching raptly, Dusty strode over to the wall where there was a large window. He pushed the window open, held out the glass, and turned it upside-down. Out flowed the conspiring fluid—with all its influences, changes, energies, and hidden powers—reduced to a pathetic puddle on the ground below.

When Dusty turned around holding the drained glass, the courtroom erupted in applause. But Dusty didn't seem to notice. Instead, he hurried across the room and gently fell on Missy, embracing her as best he could.

"I'm sorry," he sobbed. "I'm so sorry."

Missy, who could hardly move or smile, did the only thing that didn't require movement: she wept.

With one accord, the jury bypassed deliberations and made their unanimous decision. The first one out of the jury box grabbed the bottle of alcohol and traced Dusty's steps to the window. He dumped out a sampling and then handed the bottle to the next friend. One by one, the friends each poured some out until it, too, was drained. Then they willingly went to the plaintiff's table and made amends.

From up on the bench, the black-robed and white-wigged judge looked over the happy proceedings with a grand smile. One of Mr. Coy's favorite things to do was make bad men good and good men better. His delight was in taking broken things and fixing them. The only constant in his life was the change he instilled in other lives—never by force but always by love. It was not Mr. Coy's way to condemn people but rather to persuade them to change for themselves. Such was the case today: Dusty had passed sentence on himself.

With great joy, Mr. Coy watched the group mingle together, a smile on every face. After Thorne hugged his son, the bailiff looked up at the judge, and the two exchanged victorious nods. When Pauline glanced Coy's way, she gave him an appreciative grin, as if the two had never been at odds before. Ana gave him a thumbs-up, and Paige put up a dainty wave. Leo, now swarmed by former foes, managed to catch Coy's eye as the judge winked at him with pride. There was only one person missing.

Suddenly, amid all the jubilation, the large double doors at the back of the room burst open, and a strong wind rushed into the courtroom. A hush fell over the merriment as everyone turned to see who was making their belated entrance. It was a young man, his clothes dirty and face unshaven. He looked tired and gaunt, like he had just traveled across a continent and back.

The on-looking crowd stared searchingly at this unknown person—some with confusion, others with fear. There was one among them, however, who recognized the stranger instantly. With a mixture of relief and elation, Paige yelled, "Ret!"

CHAPTER 16

MISS UNDERSTANDING

As Ret came striding down the center aisle of the courtroom, there were only two people who rushed toward him: father and daughter Coy. With pure joy on her face, Paige hastened to embrace her long-lost love. Mr. Coy, however, was hurrying not to greet Ret but to restrain Paige. The moment he had seen Ret, Mr. Coy sprang from his leather chair in alarm and hurried down the judge's bench, throwing off the wig and robe of his costume as he chased after his daughter. Paige hadn't made it to the first row of the gallery when she felt Mr. Coy's firm hand grasp her shoulder from behind. Surprised, she stopped and looked back at her father, whose wary expression begged her to obey him.

There was visible eagerness to Ret's march, as if he had exciting news to share. His zeal waned, however, when he saw the Coys come to an abrupt halt. The worry that washed over their faces splashed some on his own. His pace quickly diminished until he stopped a few steps in front of them.

It required every last shred of Paige's self-control to remain at Mr. Coy's side and not in Ret's arms, which was a shame because there was something about Ret's disheveled appearance that made her heart swoon like never before. It was a rugged sort of handsomeness, amplified by seeing him for the first time in months. His hair—once blond, now bronze—was getting long, and a scruffy beard half-covered his face. His clothes, which seemed to hang more loosely on him than Paige remembered, were dusty and dirty. Wherever he had gone, he had obviously spent a fair amount of time outdoors, judging by the ever-darkening tint of his skin. And was that ash on his shirt? He seemed older, wiser, more mature. All she wanted to do for the next few hours was sit with him and listen to him talk about his recent travels and experiences. The two of them had so much time to catch up on.

"Hello, Ret," Mr. Coy said flatly, a thick awkwardness in the air.

"Hi," Ret replied, feeling a little uncomfortable.

"Where have you been all this time?" Coy asked.

"Lots of places," Ret answered, "but mostly way up north in Canada somewhere."

"As far north as the Arctic?" Coy wondered. Paige noticed an unusual amount of suspicion in her father's pointed questions.

"Uh, maybe," Ret reasoned. "I'm not sure where I was exactly." Then, confused by the way the conversation was going, Ret asked, "Why?"

"I've also been 'way up north' recently," Coy told him, "and while I was there, I saw you."

"Really?" Ret lit up at the coincidence. "You should've said hi—we could've hung out!"

"I wanted to," said Coy, "but you were with Lye." Paige stared at her father in shock. From behind, Pauline and Ana looked on with similar disbelief.

"So you saw me save Stone after Lye blew up the trailer?" Ret wondered.

"What?" Coy returned. "Stone? The trailer?"

"Then what did you see?" Ret asked.

"I saw you at the North Pole," Coy said. "You were cooperating with Lye, helping him do something."

Now it was Ret's turn to ask, "What? The North Pole? I'm pretty sure I didn't go *that* far north. And I was fighting against Lye, not cooperating with him."

"Well, I saw you with my own eyes, Ret," Coy reaffirmed. "I saw it all: you, Lye, the dog sled—"

"What are you talking about?" said Ret, almost with a chuckle at such a ridiculous story. "Are you sure this wasn't a dream you had or something?"

"Thorne was there with me—weren't you, Thorne?" Coy persisted, glancing back at the bailiff. "You saw Ret, didn't you?"

A little startled from being put on the spot, Thorne nevertheless witnessed, "I—I did."

"Well, I'm sorry, but you're wrong," Ret denied with a laugh. "You're both wrong."

"I wish I was," Coy admitted, "but I know what I saw. And didn't you just say you were with Lye—something about Stone and a trailer?"

"That's right," Ret said with sudden excitement. "Get this: Stone quit working for Lye." The happy headline didn't have its intended effect. When Coy's face revealed he wasn't buying it, Ret added, "It's true. Stone cut his ties—cold turkey. Then he went into exile. That's when he and I crossed paths. He rescued me—took me in and cared for me when I was lost. Stone has changed. He's a good man. Did you know he was actually the one who called off those—"

"Stone, a good man?" Coy balked. "Do you hear yourself, Ret?"

"Yes, it's true," Ret avowed. "And when Lye found us up there (I don't know how he did), he was angry with Stone, so he murdered Virginia." Breaths of dismay escaped the lips of several audience members. "Stone is a changed man—believe me. He could use our love and support right now, especially from you, Mr.

Coy. And he also knows what really happened to your—"

"And how do we know you're not just making all of this up?" Coy questioned, now even more suspicious on account of the sob story.

"I can prove it," Ret promised, much to everyone's surprise. Then, turning around, he yelled, "Stone! Come in here, will you?"

Upon hearing such words, Pauline instinctively pulled Ana in close. With unbridled suspicion, Mr. Coy looked past Ret at a person's shadow that was on the floor just outside the courtroom's double doors. A few seconds later, the figure of a man appeared from around the corner, so sluggishly that it was like watching it happen in slow-motion. Sure enough, there was their neighborhood foe, Lester W. Stone. With no sense of urgency, the old principal staggered into the room, his head hanging down as low as his neck would allow. He came just far enough to be inside, then leaned against the wall and slid to take a seat on the ground.

Coy was outraged to learn Ret had brought Stone onto the premises of the Manor.

"What is *he* doing here?" Coy fumed.

"I brought him here," Ret replied innocently.

"Why would you do a thing like that?"

"Because he's my friend," Ret said matter-of-factly.

"What are you talking about, Ret?" Coy asked sincerely, totally bewildered by what he was hearing. "What's happened to you?"

"Dad!" Paige snapped.

"He just brought Stone into our home," Coy rebutted. "Stone—our common enemy!"

"But this is Ret!" Paige pled.

"I know it's Ret," he said defensively. "It's the same Ret who Thorne and I saw standing on the ice that day in the Arctic, working with Lye. I didn't want to believe it, but I can't deny what I saw."

"But Ret said that isn't true," Paige reminded him.

"Maybe that's precisely what Lye wants him to say," Mr. Coy suggested. "Don't you see? Doesn't this look suspicious to anyone else? This could all be part of Lye's scheme: send Ret back to the Manor with Stone, think up some pitiful story to win us over, and then ransack us from head to toe. I wouldn't be surprised if next Ret asks me to give him the Oracle!"

"This isn't some story we made up," Ret retaliated, upset by Coy's insensitivity for the bereft man at the back of the room. "It's the truth. I saw it with—"

"—With your own eyes?" Coy smirked, hearing his own words from earlier.

Ret was dumbfounded by the welcome he was receiving. He had returned to the Manor with enthusiasm, anxious to tell everyone where he had been and what he had learned: the fourth scar, his new powers, the Northern Lights, Stone's repentance, the truth about Helen's death. He couldn't wait to announce where the next element was and then embark on another adventure together. But Ret's high hopes were dashed in an instant. Now, it felt like he and Mr. Coy were opponents.

"Why don't you believe me?" Ret asked sincerely. "Why are you attacking me like this?"

"Because, Ret, I know what I saw," Coy said.

"I told you," Ret insisted, "that wasn't me!"

"Then who was it?" Coy shot back. "A clone? Was it a mirage that Thorne and I saw? A figment of our imagination? Has Lye brainwashed you like he did Jaret? Hmm? And why did Lye chase after us so zealously once we saw you two together? He was obviously trying to hide something."

"Look, I don't know what you saw," Ret stated calmly, "but whatever it was, it wasn't real. I'm not working for Lye, I promise. Please, you've got to believe me. I know what I'm doing. There's so much I could tell you—so much we need to do. Please, trust me."

"I'd really like to, Ret," Coy lamented, "but for the sake of our safety and security, I'm afraid I can't right now." When Ret shook his head, Coy expounded, "Look around, Ret. All of these people here depend on me and my sound judgment. I'm unsure of your motives right now, and, given the present circumstances," Coy glanced again at Stone, "you might be putting us all in danger. Try to understand where I'm coming from."

Ret took a deep, unsatisfied breath and exhaled.

"Just give me some time," Coy petitioned. "Hopefully, once the dust settles, we'll both be able to see things with much clearer vision. In the meantime, however, I'm going to have to ask you to leave."

Even though Mr. Coy's indictments were valid in theory, they were completely false in reality. He was, of course, telling the truth about what he saw that day on the Arctic Ocean. His confusion, therefore, came not from what had been seen but from what had been unseen. He had no idea that the Ret he saw wasn't the real Ret but rather Lye's crude clone. And so, it was the seen without the unseen that had caused Mr. Coy's misunderstanding. But how does someone see an unseen thing? Is it even possible?

Of course it's possible, Ret would tell you. For months now, he had been seeing marvelous things that had previously been unseen, not because the things themselves had changed but because he himself had changed. Like a pencil's point being constantly sharpened or a microscope's lens being continually focused, a recurring refinement had taken place within Ret's mind and heart that granted him the capacity to see the more refined features of the world. So yes, the unseen can most certainly be seen but, as its name implies, usually has very little to do with what we can see.

Ret peered across the room at Pauline and Ana. They were staring back at him with belief—not distrust—in their eyes. They looked like they would run to him if it weren't for the iron-fisted judge in their way.

Then Ret's eyes fell on Paige. Her joy had succumbed to disaster. She was pitted against the respect she owed her father and the love and trust she felt toward Ret. Her mind was in one place, her heart a few steps away.

Adjourning the case with one final comment, Ret stared Mr. Coy unabashedly in the eyes and used the man's recent phrase to tell him, "'Clearer vision,' sir, comes with eyes closed and heart open." Then Ret turned around and strode out of the room.

"Come on, Stone," Ret mumbled caringly as he passed by the mourner on the floor.

Stone slowly rose to his feet, then stopped in the entryway and glanced back at Mr. Coy. With a face drowned in grief, he spoke a simple, "I'm sorry."

"Nice try, Stone," Coy returned without affection. He assumed Stone's heartfelt apology was yet continuation of the pretended scenario that was part of Lye's botched scheme to take advantage of the Manor. In reality, however, it was an overdue expression of earnest regret for an unrelated tragedy that had happened years ago, spoken from one widower to another.

Misunderstood, Stone turned and dragged himself after Ret.

Paige burst into tears and tore herself from her father's side. She ran out of the room and out of sight. Knowing her friend was retreating to her room, Ana followed after her to offer consolation.

The audience began to shuffle out. The remaining court staff went their separate ways. Within minutes, Mr. Coy found himself completely alone.

O   O   O

Paige awoke before sunrise the next morning. It was Saturday, and, for the first time in months, she knew where Ret would be. Without waking anyone, she snuck out of the Manor and crossed the creek, heading for a certain spot on the southern tip of Tybee's beach.

He was right where she thought he would be, sitting in his hand-made hollow in the sand. His favorite nook was in a state of disrepair these days, having been neglected for many months and washed out by high tides. But Paige knew that was one thing Ret admired about the elements: they always win in the end.

"Got room for one more?" Paige teased.

"Only if that one is you," Ret smiled, scooting over.

Snuggling next to him, she said, "How'd I know I'd find you here?"

"Where else would I go?" Ret joked. "Lye destroyed my house, and your dad kicked me out of his."

"Ret, I'm so sorry—"

"It's alright," Ret told her.

"You mean you're not angry?"

Ret laughed, "You know I don't get angry."

"Yeah, I know," said Paige, "but still. I don't know what's come over Dad."

"I'm not sure what he saw exactly," Ret iterated, "but it wasn't me. It's probably just more of Lye's mischief."

"Well, I believe you," Paige pledged.

"I know," Ret beamed, reaching to hold her hand.

"So, when are you going to tell me about your trip?" Paige asked with interest.

Ret told her everything. Through his chronicles, he took her from Tybee to the Midwest, then to New England and finally to the far North. He explained his newfound ability to control wind and all forms of energy, even demonstrating it to her by bending the rays of the rising sun and tuning in to a radio station. Paige was most impressed by such prodigious power, and she even taught Ret a thing or two about the science behind the aurorae. Then Ret dove into the tale of Stone's change of heart, which inevitably led to the true account of Helen's demise.

"So that means Lye might still have it somewhere," Paige thought aloud.

"Have what?" Ret asked.

"Mom's slip of paper," she answered. "The one that has the molecular structure of the mysterious water written on it." Ret had never considered that before.

"Maybe Stone went back to his house to look for it," he kidded.

"Where *is* Stone?" Paige wondered, searching around.

"I don't know," Ret admitted. "He came across the creek with me last night, but I haven't seen him since. He has to keep a low profile, now that Lye's after him."

"Oh, Ret, I'm so glad you told me what really happened to Mom," Paige said. She took the news very well, which was to be expected since it put somewhat of a happy twist on an otherwise tragic ending. "She did it! She figured it out! Way to go, Mom!" Paige shared her mother's indomitable spirit. "You've got to tell Dad."

"I wanted to," Ret stated. "That's one reason I brought Stone back with me—so he could tell him in person. But your dad didn't give us a chance."

"I'm sure he'll come around," Paige hoped.

"Well, I'm not just going to wait around for things to blow over," Ret said. "I don't have time for that. I've got an element to collect."

"You mean you want to go to Antarctica without Dad?" Paige wondered.

"Want?" Ret repeated with a hint of disgust. "You've got to understand, I never *wanted* to do any of this, and I still don't want to."

Paige was confused: "You don't want to collect the elements?"

"No!" Ret said broadly, making the very idea sound ludicrous. "I just want to be a normal guy—go to school, get a job, have a family. How great would *that* be?"

"Then why don't you?"

"I tried," Ret said. "That's the whole reason why I left. I tried to put it all behind me and start over in life, determined to do everything based on what *I* wanted. But I can't do it. The Oracle won't leave me alone. It's like it has given me this calling—a mission—to find the elements."

"I guess you're just the chosen one," Paige mused.

"No, that's not it," Ret quickly countered. "I'm no one special."

"But you have the scars," she pointed out.

"Everyone has scars, Paige—creases in their hands, wrinkles in their skin, birthmarks, talents, skills, yearnings. Each and every one of us has a calling to carry out—a mission to perform—but it takes effort to figure out what it is. That's why I sit outside among the elements so much. I'm thinking, pondering, meditating. I'm listening to what they tell me, and I can hear them because I'm trying to hear them."

"So the elements speak to you?" Paige asked with a tinge of strangeness.

"Yes—not really through words but feelings," Ret tried to describe. "When they tell me something, it comes as a feeling. I'm not sure if it's a real thing that you can reach out and touch, but it becomes real when it touches me as a feeling. And then I know, without a doubt, what I must do, no matter how difficult or unwanted."

"Sounds hard," Paige observed.

"It's what I learned during my time in the wilderness," said Ret. "My wants don't really matter. The Oracle requires complete submission to its higher, nobler will."

"Isn't that what Lye requires, too?"

"Yes," Ret submitted, "but Lye does it by force; the Oracle does it by invitation. It simply asks. It is patient. It works on you, tender but firm, hoping that your wants become aligned with its wants. That's why I don't believe in the idea of a 'chosen one.' We can all be chosen, but the choice is up to us. So if I am chosen, then it's not because the Oracle has chosen me but because I have chosen the Oracle."

Silence prevailed for a few moments. Ret's words had moved Paige to introspection. There was something about watching the crest and fall of the endless waves that encouraged contemplation.

"So what's my calling then, I wonder?" Paige looked inward.

"That's what you have to listen for," Ret answered. "Maybe it's to go to school and become—oh, I don't know—a doctor."

"A doctor?"

"You could follow in your mom's footsteps," Ret brainstormed. "Maybe it's to get married and become a mother."

"Mom did all of those things," Paige proudly pointed out. Thinking further, she suggested, "Or maybe it's to help you collect the elements."

"Maybe so," Ret grinned. "Actually, I think I'm really going to need your help this time since it might be a while before your dad offers any assistance."

"What did you have in mind?"

"I'd like to leave for Antarctica as soon as possible," Ret detailed. "Like today."

"Well, I don't know how to fly an airplane," Paige thought, "but Dusty might."

"Who's Dusty?"

"He's Thorne's son," Paige clarified. "He could take us in his dad's floatplane."

"Sounds like a plan," Ret agreed. "You're helping me already."

"And I'll ask Ana to come, if you don't mind," Paige said. "You know, just to have another girl around."

"Of course."

"Should we ask Leo to join us?"

"You mean the person who was responsible for collecting the element last time?" Ret recalled. "And for saving my life?"

"Good point," Paige understood. "I'll try to have everything ready by noon. I think Thorne keeps his plane parked in the creek, so we can pick you up here." Paige moved to leave.

"Wait," Ret stopped her. She looked back at him, waiting for him to tell her a task they may have over-looked. But Ret just stared at her. The morning sunshine caught her large curls and turned them to gold. She was beautiful to him, but the expression on his face signified more than that. The gaze in his eyes bespoke of gratitude for her unfailing support and understanding heart. It was for him a source of strength.

"What?" Paige blushed.

"There's one more thing I need you to do," Ret told her softly. Then he slid his hand behind her head and kissed her.

Afterwards, Paige said, "That was easy."

"That wasn't it," Ret informed her. "I need you to get the Oracle from your dad."

Paige considered the assignment briefly and then replied with a romantic smirk, "Okay, but it's going to cost you."

Ret put his lips to hers again, a price he was more than willing to pay.

.

CHAPTER 17

THINGS GO SOUTH

While Ret was waiting to get picked up by the floatplane that would take him to Antarctica, he saw Leo walking toward him from up the beach.

"Hey, Leo!" Ret hailed as he drew near. "Ready to go?"

"Go where?" Leo wondered, obviously unaware of his upcoming travel plans.

"The South Pole," Ret answered.

"Really?" Leo smiled, always thirsty for adventure. "Right now?"

"Right now," Ret informed him. "Paige should be pulling up in a floatplane any minute."

"So that's why Peggy Sue told me to come down here," Leo deduced, referring to the orphanage director. "Paige must've called her." Then, realizing he wasn't exactly outfitted for a polar expedition, he asked, "Is it too late for me to run back and get some pants?"

"Don't worry: I'm a human flame, remember?" They both laughed.

"So did you sleep out here last night?" Leo inquired, sitting down in the sand close by.

"Tried to," Ret said.

"You should've come down to the orphanage," Leo told him warmly.

"Thanks. The way things are going, I might need to take you up on that."

"I'm sorry Mr. Coy doesn't believe you," Leo consoled. "*I* believe you—'course, I didn't see what he saw."

"And that's why this is so frustrating," Ret confessed. "I'm sure Mr. Coy isn't lying, but I know it wasn't me who he saw. So it's like he's both right and wrong at the same time, and he probably feels the same way about my story."

"Maybe you're both right," Leo suggested, "but neither one of you sees it yet."

"I hope you're right," Ret sighed. "You were right the last time we talked together, you know."

"Sir?" Leo begged reminding.

"Remember when I ran into you on my way out of town?" Ret asked.

"When you heard me singing?" Leo blushed.

"Yeah, well, you told me something at the end that proved to be prophetic. You said you hoped I'd find my light in the night, remember?"

Scratching his head in a bit of embarrassment, "Sounds like something cheesy I would say, doesn't it?"

"Well, guess what?" Ret glowed. "I did! I found my light in the night—a lot of them, actually. When I went up north, I discovered the Northern Lights. It reminded me of your song, and I realized it's not so much about lights but about people. After that, everything just sort of clicked. So thank you, thank you very much."

"Glad to be of service," Leo beamed.

True to her word, Paige pulled up in the floatplane just before noon. With a handshake, Ret introduced himself to Dusty and joined him in the cockpit while Leo wedged his way into the backseat with Ana and Paige. Wasting no time, they glided from the creek into the ocean and, after a thrust from the engine, took to the sky.

Although not a licensed pilot, Dusty was very familiar with the workings of his father's plane. He set all instruments to the south, generally following the seventy-eighth meridian, and kept close to the coastlines, near enough to make an emergency landing but far enough away to prevent being identified. It was a familiar route—one that Ret had traveled before, at least in part, to find each of the elements thus far:

Earth had been hiding relatively close to home, just down the road called Bimini. Now, flying over the Bermuda Triangle, it was clear that the sea had fully swallowed the civilization known as Sunken Earth.

Fire had required a longer journey. After three stops in Peru—first to see the lines in the Nazca Desert, then to tour the mountain city Machu Picchu, and finally to float with the islands of Lake Titicaca—they arrived at Easter Island, which now was too far west for Ret to see if there was still smoke rising from its drowned-into-dormancy volcano.

Ore proved farther still, spanning two continents and jumping the ocean in between them. Although he could see neither the Amazon Rainforest nor the Sahara Desert, Ret knew the headwaters of the Amazon River were somewhere deep within the Andes Mountains that they were now following down the coast of Chile.

As for wind, well, Ret had already been to the top of the world, and now he was on his way to the bottom of it.

At this rate, Ret wondered if one of the two remaining elements might take him to the moon! But he figured this was unlikely, for each element so far was linked to one of the earth's six landmasses—further proof that the Oracle's purpose was to unify the entire planet. Element by element, the quest to cure the world was growing in complexity: the scars more puzzling, the places more far-flung, the secrets more subtle. But even though the requirements were escalating, so were the rewards: knowledge unknown by most, love proven in trial, friends in life and beyond. And so as Ret reviewed his travelogue this time around, he did so with more sweetness than sorrow—now seeing some losses as gains, now aware of the hardship that often accompanies true change.

Other riders were going through their own emotions, however:

Leo was shocked a bit when he learned their trip was being carried out without the knowledge of Mr. Coy.

Ana felt the burden a little heavier, knowing Coy and Thorne might be disappointed in her for not obtaining their permission.

Paige was the most unsettled of all, her guilt even greater for taking the Oracle from her dad without his consent. The snatch had been easily made; she knew where he kept it. Still, it bothered her.

As for Dusty, well, he didn't seem too worried about things, not even his recent jacking of his father's plane.

Ret tried to ease their concerns with reassurances of the validity of their cause. He explained to them the intricacies of the wind barb scar and rehearsed his experiences in the Canadian wilderness. He even demonstrated aspects of his power over wind and energy (which always seemed to do the trick when persuading others). He conjured a gust of air to propel the plane at a faster speed. He intercepted a satellite signal to broadcast footage from Santiago's evening news.

Then, as they neared the tip of South America, Ret prepared to introduce his fellow passengers to the aurora australis. He knew the phenomenon was ongoing but that it was impossible to see amid the light of day. So he waited, watching the sun go down, keeping his eyes fixed on the horizon, until finally—

"There!"

All eyes fled to the windows. There, not much higher above them in the atmosphere, was the green glow of the Southern Lights. Just like its northern counterpart, the aurora danced across the starry expanse like a great, flowing curtain. With wonder in their eyes, the flight crew watched the bands of illumination come and go, powered by solar wind being blown from the sun. After a few hours of admiration, sleep overtook the backseat dwellers, but Ret was happy to stay awake with the pilot. Ret relished the lights. They energized him— enlightened him. It was enough to keep his attention all through the night as they passed Cape Horn and headed due south toward the heart of Antarctica.

When morning came, the daylight shuttered the brilliant display above but revealed an equally stunning sight below. The ground was white. In every direction, as far as they could see (which was quite far), the terrain was covered in snow and ice. They had made it to Antarctica.

The landscape of earth's southernmost continent was unlike anything Ret had ever seen. Desolate and barren, it was a desert of snow instead of sand. The whiteness was so pervasive that it hurt to look at it after a while, blinded by the reflection of the sun on the ice. The plains were exceptionally flat, making the mountains seem unusually tall. Ret felt like a tiny mite atop a vast silo of flour.

"Looks cold," Ana said with a shiver upon waking up.

"Well, this *is* where the coldest natural temperature on earth was recorded," Paige observed. "A chilly 128.6 degrees Fahrenheit below zero."

"Please tell me you're kidding," Ana hoped.

Paige shook her head and added, "What do you expect when ninety-eight percent of the place is covered in a layer of ice that, on average, is a mile thick?"

"How do you know so much about Antarctica?" Leo wondered.

"I had to do a report on it once," answered Paige.

"What else can you tell us?" Ret asked.

"Well, let's see," Paige tried to recall. "The continent is about twice the size of Australia, has no permanent residents, and has been set aside by the international community as a scientific preserve."

"So no one lives here?" Ana questioned, looking out at the vacant vastness.

"Not really," Paige said. "Seven countries have made territorial claims and set up research stations, but their claims aren't universally recognized, and most of the territories overlap anyway."

"I wonder if any of them know there's an element here," Ret thought.

"Where exactly is this element?" Dusty asked, curious where to stop.

"I think it's either at or really close to the geographic South Pole," Ret replied.

After analyzing the plane's positioning system, Dusty said, "Looks like we're less than an hour away then."

Everything was going smoothly until the plane's communications system picked up a signal from one of the outposts on the ground.

"This is Amundsen-Scott Station," a scratchy American voice was heard over the radio. "Please identify yourself."

The five youth froze. All eyes were on Dusty. No one knew what to do.

"Maybe they're talking to a different plane," Dusty reasoned unconvincingly.

But then the radio repeated, "This is Amundsen-Scott," this time with a bit less cordiality. "Please identify yourself."

In a fit of panic, Dusty quickly turned off the radio.

"Let's hope they haven't actually seen us," the young pilot wished, "but only picked up our signal."

Even though Dusty had disengaged the radio in the control panel, there was still one sitting in the seat next to him: Ret. With his growing power over wind, Ret scanned the airwaves to find the former signal. He knew simply turning off the system didn't solve their potential problem. It was a good thing he tuned in again, based on what he heard:

"Amundsen-Scott alerting all stations of an unidentified aircraft heading inland across the Transantarctic Mountains."

"Vostok will attempt to establish communications," Ret overheard a Russian person say, followed by a message meant to be picked up by the floatplane. Then, "Attempt unsuccessful."

"Halley here," came a British voice. "Shall we locate Mr. Zarbock?"

Ret only knew one person by that surname. He listened even more intently.

"Señor Zarbock is here at San Martin," replied someone from the Argentine station. A few moments later, Lionel entered the conversation.

"This is Lionel."

"Mr. Zarbock, this is Amundsen-Scott. We've picked up a small aircraft that refuses to identify itself. Your orders, sir?"

"Send out a scout immediately," Lionel instructed with alarm. "If there's still no cooperation, then shoot it down." Ret's heart jumped.

"Yes, sir."

"We need to land," Ret blurted out. "Now!"

"What? Why?" Dusty asked.

"They're sending out a scout," Ret explained, "and if we don't cooperate, then they're going to shoot us down."

"How do you know?" said Leo.

"I tuned into the radio signals," Ret told them. "All of the stations on the ground are communicating with each other."

"Wait, this can't be," Paige interrupted. "Antarctica is politically neutral, sanctioned for peace. There's not supposed to be any kind of military action here."

"Not anymore, apparently," Ret said, almost certain the exception to international law had something to do with Lionel.

"Where do you want me to land?" Dusty pressed.

"As close to the South Pole as possible," Ret said.

Dusty immediately began their descent. Moments later, the promised scout arrived, flying a plane that was far more advanced than their own. It pulled up alongside them, as if to get a look inside at the unresponsive invaders.

Ret heard the pilot report, "Small plane. Two male riders, maybe more. No obvious firepower." Ignoring the scout, Dusty maintained a steady dive. "Descending fast, may be attempting to land."

So it was true: Lionel truly was in league with the nations of the world to stop Ret from filling the Oracle. Ret shook his head. Given the level of surveillance, he knew his goal of collecting the element would be greatly hampered—if not thwarted altogether—unless Lionel and his aides were certain of their trespassers' capture or demise. Ret could either cooperate and be detained for an indefinite length of time or he could fool them by staging their own destruction. It was an easy choice.

"Are there any parachutes on board?" Ret said urgently.

"I think so," Dusty replied, scouring the ground for a level place to land. "Look behind the backseat."

"Here's some," Leo announced, retrieving them one-by-one from the rear of the plane. Then, with a grave tone, he said, "There's only four."

"Perfect," Ret said. "When I give the word, I need all of you to jump out of the plane."

"Are you crazy?" Ana exclaimed. "I'm not jumping out of—"

"Okay," Ret rolled his eyes, "then you can stay here and give your parachute to me." Realizing the alternative to jumping was dying, Ana gladly put on her parachute.

The white ground of the frozen plains was getting ever closer. The scout pulled away from the side of the floatplane and fell behind it. Then it fired a few flares, obviously trying to scare the unidentified persons into submission.

"These guys aren't going to leave us alone unless we're either quarantined or dead," Ret detailed amid bright bursts of light from the flares. "If we cooperate, it'll be practically impossible for us to get the element."

"So we need to die?" Ana jumped to conclusions.

"No, you four are going to escape."

"What are *you* going to do, Ret?" Paige asked with uncertainty, strapping the parachute onto her back.

"Once you all jump," he said, "I'm going to stay with the plane until it's eventually brought down."

"You're going to jump, too, right?" Paige urged.

"I don't know yet," Ret admitted, much to everyone's dismay. "Dusty, where is the South Pole?"

"We should be flying directly over it right..." Dusty watched the map, "...now!"

"Okay, time to jump!" Ret yelled.

Knowing the skydivers would need some cover-up, Ret sent a powerful burst of wind toward the scout on their tail. The sudden turbulence sent the high-tech plane into a dizzying barrel roll, ensuring its pilot would not see the floatplane's occupants make their escape.

"Ana—go!" Ret shouted, seeing her hesitate.

"You go first," Ana begged to Paige, refusing to open the door. With a mighty gust, Ret blew the door off. With a scream, Ana was sucked out of the plane, followed by the other three.

As soon as the plane had been emptied, Ret seized the controls. He purposely caused the plane to pitch and yaw in the most brazen manner in order to make it look like he was trying to evade his pursuer.

"No cooperation," Ret heard his pursuer report.

"We gave them plenty of chances," Lionel rationalized. "They're obviously up to something. Take it down."

His decoy successful, Ret waited for the imminent explosion.

Meanwhile, his four friends were falling speedily to the earth. Although the hardest thing about parachuting may be the ground, Ana might say it was finding the ripcord. With her hair being blown all over her face, she frantically searched for anything she could pull, tumbling erratically amid the chaos.

One by one, the three others each successfully deployed their chutes, transforming their frigid free fall into a gentle glide.

But Ana's cries for help filled the freezing air. In her struggle to pull anything and everything, she somehow managed to pull the whole parachute off her back. Paige looked on with horror, her best friend falling like dead weight toward the white land below while the parachute, her only hope for survival, flittered out of her reach.

Then Paige remembered Ret. She knew he could save Ana. In search of their hero, Paige scanned the sky with optimism. In seconds, she spotted the pair of planes, still in pursuit like predator and prey. Then, with utter terror, Paige saw the scout fire a single missile that, in a direct hit, blew the little floatplane to smithereens.

CHAPTER 18

NOT YOUR AVERAGE GUARDIAN

In the blink of an eye, the floatplane was blown to bits. With a bright flash and a loud bang, a vicious fireball consumed the small aircraft, sending up smoke and raining down shrapnel. The scout passed by without remorse and then flew onward out of sight—mission accomplished.

Still descending in her parachute, Paige was experiencing the early stages of hysteria. Ana was plummeting to her death, and Ret was nowhere to be seen. Even if Ret was still alive, Paige saw no reasonable way for him to rescue Ana in time.

Then, against all odds, she saw something. Just before the flaming wreckage of the floatplane crashed to the ground, an object came charging out of it, traveling exceptionally fast along the frozen plain. When it passed under Paige, she could see it was a person, but not just any person—Ret! He was flying on a self-blown wind, speeding to save Ana.

With her screams getting louder by the second, Ret alighted on the plot of ground where Ana was likely to make landfall. Then he gathered the mass of moving air behind him and channeled it vertically, pushing it upwards with enough force to counteract the pull of gravity on Ana. When the wind met her, it quickly slowed her fall. Ret gradually lessened the strength of the wind and gently lowered Ana until she was levitating in the air just a foot or two above the spot where she should have splattered. Though the danger was over, she was still screaming, her eyes shut tight in anticipation of her impending doom.

After a few moments, realizing she should have died by now, Ana went quiet and looked around. Ret was standing in front of her with a smile on his face. Then, not far away, Ana's parachute finally made it to the ground and, upon impact, deployed.

"Did I have you worried?" Ret said playfully, setting his sister on the snow.

"Oh no, not at all," Ana pretended, glad to feel the ground underneath her feet again. "Why would I be worried?" She shot him a ruffled glare.

"Sorry," Ret told her.

"Thanks for saving me," she said with a sigh of immense relief.

Dusty landed a few yards away, the ice crunching beneath his feet. Next came Leo, whose legs weren't quite prepared for the abrupt landing. He collapsed on the frozen ground, the breeze dragging him in the snow until he detached himself from the chute. Ret looked around for Paige, and, as she approached, sent up a gentle wind to soften her touchdown.

The five youth huddled together, teeth chattering and bodies shivering from the biting cold. Despite the sunny skies, the weather conditions were inhumanely harsh, made worse by the perpetual wind. Leo reckoned the temperature was many degrees below zero, and Dusty claimed some of his toes were going to fall off. Paige kept close to Ret for warmth, and Ana feared it was going to take weeks for her to fully thaw. The bone-chilling cold was unlike anything that any of them had ever experienced or wished to experience again.

If they were to survive, the first order of business was to get warm. The task clearly fell on Ret's shoulders. He lit a fire in the center of their cluster, which immediately brought welcome heat, but he knew the group wouldn't be able to walk very well in a circle.

In the distance, Ret saw a faint pillar of smoke rising from the remains of the floatplane. From far away, he rummaged through the debris and found a large piece of the plane's metal siding. He summoned it to him from across the plain and suspended it above the group's heads.

Then he spread their small campfire underneath the metal, which distributed the warmth like a patio heater.

While defrosting, the party surveyed the area. They found themselves in a great valley. Profoundly flat and totally barren, it was encircled by a wide ring of mountains, a few of which still looked very large despite being way off in the distance.

There was only one thing that defied the uniformity of the plain. From far away, it appeared to be little more than a pile of snow and ice. Just looking at it, however, sent a numbing sensation throughout Ret's left palm. Although he wasn't sure if the feeling was caused by the wind barb scar or by the heater rescuing his hand from frostbite, he set off for the site anyway.

The rest of the group followed, marveling at how much more enjoyable the situation had become now that they weren't freezing to death. The scenery was breathtaking—bare as a bone, yes, but still attractive in its own way. Pure and pristine, nearly every square inch was of the most exquisite whiteness, practically untouched by man. Perhaps, then, there was wisdom in the extremely cold conditions of this continent, preserving it from the problems that haunted inhabited ones.

Soon, it became clear that they were being followed, not by people but by penguins. A dozen or so emperor penguins were approaching from behind, waddling after the canopied crew. It was Paige who heard them first, the snow crunching under their little feet.

"Aw," Paige's heart melted at the sight.

"Ah!" Ana screamed as soon as she looked back. She darted ahead to hide behind Ret.

"It's just some penguins, Ana," Ret laughed.

"Don't let them come near me," Ana pled.

"These guys are pretty far from the coast," Dusty pointed out, wondering how a pack of penguins had wandered so far inland.

"I reckon they're lost," said Leo.

"Oh, they must be hungry," Paige observed with compassion.

"Don't you dare feed them, girl," Ana threatened.

Ignoring Ana's overreaction, Paige stepped toward the flightless fowls, which were about the size of a grade-school child. She took from her pocket a package of crackers. Although she knew a penguin's diet consisted mostly of seafood, she figured they would eat her offering if they were hungry enough. Like ducks at a city park, the black-and-white birds gathered around Paige, scarfing the crackers and leaving crumbs on their tuxedo-like plumage.

"Great," Ana grieved, "now they're never going to leave us alone."

Ana was right. As soon as the humans resumed their journey, the penguins followed. With a fearlessness brought on by hunger, the creatures came close at times, sniffing for food. Still wary, Ana spent more time looking behind than ahead.

In time, they arrived at the mass of snow and ice, although now they saw it for what it truly was: a massive glacier. Each step toward it gave them a better perspective of its colossal size. It loomed overhead like a multi-story office building, some spots catching the sun like great glass windows. Its color was a mix of white and blue, with jagged sides and a bubbled top. Of course, their observations were based on the small portion of it they could see.

Ret bent their course toward an opening he saw along the base of the glacier. Compared to the rest of the oversized iceberg, the opening looked like a small crevice but turned out to be a large cave. They stopped at the mouth and looked inside. Mostly dark, they were unable to see the end of it.

"Well, this looks familiar," Paige remarked.

"Yep," Ana agreed nonchalantly. "Next we go through this mysterious hole in the earth and stumble upon some secret operation. Then, while Ret finds the element, the rest of us almost die—either from a civil war or Lye's little helpers. The usual."

"I think I'll wait out here," Dusty said after Ana's dismal outlook.

"Dusty's right," Ret instructed. "I think it's best if I go in alone."

"While the rest of us stay here and get pecked to death by penguins?" Ana remarked, shooing one away.

"You know what happens when I collect an element," Ret argued. "The whole place implodes."

"But what if Lye is ready for you again?" Paige remembered.

"I'd feel better if at least one of us went with you," Leo added, recalling the crucial role he had played last time in helping Ret escape the collapsing pyramid.

They had a point.

"Okay," Ret obliged, "but only one of you."

"I'll go," Paige immediately volunteered.

Sensing a bit of disappointment from Leo, Ret told him privately, "I need your help in a different way this time. Now that the floatplane is history, I need you to think of a way out of here. If things get too dangerous before Paige and I get back, then take the others and leave without us. Can you do that for me?"

"Yes, sir," Leo accepted.

Standing side by side, Ret and Paige stared into the darkness of the cave. Then they looked at each other and, holding hands, stepped into the unknown together.

"What should we do to keep warm?" Ana called out to Ret when the flames of his heater started to flicker.

"Snuggle with the penguins," Ret joked, knowing he had left Leo with that charge.

The pair hadn't gone far when they needed a flame of their own, both for warmth and for light. Ret maintained a flare-like glow a few yards in front of them, illuminating the path ahead like a floating light bulb. The place was as beautiful as it was cold, a natural ice museum with slick curves and quick chips. Long icicles hung from the ceiling while frosted crystals lined the walls. Every kind of formation was represented: round-edged, razor-toothed, water-worn, puddled-up. Frozen and refrozen, a million snowfalls lay in a thousand shapes, the product of sublimation and compaction. In fact, the ice had been compressed so densely over the years that even the tiniest of air pockets had been forced out, turning the ice a rich, royal blue color.

The further Ret and Paige went, the more obvious it was that they were traveling through a tunnel, one with a generally downward slope. The path was quite narrow in parts, and the slippery floor proved a constant challenge. Paige frequently leaned on Ret for support and came to enjoy falling because she knew Ret would catch her in his arms. Ret never lost his balance but occasionally lost his footing, causing his legs to stride and split at random, which always made them laugh. In some parts, the ice was so smooth and sleek that they could see their reflections in it, looking quite distorted and (therefore) humorous at times.

The tunnel forked on numerous occasions, splitting off in many different directions. Eventually, they came to somewhat of a clearing. Its domed ceiling and flat floor gave it the appearance of an ice rink, which was precisely what it was. Within the glacier, a small pond of water had accumulated and frozen. Ret leapt out onto the ice and began to slide. Paige followed, counting on Ret to catch her. After getting the hang of it, they skated on the ice together, without much gracefulness but with plenty of laughs. Once, Ret attempted a jump but didn't quite complete the spin and wiped out—all in good fun.

It was like being in a winter wonderland, just the two of them, gliding on the ice. Then, when they reached the other side of the frozen pool, they pressed forward in search of the element.

Meanwhile, back at the mouth of the cave, the pack of penguins was getting quite cozy with the three teenagers—well, with the two boys, at least.

"Get your beak out of my hair," Ana demanded, pushing away one bird's snout. Then, to another, she said, "And why are you so obsessed with my feet?"

"Maybe it likes toe jam," Dusty jabbed. He was petting one of the penguins who had laid its head in his lap.

"You're not helping," Ana sneered. For protection from the pesky penguins, she was sitting between Dusty and Leo. The trio had their backs against the piece of the floatplane's metal siding, which was still giving off some heat despite its rapid cool-down.

"How long does this usually take?" Dusty inquired, new to this whole Oracle business.

"A while," Leo said.

"How will we know when they've found the element?" Dusty asked.

"Oh, we'll know," Ana answered, pulling her leg away from a penguin that had decided to settle in next to it.

"Just be patient," Leo recommended.

"Yeah," Ana concurred, "maybe they'll run into Superman down there."

All of a sudden, the penguins rose up in alarm. Then, with one accord, they scurried away as if spooked by something, flailing their fins and squealing with fright.

Leo and Dusty exchanged confused glares.

Ana smiled, "Finally."

But Ana's contentment turned into concern when a noise emerged from within the cave. It was the sound of a small piece of ice being knocked off and falling to the ground. Dusty leaned forward while Leo protectively held out his arm in front of Ana.

"Ret? Paige?" Leo yelled into the darkness. "Is that you?"

The only reply was another sound—this time louder, closer.

"Hello...?" Dusty asked, his voice trembling. "Is someone there?"

Now they could hear footsteps—large, heavy footsteps—of some creature coming towards them. Rising to their feet, the three frightened youth stared in shock as the mysterious being came into the light. Man or beast?—they couldn't tell. Covered in white hair, it towered over them and lumbered toward them, the most terrifying look on its face. Then it charged.

"Ah!" Ana screamed.

Down in the ice cavern, Ret and Paige froze.

"What was that?" Paige asked.

"Sounded like a girl's scream," Ret said.

"Ana," Paige concluded with concern. "Should we go back?"

"Nah," Ret said coolly. "One of the penguins probably just licked her face or something."

With some hesitation, the two of them carried on. There was uneasiness in the air now, both of them listening for but hoping not to hear cries for help from their friends. Ret had to pull Paige along with a tad more effort now.

The tunnel was getting wider and flatter. Ret moved his flame about like a firefly, trying to learn the growing extent of the cavern. It was unsettling now that they couldn't see everything around them.

Just then, Paige heard something rush by.

"What was that?" she said with distress.

"What was what?" Ret returned, trying to remain calm.

The noise was heard again, this time by both of them.

"That," Paige pointed out. "Someone's here." They had stopped now, Paige clutching Ret's hand.

"Who's there?" Ret called out, trying to sound confident. Off to the left, he saw the shadows stir. Ret quickly sent his flame over there. On the way, however, it was snuffed out by a cold and icy wind.

"Maybe it's just a bat or something," Ret said with detectable uncertainty, assuming the flap of its wings had blown out the flame. But then, off to the right, he saw something moving—something big and white. This time, Ret sent several lights toward the spot, but again a blast of Antarctic air swallowed the flames whole.

"Uh, I don't think it's a bat, Ret," Paige told him shakily.

With a fed up sigh, Ret threw his hands down at his sides to fill the entire room with fire. His flames had hardly been kindled, however, when the whole span of them was blown out by the same, frigid wind. Ret and Paige shivered as the cold draft rushed by them.

"Ret…," Paige quietly quivered, "what's going on?"

Without warning, the room went pitch black. The little light that had penetrated the glacier was dispelled in an instant. Ret thought that was odd, and it reminded him that he could control light. He summoned some of it back and produced a glowing orb in front of them.

And there it was: the creature—standing right in front of them. Startled beyond belief, Ret and Paige fell to the ground. With terrible awe, they gazed open-mouthed at the frightening figure. It looked like a man but was much taller and thicker. As if wearing a full-body fur coat, he was covered in thick white hair from head to toe. His hands were massive, his feet even bigger, and each of his heavy breaths sent a moist cloud into the icy air. And yet, despite his haggard appearance, Ret thought he saw a twinkle in his eyes.

"Who are you?" the white giant roared without the least bit of welcome, his thunderous voice echoing against the cavernous walls. Neither Ret nor Paige said anything, too scared to reply. Annoyed, the beastly man took a step forward and bellowed, "Answer me!"

In self-defense, Ret raised a hand to conjure a fireball that he hoped would keep their antagonist at bay. Only a few sparks had shot from his fingertips, however, when the angry man lifted one of his large paws and sent a subzero wind at Ret.

"Don't you dare attack me!" he growled. The chilling blast extinguished Ret's fire and froze him to the bone. His limbs fell stiff, his hair frosted over, and his skin was turning blue.

"Please, stop it!" Paige begged desperately, wincing at Ret's immobilized state.

Finally, the man called back the air. With a desperate breath, Ret revived and fell on his hands and knees. For a few moments, his entire body experienced the pain of a brain freeze, that intense headache brought on by rapidly consuming cold food or drink. He felt Paige drape her arm across his back, trying to help. In time, the discomfort passed. Lesson learned.

"Why have you come here?" the man asked without sympathy.

"We come in the name of the Oracle, sir," Ret answered with all the bravery he could muster.

"Is that right?" the brute challenged with a defiant tone. With a sweep of his bulky arm, he lit up one side of the room. Ret and Paige gasped, for there were their three friends: Dusty sinking in a pit of sand, Ana tied to a stake with flames closing in, and Leo on his knees with his head positioned below a raised guillotine.

Then, releasing the blade of the guillotine, the white monster said, "Prove it."

CHAPTER 19

UN-EXPECTED HELP

Thorne was whistling a happy tune as he returned to work after taking a lunch break. He stepped out of the elevator and approached the skull-shaped command center, removing his cap to let the neuroscope scan his brain and grant him access. The doors had scarcely opened when a student rushed to greet him.

"Someone's just flown off in your plane, sir!" the student informed him.

"What?" Thorne asked in disbelief.

They hurried to the computer. Thorne sat down and started reviewing recorded footage from one of the onsite cameras. Outraged, he watched Dusty sneak aboard the floatplane, assuming his son was up to more mischief. Then, with shock, he saw Paige and Ana join him. Seconds later, the plane passed out of that camera's range of vision, so Thorne switched to another one nearby. He followed the plane into the creek where two more individuals boarded. Thorne zoomed in to see Ret and Leo. Then the plane took off.

Thorne phoned Mr. Coy.

"Coy, the kids are gone," he flat-out said.

"What?" Coy asked with concern.

"Dusty, Ana, Paige, Ret, Leo—they all got in my plane and left," Thorne explained.

"How do you know?"

"I just watched the surveillance video."

"Do you have any idea where they are going?" Coy pressed.

"Not a clue."

"Get down to the hangar and prepare the jet for immediate departure," came Coy's orders. "I'll meet you there."

"Should we tell Pauline?"

There was a long pause.

With dread, Coy took one for the team and said, "I'll tell her." Then he hung up.

Mr. Coy buzzed about his small private quarters in preparation for his impromptu trip. He was halfway out the front door when he stopped. A thought crossed his mind. He turned around and hurried to his closet where, tucked away in the corner, stood an old, stuffed mannequin. With a wheeled stand in place of a lower body, it was the kind a seamstress would use, leftover from when Helen sewed outfits for the family years ago. Now, it served as a necktie holder—and as a hiding place.

Mr. Coy quickly spun the faceless dummy around. There was a long stitch down the middle of its back. Mr. Coy pried it open and reached into the stuffing. In the upper left-hand side, about where a living person's heart would be, there should have been a hidden object, but it wasn't there. With worry, he searched the rest of the abdomen but found nothing. His secret stash had been infiltrated. The Oracle was gone.

Fortunately, the possibility of losing track of the Oracle was something Mr. Coy had anticipated. Not too long ago, he placed a tracking mechanism on the sphere, so tiny and clear that it was virtually impossible to see unless you knew where to look and, even then, were looking very hard. Mr. Coy turned his attention to the back of the mannequin's head, where there was also a stitch in the fabric. He reached inside and pulled out a handheld electronic device. He extended the antennae and booted up the program. It was linked to the tracker and would tell him the exact location of the Oracle, anywhere in the world.

"Thanks, Manny," he told the mannequin on his way out.

Mr. Coy hastened across the Manor's grounds toward the Cooper home. When he arrived at the front door, he paused and took a deep breath, as if he was about to deliver unwelcome news. Then he knocked.

"Good afternoon, Ben," Pauline greeted him cheerily.

"There's something I need to tell you," Coy skipped the pleasantries.

"Oh?" she replied, uncharacteristically calm.

"The kids are gone," Coy explained. "All five of them just took off in Thorne's plane."

Mr. Coy braced for the meltdown. But there was no panic to be found in the woman's face.

"I know," she said matter-of-factly.

Baffled, Coy asked, "You know?"

"Yes, the girls came and told me just before they left," Pauline said. "We discussed it briefly, they told me who was going with them, and then I gave them my blessing."

"You...you..."

"I trust them, Ben," Pauline said tenderly.

"So do I—"

"Not Ret," she pointed out.

"Pauline," Coy said in sober tones, "you would feel the same way if you had seen what I saw that day."

"Remind me again what you saw?"

"I saw Ret," Coy stated, bugged to have to review the details again, "fraternizing with the enemy."

"That's what you saw with your eyes," Pauline observed. "Now what did you see with your heart?"

Mr. Coy paused at the distinction. He bowed his head.

"It made my heart sick," he admitted softly. "In my heart, I didn't believe it."

"That's the way I felt when I saw Jaret again for the first time," Pauline related. "With my eyes, I saw a man who had forgotten me, but in my heart I knew that couldn't be true. Now, we all know Lye played a trick on us, and he may have fooled my eyes, but he couldn't fool my heart. So maybe this is another one of Lye's tricks. I'm sure it will all make sense soon enough. In the meantime, I suggest you see with your heart."

Mr. Coy slowly nodded his head. Perhaps the old maid was right.

"Have a safe trip, Ben," Pauline concluded.

"You mean you're not coming with us?" Coy asked.

"I can't leave now," she dismissed, as if the very thought was ridiculous. "I've got a cake in the oven."

"We won't be leaving for a while yet," Coy tried to buy her time.

"No, no, you go on without me," she reaffirmed, tightening her apron. "Give everyone my love, and tell them I'll have a warm slice of red velvet cake ready when they get back."

"It's a deal," Coy said, closing the door.

As Pauline returned to the kitchen, she grinned, knowing she purposely had not told Mr. Coy where the kids had gone. She peeked inside the oven, taking in the heat and aroma, and said, "Have fun freezing your buns off!"

Mr. Coy hurried to the hangar, where Thorne was readying the jet.

"Prepare for takeoff!" Coy announced as soon as he climbed aboard. He sat down next to Thorne in the cockpit, and, within minutes, they were in the air.

"So where are we going?" Thorne asked as they meandered through the sky.

"Wherever our kids are going," Coy said.

"And how do we know where that is?"

"By looking at *this*." Coy held out the tracking device. "Do you see that little dot?" He pointed at a speck on the screen. "That is where they are."

"You track your kid?" Thorne wondered, thinking the idea had merit.

"No, but I track the Oracle, and I bet they have it with them."

"You're always thinking ahead, aren't you, Coy?" Thorne admired. "No wonder you ascended the naval ranks so quickly."

"Yes, well," Coy blushed, quick to change the subject. "It looks like they're heading south along the west coast of South America. Hmm, that's strange…"

"How so?"

"We've traveled that route before," Coy recalled.

"Maybe they're going somewhere else in South America," Thorne postulated.

"No, we're done with that continent," Coy said, though Thorne didn't really understand what that meant. "Maybe they're going to—" Coy's voice trailed off in stunned realization.

"Antarctica?" Thorne finished.

Surprised, Coy said, "Well, it *would* make sense. There must have been a good reason why Lye was at the North Pole, but maybe that was only part of it. After all, there's no land up at the North Pole, but there certainly is at the South Pole."

"I say we follow them," Thorne suggested. "If we fly full-speed, we might be able to catch up to that little floatplane and head them off before they make it to Antarctica."

"I don't want to stop them," Coy overruled, remembering Pauline's wise words about trust. "I just want to be close if they need help. Let's take it slow and see what they do. I say we fly around the east coast of South America."

With a quizzical look, Thorne obliged with a prolonged "Okay." Then, while adjusting their route, he asked, "So when are you going to bring me up to speed on all of this stuff?"

"What stuff?" said Coy.

"Oracle, elements, continents, scars, Lye—I'm picking up bits and pieces, but there are still a lot of blanks."

"Don't worry," Coy smiled, "we've got a long flight ahead of us," then started from the beginning.

The two fathers flew through the night, crossing into the Antarctic Circle by mid-morning. The international research stations were still celebrating their victory over the trespassing floatplane when a second unidentified aircraft appeared on their radar.

"Blimey! Here comes another one," cried a Brit at the United Kingdom's Rothera research station. Then, turning to his superior, he asked, "Shall we let Amundsen-Scott handle this one, too?"

"I say we take it directly to Mr. Zarbock," replied the superior. "This is highly unusual." Then, just moments later, he was heard radioing, "San Martin, this is Rothera. May we speak with Mr. Zarbock please?"

The Argentine on the other end said, "Un momento, por favor." Although the Englishman didn't know what that meant, he only had to wait a few moments before Lionel came on the line.

"This is Lionel," he said, sounding as though the call had interrupted something important.

"Rothera here, sir. We've picked up another unknown aircraft. What would you—"

"Another one?" Lionel interjected. "Good grief. Thank you, Rothera. We'll take it from here." He promptly hung up.

Suddenly, a voice with a thick Spanish accent was heard over the radio in Coy's jet: "This is San Martin station. Please identify yourself." Coy and Thorne exchanged confused stares.

"Since when do Antarctic research stations demand identification?" Coy whispered to Thorne.

"Maybe it's just an extra cautious air traffic controller," Thorne said.

"Should we respond?" Coy asked quietly.

Before Thorne could reply, the station repeated its command, followed by, "If you do not identify, military action may follow."

Now thoroughly vexed, Coy said, "Since when do Antarctic research stations have military capabilities?"

"Something's up," Thorne warned. "We'd better cooperate."

"Sorry, San Martin," Coy voiced back. "Captain Benjamin Coy speaking."

Down on the ground, Lionel's eyes bulged to hear such a familiar name.

"What's *he* doing here?" Lionel mouthed to himself. Then, addressing the radioman, he advised, "Tell them to land immediately."

"Sí, señor."

With reluctance, Mr. Coy obeyed, promptly landing his aircraft at the given coordinates. Imagine his surprise when he saw who was standing on the rocky runway to greet them.

"Lionel?!" Coy exclaimed. There had been no contact between the two of them since their heated disagreement at the Cooper home months ago when Lionel wouldn't let Mr. Coy see the letter that had prompted Pauline to persuade Ishmael to take her to Waters Deep. Thorne immediately recognized Lionel from the United Nations meeting.

"Welcome to Antarctica!" Lionel said with open arms.

"Can it, worm," Coy scoffed. "Don't pretend to be our friend. We know how you ratted us out to the UN."

"I know it looks bad," Lionel said, "but I did it for Ret's own good." Coy and Thorne stared at him intriguingly. "Please, just hear me out." Starting to walk away, he bade the two men follow him inside the research station. When neither of them moved, he laughed, "You're welcome to come inside my office—unless you want to freeze to death out here." Somewhat unwillingly, the pair followed.

"It was only a matter of time before the whole world found out about Ret," Lionel began, sitting down behind a desk in a small room. "Please, sit," he told his guests, who looked as though they would rather have remained standing. A man entered the room and set three steaming mugs of hot chocolate on the desk. "Gracias, Pedro." Coy and Thorne looked at the drinks as if they were poison.

"So you thought you'd do us a favor and cut to the chase?" Coy sneered.

"In case you haven't noticed, the entire globe is in commotion," Lionel said. "The very continents are moving rapidly, for crying out loud. Ret has disrupted millions of lives, so I figured it might be helpful if I put an end to all the rumors."

"But you made Ret out to be the enemy," Thorne jumped in, an eye-witness of Lionel's UN address.

"Forgive me, sir," Lionel said to Thorne, "but I don't believe we've met?"

"Walter Thorne," he introduced himself. "I was in attendance at the UN General Assembly meeting."

"And what is it you do for the UN?" Lionel asked.

"Enough with the small talk," Coy intruded. "How was your traitorous spiel for Ret's own good?"

Ever patient with Mr. Coy's animosity, Lionel resumed, "By the time the Oracle is filled, it will have affected every human being on the planet, and already there are entire nations who are not very happy with Ret." Then, pointing at Thorne, he said, "You were there at the meeting—the government leaders were furious." It was a fact Thorne couldn't deny. "There was already talk of a bounty for Ret. Can you imagine how impossible it would have been for you to travel the world in search of the remaining elements had I not stepped in? Sure, I may have vilified Ret, but I also halted the international effort to stop him. Don't you see?" Lionel smiled, leaning back in his chair and raising his hands in victory. "I saved you a world of trouble! If it wasn't for me, who knows what would have happened? Some rogue country may have tracked Ret down by now and blown up his house or something."

"Lye already did," Coy informed him.

"No..." Lionel gasped in disbelief. "Was anyone hurt? Pauline? Ana?"

"Thankfully no," said Coy.

With a heavy sigh, Lionel continued, "Well, I may not have control over Lye, but I do have some control over the militaries of all 193 members of the UN. That's why I'm down here in Antarctica. I just came from the Arctic, where there were reports of some unusual activity in Canada's Northwestern Passages." Coy and Thorne quickly glanced at each other, realizing their submarine voyage hadn't gone unnoticed. "But since there's no continent up in the Arctic Circle, I figured it might be smart of me to hang out down here at its southern counterpart, just in case—hence the military presence."

"We were wondering about that," said Thorne.

"Make no mistake about it," Lionel carried on, "I am still a friend to Ret, still your collective ally. As you can see, I am paving the way for you and Ret, not obstructing it. Whatever you need—clearance into a country, some cover-up, extra cash—I'm here to help. Despite what you may have seen at the UN meeting, I remain your biggest supporter." Then, as if he knew about the current discord that had arisen between Ret and Mr. Coy, Lionel concluded with a chuckle, "Surely you don't take *everything* you see at face-value?"

Lucky for Lionel, his lesson hit home with the two men sitting across from him. In some eerie way, the physicist-turned-politician always seemed to know more than he let on. Still, the man had crafted a compelling argument in defense of his actions before the UN. Maybe Mr. Coy was wrong about him.

"So what brings you two all the way down here?" Lionel questioned.

"Actually, we were following Ret," said Coy, taking a sip of his hot cocoa.

"Is he not with you?" Lionel replied.

"No, he and the other kids left without us knowing," Coy explained.

"So where are they now?" Lionel wondered with a sudden surge of worry.

"I suspect they're already here somewhere," Coy told him. "We may have found them by now had you not ordered us to land."

His anxiety growing, Lionel pressed, "They weren't in a floatplane, were they?"

"Yes," Thorne answered suspiciously. "Why do you ask?"

"Oh no," Lionel mourned.

"What?" Coy urged. "What is it?"

"There was a floatplane that flew into our airspace just before you did," Lionel said. "Whoever it was, they refused to identify themselves. We repeatedly tried to warn them, but they failed to cooperate." Then, wincing, he said, "So we shot it down."

"You shot it down?!" the two men erupted.

"It may not have been the kids," Lionel tried to quiet them.

"Who else would it have been?" Coy raged.

"Let's not jump to conclusions," Lionel hushed.

"Coming from the guy who went ahead and shot down a plane," Thorne grumbled.

"I was just about to go and search through the wreckage when your jet was spotted," Lionel said. "Would you like to come with me?"

"Of course," Coy replied, as it was common sense.

"Then I'll ready the snowmobiles immediately," Lionel promised on his way out of the room.

Ever unsure about Lionel, Mr. Coy waited for him to exit the room before conferring the Oracle's tracking device. With Thorne watching intently, Mr. Coy retrieved it from his pocket, the two fathers hoping to see a single dot that would tell them the youth were still alive.

The screen was blank.

CHAPTER 20

SOLAR WIND

Ret had to act fast. Dusty was up to his chest in the suffocating sand, the flames at Ana's feet were creeping closer, and the shiny blade of the tall guillotine would strike Leo within seconds. There was no time for fear.

Fortunately, all it took to end the pandemonium was a simple wave of Ret's hand: the metal blade stopped just inches above Leo's head; the fire died before it could melt the rubber of Ana's shoes; and Dusty's pit was turned inside-out, expelling sand into the air. What had initially seemed like an unbeatable dilemma had been won without much effort.

It had been too easy. Ret marveled at the odds that each of the dangerous situations consisted of one of the three elements he had already mastered. That was when he realized the scenarios were actually tests and that big hairy white guy was probably a Guardian.

Ret and Paige ran to help their friends.

"That was a close one," Ret told Leo as he approached the guillotine, which was up against the cavern's slick, icy wall. As Ret drew closer, however, his perception of the scene changed. Leo was not stuck in the guillotine; in fact, Leo was nowhere to be seen. There was merely a reflection of him on the wall.

Confused, Ret stopped and took a few steps back. From far away, it looked like Leo was kneeling down with his neck locked in the stock, but when Ret went up close, he could see the truth: it was only Leo's reflection, an image of him projected on the wall.

Ret glanced over at Paige, who was carefully trying to cross the hot coals on her way to untie Ana.

"Paige," Ret called out to her, "they're not real."

"Tell that to my feet," she returned.

"No, I mean the people aren't real," Ret clarified.

Paige immediately looked up at Ana. All she found was a two-dimensional version of her best friend, her reflection splashed onto the wide wooden stake that was leaning against the wall.

Then both Ret and Paige turned to Dusty. The contents of the sandpit lay all around, but Dusty hadn't changed. His image was bent at the waist, with half of him on the wall and the other half bent along the floor.

Meanwhile, the white behemoth in the room had erupted in celebration, stomping out a sort of victory dance and throwing his arms in the air.

"Finally!" he cheered with immense relief. "You don't know how long I've been waiting for this day. You're here—you're actually here! The end of my assignment is at hand." The man's booming voice startled Paige, and she sought security at Ret's side.

"Is he Sasquatch?" Paige asked Ret under her breath.

"I heard that," the giant said, picking up the sound waves even from a distance. "Sasquatch, Bigfoot, Yeti—I've heard 'em all. But you, my friends, may call me Rado," he said, stopping in front of them with a slight bow, "Guardian of the Wind Element."

An obvious change had come over the Guardian. He was no longer mean and threatening but kind and welcoming. His cold shoulder had given way to a warm handshake. Gone was the monstrous snow beast, replaced by an affable stuffed animal. It seemed his imposing demeanor had been but a façade, super-imposed on the gentle giant within.

"I'm sorry if I had you scared," Rado said, "but it's what I must do to keep the element safe these days. Every now and then, someone gets too close to this glacier, and I have to scare them off. That's what I did to those three young people you left at ground level. Please give them my sincerest apologies."

"So they're okay?" Ret asked. "You didn't capture them or anything?"

"Oh no," Rado answered. "They simply ran off."

"Then how did you create their reflections?" Ret wondered.

"It was easy," said Rado. "Once I had a picture of them in my mind, I created an image of them using light. It's like how an artist splashes paint on a canvas." He lit up part of a nearby wall to demonstrate. "A little red here, some blue there, maybe some darker and softer hues of yellow—and there you have it." Ret and Paige looked at images of themselves on the wall, which, though not their true reflections, sure seemed real. "If I want, I can even make them move." Just then, the image of Ret kissed the image of Paige on the cheek. The real Paige squeaked with glee. "It's a skill you will soon have, if you don't already."

"So you trick people?" Paige questioned.

"Not directly," Rado explained. "Some people are easily deceived by what they see—real or not—especially when what they see is something they fear. But fear, like reflections, is not a real, tangible thing. It is a trick of the mind. So *I* don't trick people—they trick themselves. But it didn't work with you two. I sense very little fear in you. For most people, just seeing me is enough to scare them off—but not you. So then I moved on to the tests. Your First Father told me which elements would be collected before mine, so that stage over there," he pointed to the three scenes, "had been set for a long time. But even when your friends appeared to be in danger, you did not let your fear cripple you. Well done." Paige gave Ret a playful nudge as compliment.

"It wasn't always this way, you know," Rado continued. "Before the elements were scattered and the supercontinent broke apart, this land was peopled and plentiful—the opposite of what it is today. But, over time, it drifted farther and farther south. Believe it or not, the snow here used to melt—all of it—but not so much anymore. As the conditions became increasingly harsh, the inhabitants were forced to flee, and pretty much all life died out."

"Except for the penguins," Ret inserted, earning a laugh from Paige.

"By the time I finally found the wind element," Rado retold, "this glacier had already formed around it. Of course, it has nearly doubled in size since then but seems to have receded a bit in recent years. Must be all that global warming flimflam I hear about in the airwaves. I say bring on the heat! Let's get this place back to how it used to be."

"How have *you* been able to survive the cold, sir?" Paige asked.

"The element keeps each Guardian alive," Ret whispered to her.

"Yes, there's that," Rado agreed, "but this nice, thick coat of hair helps some, though I suppose it also has contributed to my worldwide fame." Then, as if insulted, he said, "Bigfoot—how unimaginative. And Yeti—sounds like an Italian pasta. Sasquatch? I mean, how do people think of these names?"

"How about Abominable Snowman?" Ret suggested.

"*I* actually came up with that one," Rado admitted. "I thought 'abominable' sounded pretty scary, and I hoped it would get people to start looking for an actual snowman. But I don't care what the world calls me so long as they stay away. I'm constantly roaming this glacier, checking for anyone who might be snooping around. The advent of the internet has helped immensely in recent years: now whenever people see me, I can adjust their stories and change the locations of sightings—all from the comfort of my ice box. If someone snaps a photo of me, for example, I sift through the airwaves until I find it, then scramble the pixels or just scrap it entirely. Can you believe some people actually think I'm roaming the forests in Canada somewhere?" He laughed triumphantly, "They're so confused. Isn't the wind element wonderful…I'm sorry, what was your name?"

"I'm Ret, and this is Paige."

"And do you also bear the scars, young lady?" Rado asked politely.

"No, but I do have the Oracle," she replied, wanting to contribute. She pulled it from her pocket to show the Guardian. Unexpectedly, Rado's cheery temperament faded slightly when he saw the sphere.

"Did you know there is a signal coming from the Oracle?" Rado pointed out.

"There is?" Ret questioned.

"I could see a signal coming from your pocket, Miss, and thought it might be your phone, but clearly it is not." Rado extended his hand. "May I see the Oracle?" Paige looked at Ret, who nodded approvingly, before handing over the sphere.

The Oracle looked like a golf ball in Rado's massive paw. A gentle wind began to blow up from the palm of his hand, causing the Oracle to hover in the air. He brought his other hand alongside the sphere and shined an exceptionally bright light at it from the side. A large image of the Oracle was projected onto the wall. Rado slowly spun the Oracle around until they could see the tiny tracker, now many times magnified.

"Are we being tracked?" Ret asked with concern.

"I can't tell," Rado assessed. "It's only sending a signal, not receiving one. Still, I'd feel better if it was destroyed." Rado shut off the light and then blew a frigid wind at the Oracle, which glazed the sphere in ice. Then he called the wind back, unfreezing the Oracle. A tiny spark appeared on the sphere, and the signal went dead.

"I can't take any chances around here," Rado put forth, handing the Oracle back to Paige, "especially with what happened yesterday."

"Sir?" Ret wanted to know.

Said Rado, "Lye was here."

"He was?" Ret asked.

"He snuck in while I was out roaming the area—made it all the way to the element, that clever little crook," Rado detailed. "I watched him for a few minutes before I revealed myself. He had someone with him—a sidekick or helper, maybe even a robot. I don't know what the thing is, but it was giving Lye an awfully hard time. Lye would drag it to the element, then release it to see what it would do, but it would just walk away like it wanted to find something else besides the element. Well, as soon as Lye saw me, he hightailed it out of here. Though he would never admit it, he's always been afraid of me. (What did I tell you about fear?) He left behind his uncooperative assistant, which I seized, of course, but it refused to speak. I'm not sure the thing is even real. Actually, it kind of resembles you, Ret."

"Can I see it?" Ret requested.

"By all means." Rado led his guests into an adjoining room, a massive chamber in the heart of the glacier. From top to bottom, everything was made of the purest ice. The flat floor was an ice skater's paradise, as slick and polished as glass. The high ceiling hung like a huge gemstone, the many faces of its crystal-clear ice obscuring a view of the sky but casting bits of sunbeams down below. The room was circular, with frozen walls that had been custom-carved at many different angles like in a house of mirrors.

"How do you like the walls?" Rado asked with a hint of accomplishment as he led them deeper into the room. "Carved them myself, you know."

Off to the side, Ret could see the silhouette of a person standing in the shadows. Rado stopped in front of the statue-like being and then provided his own spotlight. Paige gasped at the sight.

"It's...it's—*me*," Ret said.

"I *thought* it looked like you," Rado stated. "Is this your evil twin or something?"

"I have no idea what this is," Ret said honestly. "I've never seen it before." Then, sizing it up, he remarked, "Is my nose really that big?" Paige swatted him playfully. "You said Lye brought it here, Rado?"

"As far as I know," said the Guardian.

"Maybe Lye cloned you, Ret," Paige shared her thoughts. "That way he'd have his own set of scars." The idea had merit.

"Here, I'll unfreeze it," Rado volunteered. "Maybe *you* can get it to do something."

Like a ghost, a frosty air emerged from the clone. Ret and Paige braced themselves for the unknown, but as soon as the lookalike had thawed, it flopped to the floor.

"Hmm, it's never done *that* before," said Rado. "Hope I didn't kill it by keeping it frozen too long." Then, with an embarrassed smile, he said, "Maybe it's nocturnal."

Ret tried to see if he had some connection with the clone. He poked it with his foot, waved his hand at it, even tried to stand it up, but it remained totally unresponsive. He knelt down and examined the clone's hands. There, indeed, were the scars, just like the ones on Ret's hands.

"Well, I don't know," Ret shrugged. Then, turning to Rado, he asked, "So where is the element?"

"Right this way," Rado escorted them, leaving the clone unfrozen on the ground.

Trying not to slip on the smooth floor, Ret and Paige followed the Guardian, whose paw-like feet afforded him considerable traction. Rado stopped at the center of the room, where there was a hole in the floor. Though a familiar sight to Ret, he accompanied Paige up to the edge, where they gazed into a vertical shaft that seemed to extend all the way to the earth's core. Ret heard Paige gulp at the profound depth, and he eased her away.

Ret was about to direct Paige's attention to the wind element, which he knew from experience would be floating above the bottomless pit, but it wasn't there. He looked all around, even at varying angles, but there was no element to be found.

"Uh, Rado, sir," Ret asked. "Where's the element?"

"It's there," the Guardian reassured him. "You just can't see it yet." Then, after scanning the darkening ceiling, he estimated, "Give it a few more minutes."

Eager to utilize this precious time with one of the Guardians, Ret said, "Sir, while I was with Argo—"

"You've met Argo?" Rado roared with fondness. "Ah, that guy…how I miss the old crew. Which element did he get stewardship over?"

"Fire," Ret recalled.

"Lucky dog," Rado mumbled, glancing around at all the ice.

Ret resumed, "Yeah, well, while I was with Argo, he told me how the First Father gave each of the six Guardians something to give to me, the one with the scars."

It jogged Rado's memory: "Oh, that's right—the relic."

"Is that what they're called?" Ret asked.

"That's what your First Father called them," Rado explained. "Hold on." The Guardian held out his hand and, with the other, began fiddling with something that was wrapped around one of his plump fingers. It was hard to see amid all the shaggy white hair on his fingers. At first, Ret thought it was a ring, but then Rado started untying it. When finished, he presented a white handkerchief to Ret.

Ret stared at the hanky, not sure if he wanted to touch it.

"Don't worry," Rado told him. "It's clean."

Taking the handkerchief, Ret asked, "Did the First Father say anything about what the relics are for?"

"Not to me, he didn't," said Rado. "All he said was to give it to the one with the scars and that you would know what to do with it."

Still clueless, Ret said sarcastically, "Great." He stuffed the handkerchief in his pocket and moved on to his next question: "Do you know—"

"Wait!" Rado interrupted. "Here it comes!"

The Guardian glared up at the ceiling with childlike fascination. The sun had set over Antarctica, but a new light was dawning—a light in the night. The aurora australis was slowly twinkling to life, and already its reflection was getting caught in the ice crystals of the glacier's dome. The ceiling lit up like a kaleidoscope, continuously scattering the light to pieces and shining them on the scene below. Flecks of green appeared on the walls, whose shiny surfaces reflected the light yet again. But unlike the ceiling, which rained down its bits of light with no particular order, each different face along the round wall had been hand-crafted to reflect light at a very specific angle. Like a series of mirrors, they all directed their unique reflections to the same exact spot, just above the hole in the center of the room.

As the night progressed, the Southern Lights intensified. When new colors emerged in the sky, their reflection entered the prisms of the sparkling dome, where the streams of light were reflected over and over again before eventually being splashed on the walls below. Brilliant shades of red, yellow, and blue transformed the glacial chamber into a laser light show. Like a disco ball, the ceiling painted the room in a dazzling display of dancing lights. It didn't matter where the bits of light struck the faces of the wall, however: the faces always reflected the light they received at a constant angle. Like the dimples of a golf ball or the facets of a cut jewel, each section of the wall shined its reflection in a different direction but all toward the same location.

But where was the element? Ret searched the vertical space above the hole where he knew the element should be. He saw a magnificent glow there. It was much brighter than all the other lights in the room because this was the spot where they all met. The room had been designed to focus all the light that entered it into a single, concentrated glow. But was this the element?

"Isn't it beautiful, Ret?" Rado beamed with pride, putting his large hand on Ret's shoulder as he admired the silent spectacle.

"I don't understand," Ret told him. "Where is the element?"

"Why, it's right there," Rado said, pointing at the glow, which had just changed from a dark red to a light purple. "Don't you see it?"

"Yes, I see it, but what exactly is it, Rado?" Ret asked. "I was expecting it to be like the other elements—earth, fire, ore—something I could touch and hold. But this? This is just a...just a glow."

As if his efforts had been underappreciated, the Guardian sighed heavily and said, "Do you have any idea how long it took me to figure this out, Ret?" There was a hint of firmness in his tender voice. "What is the wind element, you ask? I might say it is the sun, or at least the energy of it. The wind element is different from the others because it resides on the sun, not the earth. All physical life on this earth—all light, heat, energy—can be traced back to the energy of the sun. *That* is the source. The wind element is but a tiny bit of the sun's energy and, by extension, is also that original source. So tell me, how would you go about collecting something like that?"

Ret was silent at the conundrum.

"Thankfully, in her infinite wisdom," Rado continued, "Mother Nature not only provided a way for the element to be blown to earth as solar wind but also created the aurorae to make an otherwise invisible medium visible to the natural eye. That's what the Northern and Southern Lights are: the transmittal of energy from sun to earth—the personification of solar wind. But how was I supposed to take something as far and wide as the aurora and get it into the palm of your hand? How could I concentrate it and confine it so that you could easily capture it?"

"I think I see your point, sir," Ret said with growing understanding.

"Just look at it!" Rado gloried in the glow. "It's brilliant, not only in the way it looks but also in the way I got it here. It requires an innumerable quantity of microscopic solar wind particles to create this marvelous glow. The wind element wasn't a large ray of light I stumbled upon one day. No, I had to piece it together, bit by bit. Even then, I still don't really know *what* it is, but at least I know *where* it is, and that was my assign-ment—not to fully understand it but to find it, protect it, and prepare it so that *you* could collect it. Such was my calling as a Guardian, and I literally moved heaven and earth to fulfill it."

Clearly, to serve as one of the Guardians of the Elements was no easy task. Little wonder, then, why Rado viewed the completion of his life-long assignment with joyful expectation.

"Did you ever want to give up?" Ret spoke from his heart.

"All the time," Rado replied right away.

"Then why didn't you?" Ret asked. "Didn't you ever feel like the Oracle was asking too much of you?"

"Occasionally. But there's really only one thing the Oracle asks for," the Guardian taught. "It asks for *you*. Sure, I had to scour the world from pole to pole, brave this bitter cold day in and day out, spend years tediously carving these walls just right, all while waiting for you to come along. I gave my life for this cause. I sacrificed myself—my *self*. That's the real test in life, Ret: self mastery."

In just a few words, Rado had summed up the last several months of Ret's life.

"Now, on with the show," Rado clapped his powerful hands. "I think you have an element to collect."

"Wait," Ret protested, "I have so much more to ask you."

"Young man, I've told you as much as you need to know," said Rado. "Now hurry up. I've been waiting a long time for this moment."

It was with bittersweet emotion that Ret stepped forward to fulfill his duty. He grabbed Paige by the hand, and together they moved toward the chasm in the floor, stopping a few steps in front of it. They stared at the element, which currently was a bright shade of green. With renewed appreciation, Ret's eyes swept the room, taking in the architectural feat that had brought the light of the aurora to ground level. Rado looked on with such sweet anticipation that Ret wondered if the Guardian knew he was about to die.

While Ret was gazing at the element, however, he saw something strange just beyond it. He shifted his focus and found a person there, standing about as far from the gaping hole as he and Paige were. Ret looked harder. When the lights feeding the element changed from green to red, the light in the unknown person's eyes also changed accordingly. Ret glanced back to see if the clone was still lying on the floor, but it wasn't there. The aurora had brought it to life, and it was now standing across from Ret, staring him dead in the face.

Ret stared at the clone, unsure of what he should do. A few streaks of yellow entered the room, adjusting the glow of the element as well as the color in the clone's eyes. Since the clone had been lifeless up until the appearance of the aurora, Ret assumed it had some sort of affinity for the phenomenon, drawing energy from it. Ret glanced back at Rado for assistance, but the Guardian simply shrugged.

"Wait," Paige whispered to Ret, her eyes fixed on the clone. "Look back at Rado again." Ret obeyed, after which Paige observed, "The clone did it, too—it moved just like you did."

Curious, Ret faced the clone. When he leaned to his left, the clone simultaneously leaned in the same direction (which was to its right). Then Ret waved at the clone with his right hand. At the same time, the clone waved at Ret with its left hand. Whenever Ret moved, the clone moved. It was not copying Ret's motion but mimicking it. It was as though Ret was standing in front of a mirror, except the reflection was a tangible thing. As if they were of the same flesh, there was no time lag between their movements, and the clone never did anything independent of what Ret did.

Soon, however, their silent version of "Simon Says" grew old, and Ret wanted to get on with collecting the element. He held out his hand and asked Paige for the Oracle. Ret was relieved when no Oracle appeared in the clone's outstretched hand. He stepped forward to the void in the floor. The clone did likewise without the least variation, and Ret could see it quite clearly now. The energy of the aurora surged in its eye sockets, duplicating the color and intensity of the lights in the sky. There was nothing original about the clone; it was solely an imitation that could do nothing of its own freewill.

Ret cupped his hands together and rolled the Oracle onto his palms. Then he raised his hands toward the element. But there was a problem. As Ret tried to move his hands into place under the element, so did the clone. Their fingertips collided. The clone was blocking Ret. With some force, Ret tried to push the clone's hands away, but the clone pushed back with equal force. Then Ret used his right hand to try and hold the clone's hands at bay, but the clone tried the same thing with its left hand.

Ret was getting frustrated. Maybe they could compromise: Ret's left hand for the clone's right hand, supposing it didn't really matter whose hands were being used so long as all the scars were represented. But this didn't work, for Ret's left hand kept bumping into the clone's right hand, and he could never get them side by side. Then Ret thought he could trick the clone, putting their fingertips together and then quickly trying to shove his hands over the clone's hands. But this didn't work either, for the clone was just as fast.

Now Ret was thoroughly annoyed. Then he got an idea. Like many times before, he put his hands together and extended them as far forward as he could until they met the clone's hands. When their fingers met, he slowly raised his wrists and lowered his fingers. The Oracle rolled from his palms and landed where their fingers touched, partly in Ret's possession and partly in the clone's. Finally, the Oracle began to come to life. It rose above the many fingers below it and started to turn in its attempt to align itself with the scars. But it never did. It just kept spinning. The sphere found itself among twelve scars—not six, as usual. It was confused and didn't know what to do, so it just kept spinning without ever opening.

"I can't believe this," Ret complained as he returned to Paige's side. "Whatever I do, that thing does it, too. It's so annoying."

"Never fear," Rado stepped forward with confidence. "I'll just refreeze this meddlesome miscreant." The Guardian blasted the defenseless clone with a terrible frost, which, unfortunately, was also experienced by Ret.

"Stop! Stop!" Paige protested. "You're freezing Ret, too!"

With a disappointed frown, Rado revoked the wind. Ret fell to his knees in pain as Paige tried to rub some warmth into his cold back.

"I'm sorry, Ret," Rado said sincerely.

"It was worth a try," Ret told him.

"The clone was frozen when we first saw it not too long ago," Paige observed. "I wonder why it didn't affect you then, Ret?"

"Probably because it hadn't been brought to life yet by the lights," Ret supposed.

"It looks like we may have to hold off until morning," Rado theorized. "If the aurora is what brings the clone to life, then it should go back to being a lifeless mold as soon as the sun comes up."

"But if we wait until morning," Paige astutely pointed out, "then the element will be gone, too."

"Good point," the Guardian submitted. "Well, I'd say we're in a bit of a pickle, wouldn't you?"

"That only leaves one option," Ret said, glaring at the bothersome clone with a face of stone.

"What are you going to do, Ret?" Paige wondered, a little worried by his definitive tone.

Ret made no reply. He strode to an open area, away from the wind element, the clone mimicking his every move on its unofficial half of the room. Ret stopped and turned to face the clone. Standing across from each other, with a considerable gap between them, it had the makings of a classic shootout from the Wild West. Slowly, the pair came together until they were face to face, their noses almost touching. Ret glared into the clone's eyes, now a bright blue color. Despite Ret's growing displeasure, there was absolutely no emotion on the clone's part, which only added to Ret's irritation.

Ret raised his right hand with the palm forward and brought it out in front of him until it met the clone's left hand. Each of their other hands followed. Then, as if with a stick of dynamite, Ret ignited a fiery explosion in each of his palms. The clone did likewise, of course, and the blasts repelled each other, flinging both of them backwards.

Ret was back on his feet in an instant. He sent dozens of fireballs at the clone, but each was met by one of its own, colliding into the invisible mirror that seemed to separate the scene down the middle. With his mind, he searched underneath the glacier until he felt bedrock. He cracked it, broke it, and sent it up through the ice. Huge slabs of rock came crashing through the floor, sending ice chips in all directions. Paige fled to Rado for protection as the same scene played out on the clone's side of the room.

Ret hurled the rocks in all directions and at varying speeds—lobbing some, rolling others, fast and slow—but each was met by a twin from the other side. With a mighty leap through the air, he charged at the clone and, just before they met, sent forth a powerful wind, which blew the clone away, yes, but himself also.

This wasn't working. It was like trying to fight fire with fire or use wind to blow out a tornado. Ret knew there had to be a difference between him and the clone—a strength to assert or a weakness to exploit. Apparently, they both possessed the same powers over the same elements, but perhaps the clone's limited genetic maturation made it more vulnerable to things that Ret wasn't as susceptible to—things like lava.

Ret mentally searched the bottomless pit below the wind element until he found a deposit of molten rock. Like a geyser, it shot up through the hole and into the air. An identical stream rose with it, being the work of the clone. Ret let his lava stream fall on the clone, well aware that the same thing would happen to him. Without resistance, Ret allowed himself to become engulfed, certain the clone was melting amid the scorchingly hot magma.

When the lava finally flowed from off Ret's face, he was dumbfounded to find the clone still intact. Now furious, Ret erupted in a flurry of vicious moves. He was giving it all he had, throwing everything he could think of at the clone. But it was all to no avail.

Paige watched from the sidelines, desperately wanting to help but not sure how to do so. From her point of view, it seemed like Ret was fighting with himself. In fact, the whole scenario looked a little ridiculous to her, like trying to outsmart your own shadow. She quickly realized Ret would never conquer himself by himself. It couldn't be done. He needed help from someone else. Even the slightest bit of aid would give him an advantage and tip the scales in his favor. But what could she possibly do?

The room had turned into a battlefield, with bangs and bursts filling the air. The lava had melted portions of the floor, only adding to the mess and confusion. Ret was growing weary. His nonstop assault was exhausting him. He looked tired and weak. Paige could tell he wanted nothing more than to collect the wind element, which he was so close to doing, but it was his clone—himself—that kept getting in the way.

Running out of ideas, Ret reached for something that he knew there was only one of in the vicinity: the blade of the guillotine. He summoned the sharp metal blade toward him. It came soaring into the room, with no sign of an identical one on the clone's side. Ret's heart took courage; he was certain he had the upper hand now. Then, when the blade reached the midway point between them, it abruptly stopped. As soon as it crossed into the clone's territory, the clone had control over it. Ret tried to push it onward, but it was met by equal and opposite force.

Ret's tactics turned frantic. His desperation was eroding his rationality. He was now flinging dagger-like pieces of ice on a wind that he blew toward the clone, hoping to put an end to its existence, but the sharp chunks simply collided into identical ones flung by the clone. Then, in his great extremity, Ret picked up an icicle at his feet and pointed it at himself. Perhaps the only way to end the madness was to sacrifice himself.

"Ret, no!" Paige cried.

Paige's plea brought Ret back to reason. He stared at the icy spike in his hand, which had nearly been turned into an instrument of death, and dropped it. Then he fell to his knees and broke into tears.

Paige flew from the Guardian's side and ran to comfort Ret, her path hedged up by the piles of debris that were strewn across the deformed floor.

Ret held the Oracle in his hand and, while looking at it, said, "Why are you doing this to me? I've done all I can do, but it's still not enough. What am I doing wrong? What do I need to do differently? What needs to change?"

Ret heard a noise nearby. It was Paige, trying to climb over some rubble on her way to Ret's side. For a split second, Ret thought she looked like someone else he knew—or had known until Lye killed her. And yet, Ret could still see Virginia, coming in from the trailer's small kitchen that day and sitting on Lester's knee, then putting her arm around him as her husband explained how it was love that had made the difference in bringing about the great change in him.

Paige arrived at Ret's side and wrapped her arm around him.

"It's okay," she told him tenderly. Ret glanced back at the clone, which was also on its knees with its hand extended but was alone. "You did your best, and that's what matters." Paige took Ret's other hand and placed it on top of the Oracle, then lovingly put her hands around his. But, to Ret's surprise, the clone's corresponding hand did not move.

Suddenly less sorrowful, Ret requested, "Move my hand again."

"What, like this?" Paige wondered.

"Look!" Ret told her. "The clone hasn't moved. It only moves when *I* move, not when someone else moves me. Quick, come with me!"

Ret anxiously rose to his feet, pulling Paige behind him. With a sudden gust, he blew a path through the debris in a straight course to the element. With haste, they ran to the edge of the chasm, on the other side of which stood the clone. Ret put his hands together, as did the clone, with the Oracle cradled inside.

"Okay," Ret instructed Paige, "now *you* put my hands under the element."

Ret relaxed his hands and let Paige take control. With her hands under his, she slowly extended them toward the element. To their great delight, they watched as the clone's hands did not follow suit but remained stationary. Unlike before, Ret was not responsible for any of the movement this time. Paige was doing something for him that he could not do for himself.

Encouraged, Paige continued until the Oracle sat directly under the element. The sphere rose above the single set of scars, aligned itself with them, and opened into six wedges. Without any interference from the clone, the fascinating glow of the wind element entered one of the empty wedges, and the Oracle reclosed.

The earth immediately reacted. In an instant, the aurora ceased to exist, and all sound was silenced for a second. The planet inhaled briefly, drawing everything inward, and then exhaled violently, expelling everything outward. Ret and Paige were thrown to the floor. The sound of shattering filled the air. Pieces of the wall were breaking off and falling to the ground, where they crashed into dust. Long cracks were growing in the floor. The great dome overhead was beginning to give way, raining down bits of ice like hail.

Ret checked on the clone. Having died with the aurora, it sat in a heap on the floor until enough of the ice had broken off around the mouth of the bottomless pit that the clone slid into it, never to be seen again.

Then Ret hurried to find Rado. The Guardian was lying on his back, a broad smile across his big face. Ret wished he could thank him.

The glacier was falling apart quickly. Ret could hear shrieks from Paige as she tried to dodge chunks of ice.

"Come on!" Ret yelled, grabbing her by the hand. "We've got to get out of here!"

Avoiding cracks and jumping gaps, they made for the doorway through which they had come. Before they could reach it, however, it caved in, sealing them inside.

"We're trapped!" Paige shouted.

There was suddenly heard a loud booming sound, like the popping of a giant light bulb. The ceiling had completely shattered and was now falling towards them in a million pieces.

Ret pulled Paige in close and said, "Hang on!" With a self-propelled wind, they were launched into the air. As they rose higher, Ret kept a steady column of fire above their heads to melt their way through the falling ceiling. They looked like an upside-down rocket as they flew out of the glacier, Paige holding onto Ret with all her might. Then Ret modified the wind to carry them to a safe place on the frozen plain.

Though she had been in the general area when the first three elements were collected, Paige had never experienced things at ground-zero before. Ret, who was mentally and physically drained himself, could tell she was shaken up, still clutching him tightly even after their feet touched the cold ground. They didn't let go of each other for a long time.

CHAPTER 22

A WARM RECEPTION

A new day was dawning in Antarctica. As the first rays of the morning sun spilled into the valley, Ret and Paige witnessed the great changes that were taking place. They watched the centuries-old glacier continue to cave in on itself, filling the air with plumes of tiny ice crystals. Echoing throughout the frigid air were the deep sounds of heavy buckling that only nature can create. Great fissures were zigzagging far across the open plain. Ret and Paige could feel the ground shaking and ice breaking as the sudden absence of the wind element sent shockwaves throughout the miles-deep icepack. The initial quake had even been felt by some of the surrounding mountains, causing large avalanches that poured immense amounts of snow and ice into the valley.

"Ret! Paige!"

The pair looked around to see who was calling their names. In the distance, next to a thin pillar of smoke, they saw Leo waving his arms at them. They immediately set off to meet him, holding hands as they trudged along the frosted ground.

Ret and Paige found their three friends near the wreckage of the floatplane, where they had built a modest fire.

"You got the element, didn't you?" Leo asked Ret right away.

"Yes," Ret replied with a tired sigh. Then, beaming at Paige, *"We* did. I couldn't have done it without Paige."

"What was it like?" Leo questioned with great curiosity. "Tell me all about it."

Leaving Ret and Leo to talk, Paige walked over to Ana. She was shivering next to the fire, surrounded by her favorite pack of penguins.

"Hey, girl," Paige greeted.

Through her chattering teeth, she said, "I think I'm frozen."

"You'll never guess who we saw," Dusty interjected.

"Who?" asked Paige.

"Sasquatch!" Dusty exclaimed. Paige just smiled.

Meanwhile, Leo was reporting to Ret: "After we got scared off by the cave monster, we came back here to keep warm. We were running out of stuff to burn

when I remembered the parachutes. It was them parachutes that got us through the night alive."

"Nice work," Ret said.

Leo continued, "'Course, I haven't quite figured a
way out of this place yet, like you asked me to."

"I'm sure we'll think of something," Ret reassured
him with a pat on the back.

It wasn't much later when the faint sound of gas-
powered engines was heard. A group of snowmobiles
appeared on the plain, hastening toward the unintentional smoke signal. As they drew closer, the identity of
the lead riders became clear.

"Dad!" Paige cheered.

"Dad?" Dusty wondered.

"Lionel?" Ret said with shock.

As soon as the rescue team arrived at the site of the
wreckage, Mr. Coy leapt from his snowmobile and
rushed to embrace his daughter.

"I'm so glad you're alright," he said with relief.
Then addressing everyone, he added, "All of you."

After a hug from his father, Dusty glanced shame-
facedly at the floatplane's incinerated remains and said,
"Sorry about the plane, Dad."

"Planes can be replaced, son," Thorne smiled.

"Ret, it's been so long!" Lionel exclaimed, placing
his hands on Ret's shoulders. "Which element was it this
time?"

"Wind," Ret answered, a little surprised to find Lionel being so friendly to him after what had transpired at the UN meeting.

"I can't wait to hear all about it," Lionel said supportively, putting his arm around his young friend. "You and I have much to talk about."

Even more snowmobilers arrived, driven by military personnel whom Lionel had asked to come along to comb through the wreckage.

The happy reunion was cut short on account of the freezing temperature and frequent aftershocks in the area. The youth, who clearly were not outfitted for their Antarctic expedition, were promptly given large parkas to wear. The adults returned to their respective snowmobiles, five of whom welcomed one of the stranded adolescents to ride in back. It was a long ride back to the research station, where there was a lot of catching up (and warming up) to do.

Lionel was quick to pull Ret aside. He explained the hidden benefits of his actions at the UN meeting and then asked Ret to fill him in on anything and everything that had happened since their last contact (which was months ago when Ret sent him a letter just before leaving for Africa).

"I know it seems like I turned the world against you," Lionel said, "but, like I said, I believe it's for our best interest. You may not have needed my help to collect the element this time, but I doubt it will be so easy next time. Don't worry, Ret. I'm here to assist you every step of the way. The real challenge will be for me to help you while making it look like I'm trying to stop you."

That didn't make a whole lot of sense to Ret, but he was presently too tired to think through it. Besides, Lionel had always been right before. It was such a relief to Ret to know Lionel was and always had been his trusted friend—so much, in fact, that the burden of finding the remaining elements was eased slightly just by knowing Lionel had promised to come to his aid at a moment's notice.

Ret left Lionel's office to rejoin the rest of the group. They were spread out across the research station's main lobby. From across the room, he saw an empty space next to Paige, who was sitting with her father on the ledge of the large fireplace, and immediately set off to fill it.

Along the way, he passed by Dusty who, with great theatrics, was retelling the last moments of the float-plane's life to his dad. Thorne listened with interest, eager to hear all about what it was like being chased by a fighter jet and then parachuting in subzero weather.

"And you should've seen Ret, Dad," Dusty said when Ret walked by. "He didn't even use a parachute…"

Then Ret strode by a couch where Ana was curled up underneath a thick blanket, surrounded by several empty cups of hot chocolate.

"Keep 'em coming," she called out to Leo, who was at the machine, working on Ana's next drink.

As Ret approached the Coys, Mr. Coy rose to greet him.

"Ret, son, I need to sincerely apologize to you," he said, sounding rather lowly. "Paige told me all about the clone. I was wrong, and I'm sorry I didn't believe you. I promise to trust you from here on out."

With a gracious grin, Ret clasped his hand on Mr. Coy's shoulder and said lovingly, "No hard feelings, sir." Coy glanced back at his smiling daughter, then walked off to let Ret take his seat next to her.

Ret sat down next to Paige, the warmth of the fire at their backs. Neither of them spoke for a few moments, preferring to let their hearts do the talking rather than their mouths. He reached to hold her hand and, while staring at it, slowly brushed the top of it with his thumb, well aware that it was *her* hands that had really collected the element this time.

"I couldn't have done it without you," Ret told her softly.

"I'm sure you would have thought of something," Paige replied modestly.

"I *did*. I tried everything I could think of, but I

couldn't do it on my own. I needed someone to help me."

"Rado could have helped you," Paige said, never one to boast.

"But he didn't," Ret pointed out. *"You* did. You cared. You came." He touched her chin and gently moved her face so that she was looking him in the eyes. "I couldn't have done it without you." Then, after a tender pause, "Thank you."

With a tear in her eye, Paige accepted, "You're welcome." She laid her head on Ret's shoulder and, for the first time, knew she had been of real help to the love of her life.

When there was nothing more to be said, Coy and Thorne readied the jet that would take them home. The five teenagers followed, each with a souvenir: Dusty had snagged a surviving door handle from the float-plane, proof of his daring feat; Leo picked up a smooth stone from the rocky runway, anxious to show his fellow orphans; Ana was clutching a steaming mug of hot cocoa, its sides bearing pictures of penguins; Paige's memento was the element, safely housed in the Oracle that she intended to return to her father; and Ret kept fiddling with Rado's handkerchief in his back pocket.

With the fathers in the cockpit, the children filed into the cabin. From the window, Ret watched how

Lionel remained on the crude runway despite the cold, waving at them even after takeoff.

"Say goodbye to Antarctica," Dusty announced.

"More like good riddance," Ana muttered, taking a sip from her mug.

It was clear from their bird's-eye view that Antarctica was already undergoing vast changes. The entire continent seemed agitated, its former tectonic path not only reversed but also accelerated. Great cracks were shooting across the ice pack like veins, causing the most turmoil along the coasts where the ice shelves were calving like crazy. Tremendous chunks of glacial ice were breaking off and crashing into the sea, creating treacherous tides. Frothy and foamy, the ocean looked nearly as white as the land's frozen tundra.

Finding themselves at the end of another adventure, Paige instinctively pulled out the Oracle to admire their accomplishment of filling one of its wedges. A green glow, the slice of solar wind swirled in its compartment, happy to be back with old friends. From start to finish—from Poles North to South—the wind element had proven to be the most difficult to procure thus far. No other scar had required quite as much sensitivity. No other element had strained rela-tionships quite as severely. Ret had never traveled so far, never felt so lonely, never been so cold. He hadn't even been able to collect the element himself.

"Four elements down," Leo said eagerly, watching Paige cradle the Oracle. "Only two more to go."

"Don't remind me," Ret sighed, slouching in his seat with exhaustion.

"Oh, Ret," Paige encouraged, "I'm sure the last two elements won't be nearly as hard as this one was."

If only that were true.